The creature had the oddest shape, Pandy thought, and certainly for a flyer: the wings were almost invisible but the tail was incredibly long. Then, with a gasp that made her miss a step and nearly tumble into the short grasses, she realized it was a peacock. A peacock, she knew, was normally a flightless bird—unless it was . . .

Hera.

"Just *try* anything," Pandy whispered, emboldened slightly by the presence of another immortal. "Just you try it."

MYTHIC MISADVENTURES BY
CAROLYN HENNESY

PANDORA
Gets Frightened

BOOK VII

CAROLYN HENNESY

BLOOMSBURY

NEW YORK   LONDON   NEW DELHI   SYDNEY

30681 3336

For Donald
Τα καταφέραμε!

First published in the United States of America in June 2013
by Bloomsbury Children's Books
Paperback edition published in June 2014
www.bloomsbury.com

Bloomsbury is a registered trademark of Bloomsbury Publishing Plc

For information about permission to reproduce selections from this book, write to
Permissions, Bloomsbury Children's Books, 1385 Broadway, New York, New York 10018
Bloomsbury books may be purchased for business or promotional use. For information
on bulk purchases please contact Macmillan Corporate and Premium Sales Department at
specialmarkets@macmillan.com

The Library of Congress has cataloged the hardcover edition as follows:
Hennesy, Carolyn.
Pandora gets frightened / by Carolyn Hennesy. — 1st U.S. ed.
p.   cm. — (Mythic misadventures)
Summary: Pandy, Alcie, Iole, and Homer hunt for the worst Evil of all—Fear—in the
dreaded underworld where Hera has been wreaking havoc and such infamous villains as
Tantalus, Sisyphus, and The Danaids have been freed from their eternal punishments.
ISBN 978-1-59990-442-9 (hardcover) • ISBN 978-1-61963-031-4 (e-book)
1. Pandora (Greek mythology)—Juvenile fiction. [1. Pandora (Greek mythology)—Fiction.
2. Mythology, Greek—Fiction. 3. Gods, Greek—Fiction. 4. Goddesses, Greek—Fiction.
5. Hell—Fiction. 6. Adventure and adventurers—Fiction.] I. Title.
PZ7.H3917Pae 2013   [Fic]—dc23   2012042330

ISBN 978-1-61963-251-6 (paperback)

Typeset by Westchester Book Composition
Printed and bound in the U.S.A. by Thomson-Shore Inc., Dexter, Michigan
2 4 6 8 10 9 7 5 3 1

All papers used by Bloomsbury Publishing, Inc., are natural, recyclable products
made from wood grown in well-managed forests. The manufacturing processes
conform to the environmental regulations of the country of origin.

CHAPTER ONE
Cliffhanger

"Iole?"

"Mmmmm?"

"You gonna open your eyes?"

"Let me think a moment . . . right . . . that would be an unequivocal negative."

"In Greek, please."

"No."

Pandy laughed in spite of herself—and their situation.

"But we're almost to the top of the cliff already," she said, looking down at the treetops, now at least eighty meters below, the green-and-brown countryside rolling away as far as her eyes could see. Except for a line of the blue Aegean due south and a thin ribbon of smoke, which indicated a fire somewhere to her left, there was nothing but tree-covered hillsides.

"All right, I'm going to correct you on this one," Iole said, her long eyelashes barely visible as she scrunched her lids tight. "*We* are not almost to the top of any-where; *Homer* is almost to the top, and I'm just going to have to take your word for it because I have no intention of opening my eyes. *We* are simply along for the ride, as it were. Like sacks of cabbage. Or sacrificial goats. You want to find Fear, Pandy? You want to recapture the biggest, most important evil of them all, Pandora Athe-neus Andromaeche Helena of Athens, only daughter of the great house of Prometheus? Then look no further: fear is trussed up like a festival-day pheasant and is swinging not half a meter from your nose in the shape of your best friend!"

"Second-best friend!" came Alcie's voice from above.

Pandy stared at the length of rope carefully wound around their waists and legs. She followed the single strand as it straightened out taut against the side of the sheer rock wall. Roughly five meters over her head, she saw the bottom edge of Homer's cloak and his bare feet searching out crevices in the cliff for a solid hold.

"If we plummet to our deaths, it won't make much difference if your eyes are open or . . ."

"Cease and desist your incessant chatter!" Iole yelled at Pandy.

"What's happening down there?" Alcie cried.

"Nothing, Alce," Pandy called back. "We're just look-ing at the sunset, glad to be back in Greece."

"Thrace, to be specific," Iole said, tightening her grip on the rope. "We're in Thrace, and stop talking!"

"Iole's opened her eyes?" Alcie asked.

"Not yet," Pandy yelled.

Just then, Homer's left foot lost its purchase in the rock, and the girls were jolted downward for a moment.

"AHHHHHHHHHHHHHHHH!" Iole screamed, her eyelids flying open.

Pandy's own scream caught in her throat as the rope tightened again.

"Sorry!" Homer called, finding his toehold, relaxing all the weight off his fingers. "I'm sorry! We're good. I'm good."

"Stop *talking* to him, Alcie!" Iole ordered. "Stop distracting him, or, by all the Olympians, I'm gonna give you such a wallop! If we live, that is."

"You and what Assyrian army?" Alcie laughed.

Pandy reached out to Dido, hanging in his own rope harness, and patted his nose to comfort him. He looked at her with love as his backside grazed the rock wall, as if to say that he forgave her for the precarious position she'd put him in. Pandy desperately wished the cliff she was hanging against, bumping her knees and bruising her arms, was the Acropolis back in her beloved Athens and that they were on their way, no matter how crazy a way it was, up to the Parthenon. The Thracian terrain was somewhat similar to the part of Greece she knew, and her heart ached, knowing she was again so close to—yet still so far from—home. It had been two days of intense walking from the harbor of Abdera where they had disembarked off the ship from Rome. "North. Go north. You can't miss the mountain," the town's innkeeper had said, and he was right. Now the ledge he'd also mentioned was in sight, which meant the famous cave of Orpheus was close by.

"You okay?" Pandy asked Iole, lifting the flap of her carrying pouch as she tried to regain a steady beat to her own heart.

Iole said nothing for a long time; she just stared reproachfully at Pandy.

"I think this is the most incredulously insane thing we have done on this quest thus far," she said finally. "And *that*, as you know, is saying something. This is more ludicrous than you becoming an old woman in Egypt, crazier than you trying to make it through the Atlas mountains with two little boys in tow—"

"I couldn't just leave them," Pandy cut in softly.

"—Crazier than all of us trying to keep the golden apple away from Aphrodite, crazier even than roaming the sewers of Rome after curfew. Right now, in your pouch, you have a perfectly good magic rope to be used on occasions such as this, yet you acquiesced when

Homer insisted on climbing this vertical death trap on his own."

"It's not that far up, Iole," Pandy countered, fumbling in the pouch. "And he begged. Said he needed the exercise. You heard him, he said it would be easy as oatie cakes. Said he needed to work his muscles in case we needed serious help in the underworld."

"But did he really need Alcie to sit on his shoulders on the way up?"

"He said it provided a good balance," Pandy said, her hand finally latching onto the sought item in her pouch. "Besides, you know she and Homer went weeks without seeing each other in Rome. This is giving them a chance to talk."

"He's not supposed to be *talking*," Iole said through clenched teeth, at last taking her eyes from Pandy's face and looking up for a moment at Homer's backside. "He's supposed to be climbing silently and with focus. What are you rummaging for? Stop rummaging! You're jostling us . . . you're gonna slip . . . *stop*!"

Pandy raised her finger to her lips for Iole to be silent, then she held up the end of the magic rope.

"You do have a point," she mouthed. "Just in case he actually does lose his grip, I want this ready. But I don't want to hurt his feelings."

"Oh, by all means. Indubitably. As we drop like

stones, let's do worry about Homer's *feelings*," Iole mouthed back, as Pandy began to whisper precautionary commands to her rope.

❦

As unbearable as the climb had been, they suddenly found themselves on solid ground as Homer lifted them, one by one, from the side of the mountain onto a large ledge.

"This ledge is bigger than it looked on the way up. It's actually more of a plateau," said Homer, as he hauled first Iole, then Pandy out of midair.

" 'Plateau'? Nice word," Iole replied, a little snark in her voice.

Homer looked at her evenly.

"Iole, I'm not stupid."

Instantly, Iole was ashamed; it was true, throughout the many weeks that the four of them had been together, no matter how valiantly he proved himself or how clearly he spoke, no matter how much he cared not only for Alcie but for all of them, no matter how sometimes brilliant his ideas and suggestions were, she'd never *quite* gotten past her image of Homer as . . . simple. In a flash, that notion was gone. And, even if he wasn't the absolute sharpest arrow in the quiver, she was being rude—and that wasn't the way she'd been brought up.

"I'm truly, sincerely, and wholly sorry, Homer," she said, choosing her words carefully. She paused and thought for a moment. "I know exactly what it is: I'm still scared from the climb and I'm taking it out on you, even after you did all the hard work. I feel like I have all this energy, and yet I want to stay perfectly still at the same time. But that's no excuse for my behavior and I know better; I promise, it won't happen again."

"Thanks," he said, with a small bow.

"Why is Alcie dancing around like my little brother with an ant in his poop cloth?" Pandy asked, watching as Alcie kicked up her heels in the twilight, Dido prancing around her. Behind Alcie, perhaps fifteen meters away, Pandy saw what should have been the cave opening; more precisely, she saw where the cave opening would have been, had it not been sealed with gray rock.

"We had what my fight master back in gladiator school used to call 'a full and frank exchange of views.'"

"A full and frank . . . ?" Iole said.

"Yeah. Right before he'd hack your little finger off, he'd tell you what he wanted to do and how he was planning do it. He'd say we were having a full and frank . . ."

"Got it," Pandy said, pulling her cloak tight around her shoulders. The wind had come up briskly since they landed and was blowing cold at such a great height; her own hair was stinging her eyes as it flew back and forth. "I would ask what views you two exchanged, but . . ."

"I told her that, like, if we lived and all, I was going to leave the import/export business and my dad in Crisa and move to Athens. And that I was going to get a nice steady job, maybe something in temple construction. Something that could support a family. I sort of asked her to be my 'girl.'"

"What has she been all this time if not your 'girl'?" Iole asked.

"I meant my real 'girl.'"

"You mean you asked her to *marry* you?" Iole said, her voice rising.

"Well . . . I asked her to be . . . engaged."

"Engaged to be *married*?" Iole nearly shrieked.

"Well, engaged to be engaged," Homer responded.

"You do mean, of course, when she's not thirteen years old?"

"She's not thirteen," Homer said matter-of-factly.

"What do you mean she's not thirteen?" Pandy said, the comment drawing her attention away from her surroundings.

"Today's her birthday, and I thought that in four years or so, we could . . ."

"Oh, great Aphrodite!" Iole said, turning to Pandy. "We forgot!"

"What do we do?" Pandy asked.

"Uh . . . come on," Iole answered, walking toward the dancing redhead.

Approaching Alcie, Iole began to sing and Pandy quickly joined in:

Happy Maiden Day to you!
Happy Maiden Day to you!

Homer joined in, completely off-key, which made Iole and Pandy wince—but they didn't show it.

Happy Maiden Day, dear Alcie,
Happy Maiden Day to you!

Homer went on in a quick monotone finish: "IhopeyouenjoybeingwifeofHomerofCrisainfouror fiveyeeeeears!"

"I'msureIwiiiiiill!" Alcie giggled as she stopped whirling and took a celebratory bow, an insane grin plastered all over her face. "Thanks, guys. I know you forgot and it's fine. I almost forgot myself until Homer reminded me. I told him the date once, months ago, and he remembered!"

"We have no gifts," Pandy said, throwing her arms around Alcie.

"You'll owe me," Alcie said, hugging back hard, as Iole hugged them both.

"Okay," Pandy babbled, breaking apart after a long moment. "We have to get moving. We have to find the cave and get inside—and there's no cave!"

"There has to be," Iole said. "This is the spot."

Pandy crossed the fifteen or so meters of plateau and began to search at the edges of the gray semicircle of rock.

"It should be right here. This is an archway, but it's sealed up! There has to be a clue. A way in, somehow."

"I smell smoke," Alcie said, turning her nose to the east.

"Is there anything in the story of Orpheus that might help?" asked Pandy.

"Nothing," answered Iole, ignoring Alcie as she sniffed the air and walked slowly toward the edge of the plateau. "Only that when his wife Eurydice was bitten by a snake and died, he came to a cave on the side of this mountain and walked down into the underworld."

"Guys, I smell smoke."

"Maybe there's another entrance," Iole said, turning to her right and walking to one far side of the plateau.

"Anything?" Pandy called.

"Nothing," Iole said, hurrying back. "Just a long drop into darkness."

"Same on the opposite side," Homer said, joining them in front of the grayish rock.

"I'm seeing lights," Alcie said, standing at the edge of the plateau. "Guys, I got lights."

All at once, Dido began to bark ferociously at the gray semicircle. There was a squeal and a crunch of rock scraping against rock, and the gray stone that sealed the cave opening began to move, becoming almost liquid. Slowly it began to swirl outward from the center into a large spiral. Then that swirl broke into several smaller swirls, which wound back on themselves. Then a large hole appeared in the middle, surrounded by large, black stone hairs. The swirling slowed slightly, then stopped abruptly. Pandy, Iole, and Homer suddenly found themselves staring at a giant ear.

"Guys, I think the lights are getting closer."

"Three questions," said a voice that came out of nowhere.

"Look," Pandy said, discovering the source of the voice.

Above the stone ear, a little to the right, was a tiny stone mouth.

"Three questions," the mouth repeated. "Three to enter."

"Guys?" Alcie called, her voice thin above the wind.

"Homer . . . ," Pandy said.

"Yeah. I'll go see," Homer said, looking at the large earhole and backing toward Alcie.

"Are you ready?" the mouth asked.

"Ready," said Pandy.

"What is the color of flesh when it has rotted away?"

Pandy looked at Iole.

"Black?" she asked.

"Is that your final answer?" asked the mouth.

"No! Wait! We're thinking," Pandy yelled, the volume of her voice causing the ear hairs to shake.

Suddenly Iole snapped her fingers and whispered something to Pandy. Pandy nodded her head.

"There is no color," Pandy said. "When flesh is rotted away, there is no flesh, therefore, no color."

At once, the earhole expanded to twice its size.

"Uh," Homer said coming back from the edge. "Like, I think you may want to see this."

"Can't," Pandy said. "Iole's brain is getting us inside."

"What is the significance of yellow?" asked the mouth.

Iole's own mouth went slack and, a moment later, her shoulders dropped. She turned to Pandy and shook her head.

"I've got nothing," she said.

Pandy turned to look at the ear. This was the way down into the realm of death. The first question had been about death, so maybe all the questions would be related somehow. Yellow. Yellow? What was yellow? The sun that Apollo pulled. No, that was life-giving. The stuff she caught in her little brother's poop cloth. No, that was watery and gross and had nothing to do with death, except that she sometimes wanted to kill her mother for making her change Xander's underclothes. Yellow. And then there was that one time, just a few days before she'd found the box of evil and started this whole mess. Her mother had told her to clean up after Xander, and she ran out of the house only to find her father standing underneath his favorite fig tree, gathering a small pile of brown leaves and complaining about all the yellow ones yet to fall . . .

Yellow leaves.

"Uh!" Pandy started.

"Yes?" said the mouth.

"You have it?" Iole whispered.

Pandy nodded, sure that she was right—but how to phrase it?

"Yellow signifies—uh—the state of something—that is between life and death," she began, looking at Iole, who stared back with growing awe. "Such as a leaf. It—is green when it is attached—part of the tree. Which is alive. It is brown when it falls and is dead. When it is yellow, it's not part of the tree—anymore—but it's also not part of the—dead part, uh, place. It's not dead yet."

The earhole expanded again; now, it was just large enough for a small child to pass through. Pandy jumped up and punched the air with joy as Iole went to hug her.

"Brilliant."

"GUYS!" came Alcie's voice from the edge.

"The final question," said the mouth. "How will you die?"

"Whoa," said Homer softly.

Pandy was stunned into silence. Iole was so horrified that she grabbed Pandy's arm. Suddenly Alcie came racing up and took Iole's other hand, dragging her to the edge of the cliff. Iole was nearly there when she broke away from Alcie with a huff and started back to the ear and Pandy, who hadn't moved.

"No!" Alcie said, catching her again and pointing down into the night. "Look!"

Iole peered down the steep side of the tall mountain and, at first, didn't register the hundred or so single flames that formed a line stretching into the distance, nor did she really smell the smoke wafting upward. What shook her out of her amazement at Pandy's final question was the singing. Hearty singing, far away, but getting closer. Women's voices. Getting closer. On their way up.

And in a flash, she knew.

If there was one thing Iole could practically recite backward and forward, it was the stories of the ancients; one she particularly loved was the legend of Orpheus, especially since she'd had the pleasure of seeing him play "live" when they had all gone back in time to the wedding of Peleus and Thetis as she, Pandy, Alcie, and Homer were hunting for Lust.

Orpheus had sought to bring his wife back from the underworld and, because he'd found his way down and had plucked his lyre so skillfully, creating such beautiful music for Hades and Persephone, Hades had granted his wish with only one condition. As he walked back up to the top of the earth, Orpheus must not look to see if his wife was following. He must trust in the word of the dark lord of the underworld. Orpheus agreed. He was almost to the top, could see daylight, and then . . . he turned around, certain he'd been tricked and Eurydice wasn't there. Aghast, he watched as her form receded back down the path, a look of anguish and reproach on her beautiful face. In the silence he heard the single word, "Farewell."

Driven nearly mad, he avoided the company of all other humans, choosing to dwell in the forests, charming the birds and animals with his music. And that's where they found him—the Maenads. A group of women, followers of Dionysus, so frenzied, so crazed, so furious that no one could or would get near them. They would dance insanely and commit terrible acts of violence, including murdering each other. And the gods help any living creature they happened to find. They came upon Orpheus alone, sitting in front of the entrance to the cave not ten meters away from where Iole stood now, and tore him limb from limb. And, as the legend went, on the night of the full moon . . . they always came back.

Iole looked up at the incredibly large, pale full moon just emerging from behind the topmost peak of the mountain, then she stared down again at the moving line of flame, finally noticing the end of a narrow pathway that led down the side of the mountain into the darkness. A pathway she and the others *could* have used to ascend, and one the torchbearers were using now.

"Maenads," she whispered.

"C . . . Come again?" Alcie said, the biting wind on top of the mountain causing her teeth to chatter.

"*Maenads!*" she screamed. But the wind had stopped the moment she opened her mouth to cry out, so her scream echoed across the valley like the call of a great bird.

At once the singing stopped below, and in the next instant a great cry went up from the approaching women. Both Alcie and Iole saw the line of flames, bright torches, begin to move with incredible speed up the winding pathway.

"And now, thanks to me," Iole said, panicked, "they know we're here!"

"Pandy!" Alcie shouted. "*We've got company!*"

The two girls ran back to Pandy and Homer; the discovery of the approaching Maenads had taken only a few moments, but in that time Pandy had stood mute at the horrible question before her. Then she started fumbling again in her leather carrying pouch.

"What are you doing?" yelled Iole.

"The bust of Athena," Pandy mumbled. "It might help."

"You don't have time!" Iole cried. "Oh Gods!"

The earhole had begun to close, ever so slowly.

"Wait!" Pandy cried, stopping the closure briefly. "Would . . . would you repeat the question?"

The small stone mouth sighed in frustration.

"How will you die?"

"*What?*" yelled Alcie, who hadn't heard any of the questions.

"Pandy," Iole said, trying to keep her voice even, "we have Maenads coming up the side of the mountain. We need to either get back down the way we came or . . ."

"Shhhhhhh!" Pandy hissed, clenching her hands in front of her. Even she could hear the cries of the frenzied women, now only a few meters from the top. "I have to think!"

How would she die? Who in Hades knew? Only the Fates knew why, when, and from what that mortal part of her would finally perish. Maybe that was it! The question was a trick for her because she was semi-immortal!

No, the two previous questions had been meant for anyone to answer; this one was as well. No one could predict what his or her cause of death would be, why it would happen. But that wasn't the question, was it? It was bigger than that.

Pandy felt that "thing" happen to her brain again, even as the light from the Maenads' torches began to glow just below the end of the path.

"Not fair!" Alcie shouted at the mouth.

"Pandy!" Iole yelled. "Say something!"

But Pandy was feeling her mind expand. The question was "how." Not what would kill her, but *how* would she die.

A smile spread across her face and she turned away from the ear, clearly wanting to express her thoughts. Out of habit, Iole and Alcie both leaned in, each knowing that they were Pandy's closest confidants. But Pandy pulled on the front of Homer's cloak, causing him to bend down so she could whisper her answer. His eyes closed for an instant, then he nodded his head. She turned back to the ear . . . as the first of the Maenads hit the top of the ledge.

"With honor," Pandy said, almost defiantly.

Three maenads were hurtling themselves across the small plateau as the earhole grew large enough for a single person to enter. Immediately, Pandy grabbed Iole and shoved her through the opening, narrowly avoiding the sharp stone ear hairs, into the blackness beyond. Homer grabbed Alcie and pushed her through behind Iole.

"Ooooof!" came Alcie's voice as she landed on the other side.

"Ow!" said Alcie, pulling an ear hair out of her arm.

"Dido! Inside!" Pandy shouted. "Go!" she ordered when he hesitated, looking at her. "I'm right behind you!"

The snow-white dog leapt into the darkness.

"Now you!" Pandy commanded Homer. The first Maenad was only two meters away.

"As if!" Homer said, lifting Pandy off the ground and stuffing her into the earhole like he was an expert sausage maker. At once, Pandy found herself enclosed in darkness with only the moonlight shining through from the other side, two ear hairs caught in her cloak. Then, even that dim light disappeared as Homer tried to squeeze through. Suddenly, Pandy heard several hysterical human barks—echoed by Dido—from the plateau, and light shone through the earhole again as Homer was pulled back from the opening. The Maenads had hold of him and were beginning to drag him off. Homer screamed for a reason unknown—something that no one recalled ever having heard; Pandy's and Iole's blood ran cold. But Alcie was up in a flash. Throwing off her cloak, she reached through the earhole, and, seeming to Pandy to grow larger than normal, blocked the light completely. She latched on to Homer's arm just as it was disappearing from view.

"Take my Homie?" she screamed at the top of her lungs. "I don't *think* so!"

She pulled on his arm with such force that he was

violently jerked away from three Maenads, each of whom had an iron grip on him . . . one with her teeth buried deeply in his cheek. It didn't matter that his shoulders were really too small for the earhole; Alcie jerked him through with two rough tugs, shearing off many ear hairs. As Homer fell on the ground, two mae-nads appeared at the opening, one's face covered in blood, the flesh of Homer's cheek still in her mouth.

Alcie turned from her beloved Homer and rose up, her shoulders squared, her back straight, her eyes huge as platters; she broke off a sharp ear hair from the stone and slashed at the maenads, baring her teeth as if they were shaving razors, hissing and screaming like she were the leader of maenads herself.

The two maenads were so startled that they backed away, bumping into the group of crazed followers that had come up behind them. Alcie, feeling in complete control of herself and the situation, brought her arm down as if to signal the end of the fight . . .

. . . and the earhole closed, leaving Pandy, Alcie, Iole, Dido, and Homer in pitch black.

CHAPTER TWO
Turning Up the Heat

It was dark and silent inside. Alcie dropped the stone ear hair as she sank against the wall to the floor; everyone heard it shatter.

No one said a word for ages. The loudest noise was that of Dido, panting hard.

Finally, Alcie heaved a tremendous sigh.

"Okay. Well, I guess I have a few questions."

That one sentence, timed and phrased just right, made Pandy laugh so hard, she thought she might lose control of her bladder. Iole started laughing, and finally they heard Alcie join in, all laughing so hard that each one found herself lying on the ground, holding her stomach. Finally, they calmed down.

"Yes, Alce?" Pandy said. "What, exactly, would you like to know?"

And that started them off again; the muscles around Pandy's mouth were now getting a little sore from being stretched in laughter. When there was no more sound to be made by any of them, Pandy took hold of Alcie's arm.

"I *would* like to know, really, how you fought off those crazies and pulled Homer away from them."

"No idea," Alcie responded. "Had no idea I had that kind of strength. I just saw that Homer was in trouble and I knew it was up to me."

"It's not without precedent," Iole said, her voice loud in the blackness. "My mother and I were walking home from the agora in Athens a few years ago and we were passing a temple to Apollo that was under construction. Some sections of a pillar were being hoisted, and suddenly the rope snapped. The stones landed on top of a woman and her baby. The woman was thrown clear but everybody thought the baby had been crushed. Then we all heard the baby crying underneath the rubble. The workers tried to move the stones but they were all too weak. The mother became frantic and she, all by herself, threw off three big hunks of pillar until she uncovered her child. It was, in a word, wild. There are other similar stories . . . I've heard them. People discover hidden strengths in times of stress. I used to think it was the gods intervening . . . but now I'm just not sure. This mother didn't have the time or wits to appeal to any god. It was all her. Just like I think it was all you, Alcie; I'm not surprised."

"Thank you," Alcie said, the last of her involuntary laughs dying away. "I just saw my future being dragged off, and I wasn't going to let that happen. No band of loonies was going to keep me from being wife of Homer of Crisa—in four or so years, that is. Right, Homie?"

Silence.

"Oh Gods!" Alcie shrieked, her cries echoing around what was obviously a very small chamber. "Homie! Where are you? Homie, are you all right?"

From a space between Pandy and Alcie there was a soft grunt.

"Light," Iole said. "We need light."

"Duh!" Alcie yelled.

"I'm only asking if we have anything to burn."

"Oh. Homie, where's your hand . . . and your arm? There!"

Alcie moved her hand up to Homer's face and felt something sticky and wet coating her fingers. Homer whimpered and moved her hand away from his ravaged cheek.

"He's bleeding," she said, rolling clots of blood in the palm of her hand; her tone changing as emotion drained from her; announcing the fact as if she were saying that the day was cloudy. "Pandy, he's bleeding. There's a lot of blood."

Suddenly Dido was up, licking Homer's face, trying to clean the wound.

"Dido, no," Alcie said.

"Dido, yes!" Iole countered. "Dog saliva has many antiseptic properties. It'll be good for Homer."

"Dido, lick!" said Alcie.

"Go ahead, boy," Pandy urged, hearing the dog flop down to the ground as he cleaned Homer's face.

Frantically, Pandy took stock of everything they were carrying. Only one thing was capable of burning; she didn't want to give it up, but they needed light—to see Homer and to move forward. For the second time that day, she pulled the magic rope out of her carrying pouch.

"What are you doing?" Alcie asked.

"Quiet a sec," Pandy said, her mind weighing the options. This rope would do almost anything Pandy told it to: what if she told it *not* to do something? There was only one way to find out. With an end of the rope in one hand, she concentrated her power over fire into the forefinger of her other hand. As her finger began to instantly glow orange, then red, then whitish, Iole and Alcie were just able to make out the look of intense concentration on their friend's face.

"Rope," she said, touching the end of it to her white-hot finger, "flame, but don't burn!"

The rope caught fire and Pandy watched the slow creep of black work its way down from the end. Immediately, with her mind diverted to cooling her finger down,

Pandy thought she was watching the rope destroy itself and raised her hand to dash the flame on the floor.

"Wait!" Iole said. "Wait. It's slowing. I swear by Aphrodite, it's slowing, Pandy."

Sure enough, the rope was staying aflame, but only a small part was on fire and it was holding steady. The light was enough to illuminate Iole and Alcie, tangled in their robes, and Homer, lying against the wall of a tiny round room.

"Dido," Pandy said softly. "Move away."

Dido raised his white eyes to his mistress, his mouth ringed with red, and padded a short distance away. Bringing the light to Homer's face, they could all see that he was pale and his left cheek was still gushing. His flesh had been torn to the bone and several teeth were exposed. Alcie raised her hand again in a vain attempt to staunch the wound.

"Alcie, no," Iole said.

"I have to stop the blood," Alcie muttered.

"Not you, honey . . . Pandy."

"Me?"

"Your finger," Iole said, looking at Pandy. "You need to cauterize . . . to *seal* the wound. You can stop the blood."

At once, Pandy knew Iole was right. She felt revulsion at having to get anywhere near the horrible tear, but Homer would certainly die of blood loss and there was no way she was going to let that happen . . . especially now that he was engaged to be engaged to her best friend. Her finger was barely back to its normal color when her power heated it again and soon it was a glowing brand. She handed the burning rope to Iole.

"Ready, Homer?" she asked.

Homer reached for Alcie's hand.

"I'm right here," she said, holding his fingers tightly.

Homer closed his eyes and nodded.

The first touch of her finger to the exposed flesh made Homer jerk his head backward, knocking it into the wall. Alcie screamed; Iole threw her arms around Alcie and held her close as Dido whimpered. Then Homer tensed his whole body, clenched his jaw, and nodded his head again. Pandy slowly worked her finger around the edges of the entire wound, the searing flesh causing a horrible smell. Alcie began to sob, and Iole thought she was going to faint at the sickening stench. Homer didn't make a sound, but tears flooded down his cheek; when they hit Pandy's finger, there was a slight burst of steam. Alcie gripped Homer's hand like she was holding on to a life rope in the sea. At last, Pandy pulled her finger away and took the rope from Iole; holding it close to his cheek, they could see that there was no blood flow at all, but the wound was immense.

"I got it," she said, cooling her finger down again. "I got it all."

Homer lay still for a moment, then lifted his head.

"Is it as large as I think?" he slurred, ever so slowly.

The three girls looked at each other.

"Nope," Alcie said. "You'll be healed in a week. Never know it happened."

Homer looked at Iole.

"You won't lie to me out of love," he said, squeezing Alcie's hand gently as she looked at him. How did he know she'd lied to him?

"It's bad, Homer. It's very bad," Iole said. "I'm worried about infection."

"Okay," he said, cautiously relaxing all his muscles. "Now I know."

Dido let out a long whine.

"Go ahead, boy," Pandy said, knowing the mind of her dog.

Dido got up and padded back to again gingerly lick Homer's face.

Alcie took a spare toga from her carrying pouch and ripped many long strips from the bottom.

"This has been washed so many times; it's worn but it's clean," she said, gently moving Dido aside and wrapping the makeshift bandages around Homer's face to cover the wound. "When we get down to Hades' palace, Persephone will have something to put on it. Some sort of oogly-boogly potion or poultice or something. Homie, hold your head up . . . Homie?"

But Homer had slipped into unconsciousness.

"I'm surprised he lasted this long," Iole said. "I would have passed out when I saw Pandy's finger coming toward me."

"Well," Pandy said, "we can't move him and we can't move forward until he's awake."

"We gotta give him just a little bit, Pandy," Alcie said, cradling his head.

"Who were those insane she-dogs?" Pandy asked, then she held up her hand. "Wait a sec . . . rope, stay lit and hold yourself upright on the floor."

She placed the end of the rope on the floor and it stayed upright, flame burning brightly, the rope not burning at all.

"Okay, who were they?"

"Maenads," Iole said. "Followers of Dionysus and murderers of Orpheus. They come here once every full moon to reenact his death and dance around, hurting themselves and each other till they drop . . ."

Iole's voice drifted off, and Pandy and Alcie could see that Iole was concentrating intensely on something else. Her eyes drifted to Dido, his head resting on top of Homer's chest.

"Dogs," she mumbled. "Dog."

"Is she gone?" Alcie asked. "Have we officially lost the brains of the operation?"

"Iole?" Pandy said.

But Iole was recalling two other myths. One, the tale of Psyche and how her love for Eros as a youth had led her on this same path they now traveled. The second, the story of Aeneas, a young son of Aphrodite. His great adventure also led him into the underworld. Both had different experiences, but both had encountered one thing—one terrifying thing—that had forced them to think fast, acting only by their wits. She had read of how both had handled this terror and knew exactly what she had to do. Without warning, Iole began rifling through her carrying pouch.

"Great," Alcie said, looking down at Homer. "We have no brains and no . . . no . . . what's the word?"

"Brawn," Iole said, her nose buried deep in her pouch. "The word you're looking for is 'brawn,' and you haven't lost either of us. I need fruit. Athena's enchantment gives us all unlimited supplies of dried fruit and flatbread, but ever since my bag lost its magic in Persia, it only gives me incalculable quantities of dried apples and grapes. I need a variety."

"What in Artemis's name are you doing?" Pandy asked.

"You'll see. Fruit, please . . . you too, Alcie. I need figs and apricots . . . something very sweet. And I need a little water; my water-skin is nearly dry. Oh, and I need the map."

Alcie called to Dido, had him lie on his side, and gently placed Homer's head on the dog's tummy. Then she and Pandy handed over mounds of dried figs, plums, cherries, apricots, peaches, nectarines, and berries. Alcie handed her water-skin to Iole while Pandy gave her the blue bowl that was their map.

"Pandy, help me mince these pieces of fruit," Iole said rather forcefully, tearing the sticky morsels to bits. "Alcie, grab some flatbread and crush it into meal, the finer the better. Do it over the bowl."

As Alcie made flour of the bread, and Pandy continued shredding the fruit, Iole poured water from the skin into the bowl. When the bowl was full to the brim, Iole dug in her hands and began to mix and mash everything together. Suddenly she realized there was silence in the tiny chamber. She looked up and saw Pandy and Alcie staring at her as if she were as mad as a Maenad.

"I'm making a cake."

"Oh, Iole!" Alcie cried, genuinely touched. "That is *so* sweet! But really, I don't need it. You can make it up to me when we get back to Athens. Or—tell you what—you can give me an extra-big Maiden Day cake next year!"

"Iole," Pandy said, "we don't have the time for this. As soon as Homer wakes, we're gonna . . ."

"It's not *for* you," Iole heaved, glancing up at Alcie. "Okay . . . all mashed together into a heavy batter-y consistency. Good. I think."

Then she dumped the contents of the bowl onto the ground and formed the lump into a round cake.

"He won't mind a little dirt. Very well. Pandy . . . blow."

"Huh?

"It needs to bake. We need heat. You can bake it with your hands or your breath or your feet. Anything. Only, please, bake the cake."

"You're a—genius," Homer said quietly, still lying flat on the ground, his eyes closed. His words were labored but clear.

"Homie!" Alcie squealed. "You're awake!"

"Thank you, Homer," Iole said. Then realizing that Homer knew exactly what she was doing and why, she smiled. "You're not so bad yourself. Pandy . . . please?"

Pandy shook her head, clearly not understanding. But she filled her lungs to capacity and held her breath as she superheated the air inside her. She bent, getting close to the lumpy, mushy round and blew softly but steadily all around the cake.

"Oh, careful!" Iole said, wrapping her hands in her cloak to turn it. "Don't burn this side."

It took two more breaths to fully bake the cake to a golden brown. While it was cooling, the three girls

31

helped Homer to sit more comfortably; Alcie petted and patted him like he were made of glass. Homer felt himself growing more and more uneasy with all the attention; now that his wound has been treated he wanted the focus somewhere else.

"So, like, what's with the ear?" he asked.

"Yeah? No one's gonna tell me that Orpheus had to get through this," Alcie said, pounding on the rock where the earhole had been.

"It's not in the legend," said Iole.

"My guess," Pandy mused, "is that after Orpheus came back up and was killed, Hades put this in place to keep the Maenads—and anyone else who didn't have a really good reason—from getting in."

"You mean anyone who isn't clever enough to answer three obscure, obtuse, and obfuscatory questions," Iole remarked.

"Obviously," Alcie answered. "What you said."

Iole poked her finger into the top of the cake.

"Right then, cake's cooled," she announced, stowing it inside her pouch. "Hard on the outside, soft on the inside."

"And you're not going to tell us who it's for?" Pandy asked.

"Nope," Iole said, squeezing Homer's arm. "The brains and the—*brains* of the operation know. For now."

"Okay," said Pandy, rising to her feet but tamping

down her curiosity. "We'll play it your way, brains. So, we start moving."

"Agreed, provided Homer can move," Iole said.

"Homer can move," he said, picking himself up off the floor.

They moved toward a pitch-black opening in the chamber directly opposite the ear—the only space not illuminated by flame. Without any warning, they were descending on a fairly steep pathway.

"Stop," Pandy cried. "Rope, tie yourself around my waist and light at least one meter ahead and to the sides."

Instantly, they saw a rock wall to their left, a narrow path in front, and nothing to their right. There was only the black space of an abyss. Iole was closest to the edge; one more step and she would have plummeted into Zeus-only-knew-what. Pandy reached into her pouch and brought out a walnut. She tossed it into the darkness. No one heard it land.

"I think I'll walk over here," she said, falling behind Alcie and Dido.

"Nice going, P," Alcie said. "Good call."

"Blackness I can handle," Pandy said. "But that just looked *too* black."

CHAPTER THREE
They Met a Man...

They walked downward for what, to Pandy, seemed like a week. She knew, because they weren't actually in Hades' realm (and according to Alcie, time had no meaning in the underworld), that the day counter on the map was still operating. But how many days could have passed while they were walking? The flame at the end of the magic rope was still burning brightly, but there was no char . . . nothing to indicate any time passage at all. The right side of the path, which had started out as the edge of a bottomless abyss, had become a vertical wall of smooth rock that went up into the darkness, just like the opposite side. Pandy felt the walls closing in every once in a while, then forcefully willed herself not to be claustrophobic.

"We have to be getting close," she sighed during a momentary lull in the conversation during which Iole was trying to explain to Alcie why Socrates had decided to drink the hemlock while Alcie argued that the scholar was simply a doofus for not turning around and running at his first opportunity.

". . . because he was a dummy, that's how I see it!" Alcie was saying. "And yeah, I think you're right, P. I'll bet you a carob-covered mint-leaf oatie cake we've been walking for at least eight of the nine days it takes to get down to the underworld. But I'm just goin' by the blisters on my feet."

"No," said Homer, who'd been nearly silent during their walk—no one could blame him; talking with his left cheek gone wouldn't have been an easy prospect. But now he spoke up. "Not eight. Only three."

"You sure about that?" Pandy asked, stopping in her tracks, the flame on the end of the rope swinging in the air like a tiny lantern.

Homer nodded.

"But how can you be certain?" asked Iole.

"Because this is what my face feels like with a three-day-old beard—the right side of it anyway. I know exactly because every time I try to grow it, I can only last three days before I go nuts and have to shave—and I just realized I'm starting to go a little nuts. Also, I've had you change my wrappings once a day, Alce. And you just changed them a little while ago. Three changes, three days."

"My Homie's beard doesn't lie!"

"Brilliant," said Iole, her respect for Homer growing exponentially. "And that would mean that it's some time before midnight—and three twenty-four-hour periods have passed. So the day counter on the map would read seventeen days left. About to be sixteen. Flawless deduction. Nice going, Homer."

"That's my guy," Alcie said.

"Yeah, it's smart." Pandy sighed again, slumping against the rock wall. "But that means six more days of walking. I'm gonna have ten days to find Fear."

"I'll take the lead," Homer said, moving forward.

"But I have the light," Pandy countered. "You can't see where you're . . ."

"Shouldn't be a problem. The path has only gone straight down, no twists or . . ."

Thump!

At that instant, Homer smacked his forehead into something hard and fell backward, landing at their feet, again completely unconscious. As Alcie rushed to Homer, Pandy held up the flaming end of the rope and saw a smooth, rounded wall. A dead end.

Suddenly, from the other side of the wall, Pandy, Alcie, and Iole heard a voice.

"Stop! No! Oh, seriously? Seriously? NO!"

And then the curved wall began to move backward; Pandy realized it was rolling. It was a giant stone, perfectly round.

"Aw, c'mon!" said the voice. "NOOOOOOOO! No . . . nupf . . . pffff."

There was silence as the stone picked up speed and rolled away, down into the darkness.

"Alcie, stay with Homer. Dido, *sit*. Iole?"

"Right with you."

The two girls moved farther down the path, the stone gone but the grinding sound it made as it scraped the walls echoing all around them as it faded. They had only walked perhaps two meters; Pandy took her next step forward . . .

"Oooof!"

Pandy jumped backward and held her flame higher.

"Not up there. Down here, silly."

Bending to the ground, Pandy and Iole saw first the legs, then torso, then arms and head of a man completely flattened into the dirt. It reminded Pandy of Sabina's tart crust after the old house slave had mashed and thinned it out with her rolling stone. But as the girls watched and Dido barked, the man's lips plumped back into fullness with a tiny audible *pop*, then his cheeks puffed out with two bigger *pops*, then his chest—*pop*—arms, legs—*pop pop*—and so forth until finally, after sounding like corn popping in a pan on a fire, his belly rose up with a *boing* and he was fully fleshed out.

"That always hurts. And I'm always surprised just

how much that hurts." He sighed. "Okay, a little help getting up maybe? Don't need any help from the dog, thanks—but girls? Maidens? A little help?"

Pandy began to extend her arm, but Iole held her back.

"We don't know who—or what—this is!" she said.

"Oh, seriously?" the man said, raising his head a little. " '*What*'? You call me a '*what*'? I know I haven't seen myself in a glass for ages, but when I was alive I was accounted as a rather handsome fellow. Nothing to frighten anyone, at any rate. C'mon! Look, I know I just got the big smasheroo by my stone and it might be a little disconcerting to see me still talking and all, but if you help me, I could put in a good word for you with some very high-ups below. I know people—gods even."

"Your stone?" Iole said.

"Yeah, my stone, oh, she-who-is-hard-of-hearing. My little burden. My little curse. I've been pushing that baby up the same stupid hill for I don't know how long now. I'm even thinking about giving her a name; something short—like Sue or Sal. Sal Stone—the one that always gets away."

As Pandy and Iole each realized with a jolt exactly who they were talking to, Alcie and Homer walked up; a nice bump was forming on Homer's forehead.

"Who's this?" Alcie asked.

"Sisyphus," Iole and Pandy answered together.

"No way!" Homer said.

"Ta-da!" Sisyphus said, raising himself up on his elbows. "In the flesh! Kinda."

"The guy who was punished in death by always having to roll a big rock up a hill . . . ?" Alcie began.

". . . only to have it roll back on me whenever I get close to the top," Sisyphus finished. "Yes, and thank you, Miss Rub-It-In. But let that be a lesson to you, young ones: when Zeus tells you to keep a secret, best to keep those hummus-holes closed! It's all I'm sayin'."

"But the entrance to the underworld is six days away," Pandy said. "How did you escape?"

"Yeah? Figs!" Alcie exclaimed, forgetting her promise not to swear. "What are you doing up *here*?"

"Are you kidding? It's complete chaos down there, you'll pardon the pun. The gates of Hades were wide open. Cerberus was busy chasing other spirits who're trying to leave, and Charon was napping by the Styx. So it was a very simple matter to roll old Sue onto his boat and ferry myself across the river. Nearly sank that rickety pile of wood, but I made it. I got the Hades out of Hades."

"Something's really wrong down there," Pandy said.

"Yeah, well, if you all hadn't been standing in my way, that *wrong* coulda been my *right*," Sisyphus said. "And now if you'll pardon me, I gotta go find my rock."

He started off down the path toward the underworld, then he turned back.

"Just outta sheer curiosity," he said, "how far away am I? Y'know—from the top? From fresh air—and living trees—and pretty . . . people. How far?"

"Three days," Alcie answered.

Sisyphus heaved an enormous sigh.

"Three days from a clean getaway. Ach—maybe next time."

He turned and strode quickly downward, following his stone into the blackness. Amazed, Pandy, Alcie, Iole, and Homer looked at each other.

"Well, *he's* creepy!" Alcie said at last. "Reminds me of those men who used to visit the house a few days after the Olympiads if my father lost a wager."

"I concur," Iole said. "But it's what he said that concerns me."

"The gates are open and it's crazy inside," Pandy said. "What do you think has happened?"

"No idea," Iole said.

Alcie took a step down toward the underworld, then thought better of it when she remembered that Pandy had the flame. She stood aside as Pandy moved forward.

"Lemons!" Alcie said, fully aware that she'd just uttered a swear word. "We better get our backsides down there and find out!"

CHAPTER FOUR

Swimming in the Styx

The flame at the end of the rope had grown much smaller—evidence that the air around them was becoming thick with death. Evidence that they were getting closer to the end of the path. Six more times Alcie had changed Homer's wrappings and six more times she, Pandy, and Iole had looked, with sinking hearts, at the wound. Even though Pandy had cauterized the flesh surrounding the gaping hole, even though they had tried to keep it clean and covered; certain sections were now black, as if the flesh was dying ("rotting away," Pandy remembered from the first question of the gate-keeping ear), and other sections were oozing a greenish-white gooey substance. Dido had stopped licking days earlier and no one blamed him. No one had said a word to Homer, but he knew something was terribly wrong; he'd resisted the urge to touch his cheek to find out for himself how bad it was. Over the last two days, he'd grown silent and pensive; even Alcie knew better than to try to jolly him out of his depression and pain. Then, somewhere in the middle of their ninth day walking, Iole's legs simply gave out. Walking beside Pandy, she groaned as her legs buckled from underneath her. She sat in the middle of the path and started crying.

"I can't take another step," she sobbed, laying her head on Dido as he sat next to her. "I'm so sorry, Pandy. My legs . . . they're numb. Can't we just rest for a moment?"

Pandy was about to sit down next to Iole and give her a big hug. Once again, Pandy realized how much her friends were sacrificing, how much was being asked of them, and how great their efforts were—and all to help her. Before she could sit, however, Homer swiftly scooped Iole up and onto his shoulders. That single act of selflessness, knowing he was already in agony, made Alcie weep, which in turn made Pandy cry. At last, Dido began to howl. They continued along the path—the only one not bawling was Homer.

Then—only a short time later and without any warning—the flame flared up, growing twice as bright as it had been, as a very soft breeze blew across their faces and they heard the unmistakable sound of rushing water. Up ahead, the blackness was pierced by a dim light.

They emerged from between the rock walls of the path and out onto a long, shallow beach bordered by a flowing river. It *did* seem as if there were a sky over-head; Pandy could swear she saw the faintest hint of clouds against the night. She knew they were thousands of meters underground, yet the terrain was the same as it was topside: rocks, a river, scrubby bushes, a beach, cliffs—only completely lacking color. On the opposite shore, they saw a huge, black wall with an enormous gate lit by four blazing sconces, each one as big as Sisyphus's stone.

"Rope," Pandy said, as Homer set Iole on the ground, "thank you for your service. No more flame."

The rope extinguished itself without even a puff of smoke, and Pandy tucked it neatly away in her carrying pouch.

"Ah, I remember this all so fondly. Not!" Alcie said, then she pointed to a rather rocky section of the beach. "Right over there—that pile of rocks? That's where I regained *el conscioso* right after Hera killed me. Hey, where's Cap'n Charon?"

"Look!" Iole said, pointing.

Farther up, they all saw two other mighty rivers flowing into the one that lay before them.

"One is the Acheron, the river of woe," said Iole, almost reverently. "And the other is the Cocytus, the river of lamentation."

"Did *not* know that when I was here before, but then, I was having too much fun. Fun, fun times," said Alcie sarcastically. "Where's Charon? Where's the boat bully, I wanna know."

"And this . . . this is the Styx," Iole said in awe, looking at the flowing water only three meters away. "Pandy—it's the *Styx*. We've seen some amazing things—but this! Into this river Thetis dipped her son, Achilles—whom you will all remember *I* helped her to name—to make him invulnerable; holding him by his heel so that *that* was the only place on his body where he could be killed. The Styx is *that* powerful. This is the river of unbreakable oath by which the gods themselves swear! If Zeus himself made a promise and swore by this river, even he couldn't break it no matter what it was."

"Well," Pandy sighed, "he didn't. Not to me, anyway. All right, those are the gates to Hades. And they're wide open, just as Sisyphus said. Now how do we get across?"

"Where's Charon?" Alcie said, scanning the river. "He's not here, he's not on the river, and his boat's gone."

"Maybe he escaped?" asked Homer.

"Don't think so," Pandy said. "We didn't meet anyone else on the path. The dead just get 'sent' here, but humans and any spirit who leaves—like Eurydice—have to take the path. I think."

"Most times, you bet," said Alcie, remembering how, when she'd left the underworld before, Hades had actually materialized her into a tree in Baghdad.

"And speaking of the dead, where are they?" Iole asked.

"Huh?" Alcie started.

"This shore, according to every legend I've ever studied, is always crowded with the dead, waiting to be ferried across. There are stories that say some spirits, those who weren't buried properly with coins on their eyes to pay Charon, or those with not enough of a payment, are forced to wander this beach for eternity. But I see no one."

"Iole's right, Pandy," Alcie said. "I don't see dead people."

"That's because they're all out there," Pandy answered.

Alcie, Iole, and Homer followed her gaze.

Even in the pale light of the sconces, they could now see that the Styx was full of various shades and transparent forms; some swimming, some floating—all trying for the far shore. Pandy saw a few shades actually drag themselves out of the water, but as they watched, it became clear that the current was too much for most, and hundreds of spirits were being towed underwater and downriver—wherever it went.

All of a sudden, Alcie's arm shot out.

"There!" she cried. "Charon!"

Alcie was pointing toward an impossibly thin man stomping about at the water's edge on the opposite beach. His boat was nowhere to be seen, but he still had ahold of the long pole he used to steer, push, and pull the ferry across the river. At the moment, he was trying to drive the dead who'd managed to get across the Styx back into the river if they didn't have the proper payment.

"Oh, yeah, you deranged old hydra," Alcie said acidly. "I'd know you anywhere. *That's* how he treated *me* until I bopped him one."

As Homer and the girls watched, one spirit, on the verge of dragging itself out of the water while being poked with the pole, grabbed the other end and forcefully pulled a very surprised Charon back into the Styx. The spirit, after standing on the shore, conked Charon on the head with his very pole—then tossed it into the river, where it got caught in the shallows.

"Score one for the dead guy!" Alcie said with a whoop.

"We still have a problem," Pandy said.

"How do we get across?" said Iole, finishing Pandy's thought.

"Same as them," Homer said. "Come on."

As he headed toward the water's edge, Alcie caught him.

"Hang on, handsome."

"Homer, this is the Styx and we don't know what could . . . ," Iole began.

"I get it, Iole. Okay? I do," he said, cutting her off. "But while you all have been watching the ferryman, I

46

have been assessing the options. That's what I trained—
for a few moons, anyway—in gladiator school to do when
faced with a no-win situation. Here, there's only one
way. There's no boat and no bridge. The water's not hurting the spirits, and we have no choice."

Pandy looked at Alcie and Iole. After a moment, she
shrugged.

"When Homer's right, he's right."

"Just try to keep your head above water," he cautioned. "Y'know, just in case. And don't drink any of it."

"As if!" said Alcie.

Pandy went to step into the river first, but Homer
gently pulled her back.

"I'm leading this," he said forcefully. "Iole, you're
behind me, then Pandy and Alcie will bring up the rear.
She's just a little stronger than you, Pandy, and we need
our anchors on each end. Everyone, hold hands."

Homer stepped into the mighty Styx and everyone
immediately looked at his face to see if there was a
change—any pain—anything.

"It's fine," he announced. "A little warm actually. Stay
against me if you can; I'll try to block the current . . . and
the bodies."

"Dido, come!" Pandy called as Dido began to bark,
running to the water's edge and then backing off.

"Oh, he's not liking this one bit," Pandy said. "Come
on, boy. Follow us."

All at once, Dido's gaze became focused intently on the river—at least that's what Pandy thought; she couldn't really see his irises in the dim light. It was as if he was calculating something very tricky.

"What's he . . . ?" Alcie began.

Then, without warning, Dido ran headlong toward the river. But instead of landing in the water, each paw landed on top of a spirit body floating by. Dido raced across the Styx as if he were following a path of stepping stones, making certain to lift his paw off before the spirit went underwater. Within moments, he was on the opposite shore, barking triumphantly.

"Youths and maidens," Pandy said when she could talk again after being stunned into silence, "I give you— *my dog*!"

"What a performance!" Alcie crowed. "He could do two shows a night with Wang Chun Lo."

"Okay," Homer said. "He can do it, we can do it."

They waded out into the flowing water—it was warm, very warm—and found they could stand. At its deepest point, Pandy could just touch the river bottom with her big toe. Halfway across, Iole thought she had a firm footing on a rock, but her foot slipped on the slimy surface, and her head went under.

"Iole!" Pandy cried as she and Homer lifted Iole's head out of the water. "Did you swallow any of it?"

Iole blinked and shook her head.

"I'm fine!" She smiled. "Moving on!"

Pandy smiled back—but in that moment, she noticed that the firelight from the sconces stopped glinting off of Iole's hair. Iole's long black hair was now fully soaked—and dull; as if someone had coated it with cold sheep's fat. They were nearly on the opposite shore when she felt Alcie go under—then pop back up.

"Here!" Alcie said. "I'm right here."

Finally, Homer stepped up and onto the riverbank and hauled Iole next to him. Pandy found her own footing, then crawled the rest of the way onto the soft dirt as Homer lifted Alcie up and out of the Styx with one arm. After only a moment, Pandy got to her feet. She looked at the forbidding black gates, tall and seemingly covered in a dark pitch—and open.

"Okay," she said, turning back to her friends. "No time to lose. It looks like . . ."

Then her voice faltered.

Alcie's eyes were huge and Homer's mouth was agape. They were staring at her with the same look, she was certain, of shock and disbelief that was on her own face as she looked at them.

Alcie's skin from face to toe was the color and shine of copper. Her reddish hair now actually *was* copper, the curls and waves made of a thin copper wire. Homer's hair was still blond, but his skin had taken on a blackish-blue sheen—as if he was covered in iron.

Pandy looked at her own hands, arms, and legs; they were a deep, rich bronze that glinted in the firelight. It was only after they realized that each of them was shining like metal did they look at . . .

Iole.

She wasn't standing slack-jawed, as they were. She wasn't examining every inch of her skin as they'd begun to do; she didn't even register surprise. She looked from one to the next, her eyes rather vacant and her skin dull. Iole definitely wasn't shining. In fact, she looked like she'd been covered in gray chalk.

"What in the underworld happened to us?" Alcie said, looking at the fine copper hairs coming out of her forearm.

Without thinking, Pandy looked at Iole, who she knew would have some sort of answer. But Iole just gazed back at Pandy as if the question hadn't even been asked. To her amazement, Pandy didn't panic; she just began to deduce.

"It's the Styx," she said. "It has to be. We went in, we were fine. We came out and . . . this."

"Like Achilles," said Homer.

"Exactly!" said Alcie.

"But not exactly," Pandy countered. "His mother, Thetis, just held him by the ankle and dipped him in for, like, a second. That's what made him invulnerable everywhere but his heel. But we were in there for . . . what?"

"A lot longer," said Iole.

"Arrows would bounce off Achilles like his skin were made of metal," said Homer.

" 'Like' it were metal," Pandy said. "Only our skin *is* metal! Great Zeus, I'm *bronze*!"

"But I can still pinch my flesh," Alcie said, grabbing the skin between her thumb and forefinger.

"Then it must mean we only have some sort of metal coating," Pandy answered.

"Is it going to make us sick? Will it ever come off?" Alcie asked. "Are we going to stiffen up like boards? Are we gonna die?"

"Alcie, calm down," Pandy said. "If it didn't hurt Achilles, I don't think it's gonna hurt us. Besides, there's nothing we can do about it right now."

"Why isn't anyone else affected?" Homer asked, looking at the spirit bodies floating in the Styx.

Before anyone else could think of an answer, Iole shuffled her feet.

"They're dead. We're not."

"But why do we all look different?" Alcie asked. "Why aren't we all the same metal?"

"It just picked what we were most like," Iole said matter-of-factly.

"*What?*" Alcie cried.

"She's right," Homer said. "I'm iron—because of my strength."

Pandy had stopped paying attention to their predicament and was, instead, focusing on Iole—and why she was using such short, simple phrases. It was completely unlike her.

And it was at this precise moment that Charon ran up on his skeletal legs, brandishing his pole—which he'd fished out of the water—and swinging wildly, trying to force the foursome back into the Styx. With one hand, Homer lifted the frail ferryman by the waist and threw him into the middle of the river.

"Okay," he said, after a pause. "But you know I could have done that even before I was covered in iron."

"The metal relates to our strongest trait. Alcie, you're copper because . . . because . . . ," Pandy started.

"What?" Alcie snapped. "Because I conduct heat well over an open flame? That would be *you*, Pandy!"

"No," Pandy said. "But you're close. Because you're fiery. And quick tempered."

"I AM not!" Alcie yelled. Then she closed her mouth. "Okay, you're right. But what about my hair?"

"Wet," Iole said.

"You slipped and went under," Pandy said, with a sideways glance at Iole. "Your hair got wet."

"Oh. Yeah. So why are you bronze?"

"I have no idea."

"Because you're a combination," Homer answered. "You're a rare mixture, Pandy: mortal and immortal."

Alcie and Pandy stared at him.

"It's my best guess."

Suddenly, Alcie shrieked.

"Homie! Your face! Your cheek—it's perfect!"

Homer reached up, touched his cheek, and felt nothing but smoothness. His skin was cool and a little hard, but his iron-coated flesh was nicely healed.

"Well, that's a groovy bonus," he said. "Guess I won't be spilling food out of my face every time I chew."

Out of nowhere, Dido padded up and put his forepaws on Pandy's waist.

"Hey, ghost dog," she said, kissing his face. "You didn't get wet, did you? Huh, boy? No metal for you, right?"

Then she saw the gold specks glinting off his paws.

"Look," Pandy said. "If he'd gone all the way into the water, I'd have a golden dog."

Then everyone turned to Iole; her skin gray, her hair dull.

"Gods," Alcie said softly.

"She's lead," Pandy muttered, the terrible certainty dawning on her. "Iole is lead."

"But that makes absolutely no sense," Alcie said, her voice rising again. "*She*'s the smartest! *She*'s the brightest! *She* should be gold! Her brain is the size of the Aegean Sea! It's dense, like my mother's lamb stew! It's thick! It's . . ."

"Heavy," Pandy said. "It's thick and dense and heavy.

And Iole went underwater too, remember. The power of the Styx came into contact with Iole's brain—which is the most important part of her—and probably didn't know what to do with it. It's so dense, it thought her brain was lead."

"And now," Alcie said with a gulp, "it is."

"No, it's not," Pandy countered. "She just has a dull lead coating. Her brain is fine. It's just buried. We'll fix it. I don't know how, but we'll fix all of this."

Iole looked from Pandy to Alcie to Homer. In the darkest corner of her brain, a tiny voice was screaming at all of them. Screaming that she knew exactly what they were saying; that she had every word she'd ever learned right on the tip of her tongue, but somehow she couldn't get her tongue to work. To Iole, it was as if she were sitting alone in a chair in a small room with a single candle; every piece of knowledge she'd had was written on tiny pieces of parchment, scattered about her on the floor. And outside was the cold, black, terrifying emptiness of the entire universe.

CHAPTER FIVE

Good Dog

"What are we gonna do?" Alcie asked Pandy quietly as they walked ahead of Homer and Iole toward the massive gates of the underworld. Dido, as if he could sense something wrong, was trotting alongside Iole.

"About what?" said Pandy, focusing more on the ooze that covered the gates from top to bottom. At first, she thought it was pitch or mold or slime. Now, she was certain it was blood.

"About our simpleton?" Alcie said.

Pandy stopped dead in her tracks and whipped her head around to stare at Alcie. Alcie had a half smile on her face and Pandy knew instantly that Alcie was just as scared as she was about Iole's condition, and she was putting on what she thought was a brave face, making a ridiculous joke. But in that second, Pandy didn't care that Alcie was frightened and wasn't about to tolerate any jokes at Iole's expense. It didn't matter, at that moment, that she knew there was no real malice in Alcie's heart. She, herself, was beyond scared at Iole's condition—at the condition of them all—and she snapped. She searched her own brain for the cruelest, most hurtful comeback she could think of. Then she put her hands on her hips, just the way she'd seen the mean girls back at the Athena Maiden Middle School do before they delivered a devastating barb.

"I don't know what to do about 'our simpleton,' Alcie," she said, making sure that Alcie was the only one who could hear her. "You're the one who likes him so much!"

Alcie was so stunned that her right knee actually buckled; every ounce of humor, wit, and sass drained right out of her.

"I wasn't talking about . . . ," Alcie whispered. "I didn't . . . I didn't mean to be . . ."

The next instant she burst into tears. Pandy was aghast at her own words and threw her arms around Alcie.

"I'm sorry. I'm sorry. I'm sorry," she cried, beginning to sob into Alcie's hair, feeling the copper wires press into her cheek. "I know you didn't mean it. I didn't mean it either. Homer's wonderful; you know I think that. But I don't *know* what to do about Iole—or any of us."

Homer, not having heard any of this, but for reasons

he couldn't say, slowed Iole's gait and let Pandy and Alcie have a moment.

"*I'm* sorry," Alcie sobbed. "I don't know where that came from."

"It's the same reason we laugh when something, anything is really awful," Pandy said. "It's like we need relief."

"Wow," Alcie said, finally stifling her cries. "What *you* said—that was really good. That was worthy of Helen and Hippia."

"Somehow," Pandy said, remembering the two most horrible girls at school, before they'd been changed into legless black salamanders, "that doesn't make me feel better."

"Well, I'll tell you how I feel," Alcie said, walking over to Iole and wrapping her in her arms. "I feel less like copper and more like glass. Very, very fragile. Iole . . . I love you."

"I love you too," Iole said with a smile.

Suddenly, they heard a mad, incessant barking in the distance beyond the gate. Then a second bark— another dog—joined in, and then a third. Three distinct and ferocious barks, all yelping at once and all getting closer.

Looking down the road, which led off beyond the gates and into the underworld, Pandy could see only a fine mist concealing nearly everything.

"Cerberus!" she cried.

Dido took off at a run; Pandy knew her dog wouldn't stand a chance against what lay ahead.

"DIDO, COME BACK HERE NOW!" she screamed with all the force she could muster. Dido stopped and gave a quick glance back to his mistress.

"HERE. NOW!"

Dido ran back to Pandy. Thinking fast, she fished the magic rope out of her pouch.

"Rope," she commanded, "hold Dido *here*."

The rope moved so fast, no one actually saw it. The next instant, Dido was bound, twitching but immobilized—including his jaws—a good distance from the gate and the approaching terror. Instinctively, Pandy looked for a place to hide them all. But Iole stepped toward the gate.

"I have something for this," she said. "Don't I?"

Without warning, a black shape bounded out of the mist and tore straight for them. Homer shoved Iole aside just as three black snarling dog heads—attached to a single enormous body—flew out of the gates, heading directly for Iole's throat. Homer raised his iron fist and swiped hard at the heads. He sent two off in one direction unfazed, but the third head managed to land a bite on Homer's right thigh. Then, there was a sickening shriek and the entire beast sprang back as if it had been mortally wounded. Homer looked down and saw a deep bite mark in his leg, but there was no blood and no pain. There were, however, two huge canine teeth sticking out of the wound.

Cerberus's three heads began to howl as his whole body felt the pain and spun in wild, thrashing circles; then he flopped on the ground and covered his injured mouth with his paws, trying to rub away the agony of his missing teeth.

Homer had been standing stock-still, but when he took a step forward, Cerberus leapt to his feet again, his two undamaged heads snapping and snarling. He paced back and forth toward Homer.

"Well," Alcie said at last, "you three could get by him all right. But copper dents really easily. I threw a cooking pot across a room once when I was little; looked like a piece of flatbread."

"I have something for this," Iole said, her brow furrowing. In that tiny, dimly lit room in her brain, a shard of parchment blew up off the floor and danced in front of Iole's face. Written on it: *feed the dog*. In her mind, Iole snatched it out of the air and ran to the doorway. But she was surrounded by space. Staring into the void, she realized that what she'd taken for inky blackness was really a dark, dull gray—the color of lead, or a brain. But it didn't matter. She was buried in the deepest crevice of her mind: there was no way this bit of a memory could get free on its own and work its way to the surface.

"Iole," Pandy said. "The cake? Did you bake the cake for Cerberus?"

"I did!" Iole cried, breaking out into a smile. "That's who I made it for!"

She pulled the dried-fruit cake out of her carrying pouch and broke it into three parts. She began walking toward the barking, whimpering dog.

"Let me," said Homer.

"No," Iole said, skirting around him. "I baked it; I can give it to him."

She tossed a morsel of cake onto the ground in front of the injured head. Bending down to lick it, the one head forced the whole creature to lie on the ground.

"Go!" she said, turning to the others and nodding her head toward the gates.

"Pandy?" Alcie asked, her voice shaky.

"She knows what she's doing. She's still Iole, Alce—somewhere down deep. Rope!" Pandy called. "Lead Dido behind us."

As Pandy, Alcie, Homer, and a struggling Dido skirted by, Iole steadily approached the dog, her hands outstretched to the two heads with their full sets of teeth bared, lips twitching and curling.

"Good dog," she said. "Look what I have for you. So yummy!"

The two heads began to sniff the air, catching the scent of the cake. Each stopped snarling and began to pant with anticipation. Iole was now within striking distance of Cerberus, but instead the two heads gently took the pieces of cake from her hands and started to munch. As Iole sidestepped toward the gate, one head turned to watch her; it would have started to bark again, but couldn't because of the dried fruit stuck to the roof of its mouth.

Suddenly, from above, a large chain was draped swiftly but gently over the three heads and fastened snuggly around the creature's neck with a fat, adamant lock. Iole caught the scent of roses and lavender and looked up to see a beautiful young woman dressed in shades of gray with luminescent flecks of pink and fuchsia.

"Hi!" the woman whispered. "You're Iole, right?"

"Right."

"Hiiiii! You're the one I haven't formally met yet," the woman said, then she turned back to Cerberus, fastening the end of the chain to a hook on the gate. "Oh, I *hate* doing that! We usually never have to chain him up. Isn't that right, Cerby? Such a good doggy!"

All three of Cerberus's heads were now too busy trying to get the dried fruit off their tongues to pay attention. The woman bent down and patted his head lovingly.

"This will only be for a little while, I promise," she purred to the creature. Then she stood and, with the biggest smile possible, enveloped Iole in a tremendous hug. "I just feel as if I know you already! When Alcie was here, well, she practically did nothing but talk all about you! How smart you are. How you come up with words that she's sure don't even exist, but you make them sound so wonderful!"

Then the beautiful woman bent down and whispered conspiratorially.

"How she wishes she were more like *you*!"

"Okay," Iole said, loving the smell of lavender coming off the woman's hair.

"I *know*, right! As if she isn't completely fabulous just as she is. It's crazy, I know! So . . . hi . . . I'm Persephone, but you're such a biggie-brain, you probably already knew that."

There was a blank look on Iole's face that made Persephone stop talking, utterly confused. Persephone giggled after an uncomfortable moment of silence. Then she sighed and looked off after Pandy and the rest, her mind placing names with the faces of the others.

"You *are* Iole . . . right?"

"Yes."

"And you're the genius," she said, then paused. "Right?"

"Okay."

"Hmmm," Persephone said under her breath. "Not really seeing it. Yes, well, the others are over here. Let's . . . um . . . let's go to them. Now. Wow."

With Iole following, Persephone crossed quickly behind the gate to where Pandy, Alcie, Homer, and Dido were patiently waiting. Without any formal show of respect, Alcie ran to Persephone and threw her arms around the goddess.

"Hi, honey," Persephone said, although her tone betrayed a bit of urgency, as if she wanted to be welcoming but had suddenly realized she was needed elsewhere.

"Hiiiiiiiiiiiiiii," Alcie answered.

"Hey, cutie," Persephone said, hugging Pandy. "Fancy meeting you here in the Fields of Asphodel. How's the shoulder?"

"Fine. I have the Eye of Horus around my neck and it's almost completely . . . ," Pandy began, then stopped. "How did you know about my shoulder? Were you there when the Apollos healed me in Rome?"

"*They* healed you?" Persephone snorted. "I *so* don't think so. Uncle Apollo is good with hangnails and things like that. But your spirit was teetering on the brink of life and death. You needed *me*! Me and Proserpine, that is. We just brought you a little hope in the darkness. Just a little healing touch."

"Hope is still in the box," Iole said.

"Uh, *yes*. That's *right*. Very GOOD," Persephone said, her voice getting louder with each word as if she were talking to someone who was deaf. Then she turned back to Pandy. "But there's a little hope that always comes with springtime, and that's where I come in—box or not. Is she really the *smart* one? I mean, I was kinda expecting Aristotle in girl form. Anyway, I must dash off—Alcie, why is your hair crinkly?"

"Because it's made of copper."

"We have a little problem," Pandy said.

"You think you have problems!" Persephone cried. "You have *no idea* what's going on around here. Cerberus was deliberately lured away from the gate. There are non-heroes wandering the Elysian Fields. No one is guarding Tartarus. Most of the punished have just been able to walk away from whatever torment they'd been cursed with. I think Charon's boat is sunk. And it's all Hera's fault. She's here—I think Mom's with her—and she's turning the underworld upside down, you'll pardon the pun. I'm running around like crazy trying to right all the wrongs, but I can only be in so many places at once. Wait! If Charon's boat is sunk, how did you all get across the Styx?"

"That's the problem," Alcie said. "We swam and . . ."

"*Stop!* Stop right there! You *what?* You went in the water?"

"We had to," Iole said.

"*From one side to the other?*" Persephone croaked. Then she looked hard at each of them. "Alcie, your hair *is* copper."

"I know."

"I KNOW!" Persephone yelled. "Pandy, your skin is bronze. Homer—what are you? You're black—no—you're blue!"

"Iron."

"But—but—you all feel nice and fleshy and human to hug," Persephone said, now way beyond confused. "A little cool, maybe."

"We seem to be fine," Pandy said. "We think the Styx just brought out our strongest traits and gave us a metal coating."

"But Iole's brain . . . it's lead," Alcie whispered.

"No way!"

"Well, it's got a lead coating," she countered. "At least we think so."

"Iole's still in there," Pandy said. "It's like she's fighting to remember everything she knows. She baked a cake to distract Cerberus before we crossed the river and she was fighting to remember to give it to him."

It was then that Persephone did something highly unusual. She stopped talking and focused. She circled and stared at Iole like she was a puzzle, and Persephone knew she alone had the missing piece. Iole just looked bewildered.

"Perseph . . . ," Pandy began.

"Quiet," Persephone whispered. "Thinking. Many thoughts. Takes work. Need quiet."

"Sorr—" Pandy said.

"Okay, I'm done," Persephone cried, waving her hands wildly as she cut Pandy off again. She looked around as if someone unseen might be watching. "Oh, Buster will probably have my head for this. Yes, I can grow a new one, but so not the point. All right . . . memory troubles, huh? A coated brain? Well, gods know, I've got a thousand things to do, but first we're gonna get the little lady a drink. Great Zeus, I hope this works. C'mon!"

CHAPTER SIX

Lethe

Persephone began walking down the main road into the underworld with such speed that soon she was almost out of sight, with Alcie hollering for her to please wait. The rest of the group could not match the step of her long goddess legs, and several times she outstripped everyone, including Dido, who'd been unbound as soon as the gates were out of sight. Pandy and Alcie had to keep calling for her to return, until she finally decided to simply float alongside the group.

"Walking slowly bores the undergarments off me." Persephone yawned. "But you mortals all just take your time."

"Rude," said Iole.

"Now, uh . . . now, Persephone," Alcie called up to the goddess, hovering a meter off the ground, her brow now furrowed, "you know she didn't mean that."

"Trouble is, she did mean it," Persephone sighed.

"And she's right. Sorry. I'm thinking we have to hurry, though, before she says something very honest to someone who won't understand her condition. I might suggest picking up the pace. I'll keep you from getting weary, I promise."

"Of course, great Persephone," Pandy said, putting on her sweetest voice, "you could just float us along with you."

"Sorry, cutie-pie, can't be so obvious with my assistance."

Everyone began to jog, Alcie and Iole's metal hair making a soft scraping sound as it hit their backs with each stride.

Since they had left the gates at least fifteen minutes before, as near as Pandy could calculate, Pandy had glimpsed several shades lurking in the grassy fields, which stretched on either side of the road as far as the eye could see. The farther along the road they got, the more spirits and shades she saw. But nobody was actually doing anything. In fact, every shade was simply standing, not frozen but rather loose, with eyes that occasionally followed the group's progress but mostly just stared out into the middle distance. She looked to Persephone, who was now miming that she was riding a very large horse, pretending to rein it in from side to side, and making clopping and whinnying sounds by sputtering her lips together.

"Persephone?" Pandy called up. "Where are we again?"

"And where are we going?" Alcie asked.

"Whoa!" Persephone said to her invisible beast, pulling back hard on the nonexistent reins. "Good horsey! Well, I have *theee* most fantastic but probably fatal idea—for Iole that is. But first we have to cross through the Fields of Asphodel, which is where we are now and 'where live the shades of lesser heroes and lesser spirits,' according to my Buster—Hades. Basically, it's the final destination for average, common folk . . . but for Zeus's sake, don't tell *them* that! They get snarky!"

"Persephone?" Pandy called again; Persephone was now pretending to be at a dance and twirling around in the air. "You know why I'm here, right?"

"Naturally," she said, stopping mid-spin. "You put the sixth Evil, Greed, back in the box when you were in Rome. Good going, I might add, and thanks for giving Zeus an excuse for a family reunion. Buster and I never get out of this place when I'm here, and Mother won't let me out of her sight when I'm on Olympus. So I owe you big time, Pandy-poo. You allowed Buster and me a nice little vacation! Now, if you're here and you're not dead—you're *not* dead are you?"

"No," Pandy replied.

"Of course you're not, silly. But you *are* here, and

that means that the seventh Evil is somewhere in the underworld."

"She's so smart," said Iole.

"I know," Alcie agreed.

"I KNOW!" Persephone cried.

"And you all know, I'm sure, that Zeus would be ginormously unhappy if any of us helped you find and capture it—which is why I can't just float you any-where, Miss Smarty-Toga—still, the way I see it, helping someone—and by someone, I mean Iole—get her thinker back on track is not really helping you find the Evil, am I right? So, no harm, no Olympic Games foul. Besides, the only one who might actually know where Fear is hiding is Buster and, if I were you, I'd head to the palace when we're done and wait for him. But that's just me."

"But he never *left* the palace when I was here before. At least I think don't so. If he's not there . . . ," Alcie began, realizing that things really were disturbed in the underworld.

"Hera has also freed Briareus, Cottus, and Gyges, the three hecatonchires that have guarded that gates of Tartarus since time began," Persephone answered. "Thanks a lot, Mother's best friend."

"Hecatonchires?" asked Alcie.

"Big word," Iole said softly.

"Giants with fifty heads and one hundred arms,"

Persephone said. "And between you, me, and the oil lamp, I just can't see why they would want to leave the underworld even if they were free; the pay is good and they have a great health and dental plan. Anyway, Buster was able to catch Cottus and Gyges rather quickly; apparently it was easy: he just followed the path of half-mashed, moaning, screaming mortals. But he's only now just managed to get ahold of the third, Briareus, and word is he's on his way back home. How's everybody feeling?"

"Not winded at all," said Pandy.

"I'm fine," Homer answered.

"Feelin' good, feelin' strong," Alcie sang out.

"I like running," Iole finished.

All at once, Pandy felt herself being watched. She spun her head right and left, looking for whoever was spying on her, on them all. Nothing. The mass of vapid shades standing in the fields was thinning and still they didn't seem at all interested. She ran backward for a bit, thinking that she'd passed someone or something whose eyes were now locked onto her. She stared upward into the vault of the "heavens," which were brightly lit and yet the light was a dull, matte yellow and obviously artificial. There was nothing from horizon to horizon.

And then she saw it.

A small bird circling so high above that for a moment

Pandy thought she'd gotten something in her eye. She blinked, but the bird was still there, circling and swooping slightly lower, allowing Pandy to take note of its body. The creature had the oddest shape, Pandy thought, and certainly for a flyer: the wings were almost invisible but the tail was incredibly long. Then, with a gasp that made her miss a step and nearly tumble into the short grasses, she realized it was a peacock. A peacock, she knew, was normally a flightless bird—unless it was . . .

Hera.

"Just try anything," Pandy whispered, emboldened slightly by the presence of another immortal. "Just you try it."

But her legs had grown weak, not from fatigue but from fear.

"Persephone," she called. "I have to slow down just for a bit."

"No, you don't," the goddess replied. "Don't you know that a moving target is harder to hit? Besides, that's not Hera."

"Hera? Where?" Alcie squeaked.

Persephone delicately pointed upward to the peacock now streaking away from them in the direction they were trudging.

"How do you know?" asked Pandy, her voice shaky.

"Trust me on this one, youth and maidens. Oh,

certainly, that was a bird she enchanted to keep her apprised of your whereabouts, but you won't have any trouble recognizing Hera when you do finally see her."

"Why not?" Pandy asked.

"Well, after the feast in Rome, when Zeus found out about all her plans and schemes and finally caught up with her, he gave her backside such a thunder-cracking walloping . . ."

"We saw it!" Alcie chimed in with such glee that Persephone was thrown for a moment.

"We happened to be passing by the insula at the exact moment both she and Juno were being punished," Pandy explained.

"We saw her butt!" Iole guffawed.

Persephone just gaped at Iole for an instant.

"Uh-huh. Okay then, well you can imagine the damage a spanking from the Sky-Lord might do. So when you see Hera, you'll know her by the bandage across her butt!"

❦

Moments after Hera's winged spy had disappeared beyond the horizon, the light in the sky—wherever it was coming from—dropped sharply and the terrain changed from endless stretches of grassy meadows to shorter grasses with patches of pebble-strewn dirt in places.

"There it is," Persephone said, interrupting her own monologue in which she was relating how she was going to surprise Hades on their next anniversary with a romantic vacation to a land in the far-off Orient where they "stuff little shrimps in dough balls and fry them very fast in hot oil. Yum yum!"

"There what is?" asked Pandy, stopping her jog and bringing the group to a halt.

"The border."

"I didn't see a sign," said Alcie.

"How's this, doubting Alcestis?"

Persephone waved her hand, and immediately two large stones appeared on the side of the road. The stone on the left bore the words, NOW LEAVING THE FIELDS OF ASPHODEL. COME BACK SOON! Into the stone on the right was cut, NOW ENTERING EREBUS. POPULATION: YOU CAN'T COUNT THAT HIGH. ENJOY YOUR STAY . . . FOREVER.

"What's the difference?" Pandy said, feeling the temperature drop just slightly.

"Not much, really," Persephone answered. "It's like the Fields, only darker, a little cooler. This is stop number one for the dead; they come here before they're judged on their lives and then sent to their final destinations. Almost no one resides here. Only a few despicables that Buster didn't want to torment in Tartarus; some very clever tortures those. But it's pretty desolate. C'mon, feet up and we're off!"

They had only jogged perhaps another fifty meters when Pandy saw the tail end of a line of shades that paralleled the main road and stretched far off into the dimness. The spirits, in single file, looked to be very much alive, only now somewhat transparent. Some were talking animatedly, some were weeping, some were greeting comrades up or down the line, some were dabbing at wounds. None of them had the glassy, uncomprehending look of the spirits they'd passed in the Fields.

"They have to line up?" Alcie asked.

"If they want to drink, you betcha."

"Drink?" Homer piped up. "I could use a drink."

"Not for you, you supremely buffed-up youth," Persephone replied. "This is a good sign, though. It means we're getting close."

As they jogged by, Pandy saw the line move the tiniest bit, but the next instant another shade of someone who had just "passed on" materialized at the end, so the line never shortened at all.

"That's a lot of dead people," she mused.

"Disease, famine, neglect, abuse, someone steps in a chariot rut and lands the wrong way, someone strays off the path in the forest and gets eaten by a lion, someone doesn't like the way his best friend looked at his sister." Persephone sighed. "A thousand and one wrong turns, mistakes small and large, and we add to our happy little family. And, of course, there's always a war raging somewhere. And old age, can't count that out."

Suddenly, the line stopped just short of a large pool surrounded by black stones.

"Stop here," Persephone said. "Watch."

As they stared, the spirit at the head of the line, a young woman of twenty or so who'd been chatting brightly with an elderly soldier standing behind her, walked up to rim of the pool and knelt, dipping her hand in the water and bringing a small taste up to her mouth. Instantly, her smile faded, her mouth became slack, and her body went loose.

"Wait for it . . . ," said Persephone very softly.

Then the woman's chest heaved up sharply and a long, heavy sigh—almost a moan—passed over her lips. Pandy's blood turned to ice water. In her entire life, she thought she'd never heard anything so heartbreaking, desperate, and agonized. Without warning or knowing quite why, tears welled in her eyes.

"What was that?" she asked.

"That, my sweet fig tartlets," Persephone said, wiping a small tear off her own cheek, "is the sound of loss."

"Loss," echoed Iole.

"But what just happened?" Alcie demanded . . . in a tiny voice.

"The pool is the stopping point of the river Lethe—also fondly known in these parts as Oblivion—where almost all the newly dead souls drink to erase their memories of living. What you just saw was the vanishing of every single memory in the woman's mind. If she has children, she doesn't know it. First love? Gone. The alpha she got that one time on her algebra test? Not there. Not one single memory of her life resides in her head. And her mind watched everything leave, before it shut down. That was the sigh."

"Gods," Pandy whispered.

"I know," Persephone whispered slowly in return. Then she shuddered as if to shake off the bitterness of the moment. "Yeah, well, it's why I don't get out this way much."

"Then why does everyone drink from the pool?" Alcie questioned. "Don't they know what's going to happen? Aren't they watching?"

"Because most people want to forget, sweetie," Persephone said, smiling—rather sadly. "You—any of you four—won't look back on your lives with regret, thinking about adventures you could have had, how exciting it might have been. And, if I were a gambling goddess, I'd say that P here won't even regret taking the box to school when all is said and over. Look at the lives you've lived thus far. Look at what you've all done. Sure, you've had a rough go of it along the way—and you might be killed at any moment in any of several gooey, gory ways that I can think of. But you've accomplished more in the last few moons than any ten mortals in ten lifetimes will have done combined. The spirits in this line don't want to spend an eternity reflecting on missed opportunities, days of drudgery and routine, words like 'can't' and 'shouldn't' that filled their lives. They race to the line as soon as they arrive. And then there are some that just stand in line because everyone else does. The sheep. By the time they drink, it's too late."

"And you want Iole to drink from *Lethe*?" Pandy queried incredulously.

Persephone stared back at Pandora, just as dumbfounded.

"Okay, I get that *she*'s supposed to be the one with the big thinker," Persephone chortled, pointing to Iole. "But tell me you're smarter than *that*! You can't seriously believe that *that* was my idea! C'mon, she's barely got any memories in there as it is. You think I want to drain her?"

"Uh . . ."

"Besides, I'd just like to see you try to take cuts in that line. Seriously. No, my little buckets of sweet cream, we are going *this* way."

CHAPTER SEVEN

Mnemosyne

Persephone turned her back on the line, now facing the other side of the road and a second large pool, which had somehow gone unnoticed by all of them. This pool was ringed in large flat white rocks, and there was a small silver goblet resting on top of one. There were several people gathered around, kneeling, but Pandy could tell almost immediately that there was something different about them. They were all women and there was no transparency. They looked solid, real flesh and blood, not dead at all.

"They're not," Persephone said with a wink, reading her thoughts. "They're as alive as you and I. Well, not as much as I . . . me . . . but you get my drift."

"They're alive? How did *that* happen?" joked Alcie. "You guys don't normally make mistakes down here."

"No mistake, Miss A. The pool is Mnemosyne. The only spot in the entire underworld where humans can pop in for a little bit without the the stress and strain of knowing they're gonna have to stay."

At that moment, another mortal woman materialized by the pool. She was warmly welcomed by the others. Pandy noticed that all the women were dressed similarly in long, loose, full robes. Several were wearing ceremonial headdresses.

"And when I say humans," Persephone continued, "I mean priestesses of a very special order who wish to be initiated into the 'mysteries.'"

"The who-steries?" Alcie coughed.

"The mysteries."

"What are those?" Pandy asked.

"If I told you, it wouldn't be a mystery. And I'd have to kill you."

"Seriously?"

"Yes," said Persephone.

"Uh, *excuse* me . . . ," Alcie cried.

"No, silly." Persephone giggled. "I wouldn't *have* to kill you. But I had you both going there for a moment, didn't I? To tell you the truth, I couldn't tell you what they really are even if I wanted to, because I just don't know. No one does, mortal or immortal. Only them."

As she spoke, Pandy watched one of the women bend down, dip the silver goblet into the water, and raise it to her lips. The other women joined hands and gazed intently at the initiate. The woman dropped the cup where she knelt and began to sway slowly back and forth. Her eyes rolled back in their sockets and her breathing became labored. Two other priestesses rushed forward to hold her arms as she began to twist and thrash, cooing into her ears inaudible but obviously soothing words. After a few minutes, the initiate began to calm down and shortly she was very quiet. Her eyes rolled forward and as her breath evened out, an enormous smile spread across her face. The other women nodded and laughed in agreement as they shared a very special and sacred secret. Then one of the women, one who'd been holding the initiate's arm, dematerialized in the blink of an eye. The priestesses together chanted some mystical words, and Pandy thought that it was some sort of communal farewell.

"What I can tell you," Persephone said, grabbing everyone's attention away from the chanting women, "is that Mnemosyne means memory. Personally, I think that's really all the 'mysteries' are: every memory from everyone *ever*, from the time before Chaos, contained in that pool and passing into the priestesses when they drink. I wouldn't be surprised if there were some sort of tube under the road that connected the two pools, draining all the mortal memories captured by Lethe and dumping them in Mnemosyne, but that's just my theory. Anyway, the way I figure it, if Iole's memories are anywhere, they're in that pool."

"But wouldn't that mean that Iole will be filled with all the memories, just like those women?" Pandy asked.

"Don't know," Persephone said with a shrug. "Maybe, maybe not. Those women are trained practically from the time they can talk to prepare for that one sip of water. It's basically the only thing their lives are about. They don't know exactly what's coming, but they know it's gonna be humongous, and they're ready. But this is gonna hit Iole like Zeus's hand on Hera's backside. So one of two things will happen: Iole's own memories will find her—if they're there—and her brain will accept only what it's supposed to, or her head will explode."

"Seriously?" said Pandy.

"Yes."

"My head?" Iole said, looking from Pandy to Alcie to Homer.

"Okay . . . ha ha, another joke." Alcie laughed nervously. "Right?"

"Nope."

"Is there another way?" Homer asked.

"Something else?" Pandy cried. "Something we haven't thought of?"

"First of all, *you* all haven't thought of anything," Persephone said. "This was my idea—something you all might remember when deciding whom to patronize first on the next feast day. And second, no, I don't see another way. Look, she certainly doesn't have to drink, if you don't want. She can stay this way for the rest of her life if you all think it's best. It will save her from standing in that long line across the road; she can just head on over to be judged . . ."

"No!" Pandy cried. "If there's a chance . . ."

"She's got to do it!" Alcie agreed. "Iole, you have to do it!"

"But my head . . . ," Iole said flatly.

Persephone grinned and took Iole gently by the hand, leading her over to Mnemosyne. At the sight of the goddess, the priestesses all instinctively drew back and bowed deeply.

"Yes, yes, I know, I know." Persephone smiled beneficently at them. "Worship, worship, yes, yes."

She gently guided Iole to the edge of the pool. One of the priestesses, who only then realized what Iole was going to do, let out a small cry of protest. Persephone shot her a look that, literally, aged the woman thirty years. The woman now sported gray hair and a face full of wrinkles. And a closed mouth.

"Spring can really bring you down the most, huh?" muttered the goddess of springtime.

She dipped the silver goblet into the clear water and held it out to Iole, who took it unquestioningly. Pandy found both Homer's and Alcie's hands and held on tightly.

"All down," Persephone said. "There's a good maiden."

Iole drank the entire contents in one gulp. She stood staring from Persephone to her friends and back again. Then, without warning, Iole started shaking.

"She's gonna explode," Alcie whispered.

Iole took a step backward, dropping the goblet. Her tongue seemed to swell in her mouth and she began to choke. Homer was the first to reach her, but Persephone commanded him not to touch even the hem of her toga. Iole's eyes turned as red as blood, and a thick gray foam poured from her mouth.

"She's dying!" Pandy cried.

"Maybe," said Persephone, holding them all back as they rushed to help their friend.

Iole collapsed on the ground in a heap. That's what Pandy, Alcie, and Homer saw. That was all they knew.

Iole, however—who had been sitting slumped in her chair in that small room for such a long time, surrounded by millions of pieces of parchment and the terrifying void that was her mind—suddenly bolted upright. Something was coming. Something big. No . . . no, better word: gargantuan. Yes, better. And it was something, she knew, not to be feared. She ran to the door of the room, floating in the dark gray abyss, trying to catch a glimpse of whatever it was, this gargantuan . . . leviathan. Where did *that* word come from? She turned back into the room and saw the pieces of parchment had begun to rise up off the floor and were swirling through the air. Each one drifted into the candle flame, which had been her only comfort for ages, and ignited with a flash. Then she saw the ashes from each piece drop into a small silver funnel, floating in midair, and emerge at the bottom as drops of clear liquid, which ran with ever-increasing force into a small silver goblet standing upright on the seat of the chair.

The room was ablaze with millions of thoughts and memories, every bit of information that had ever entered her brain, sparking and liquefying, emptying into the small cup that never filled. She walked straight through the . . . what was the word? Her word? Maelstrom! She walked through the maelstrom, the bits of parchment whooshing around her with lightning speed, toward the candle flame. There were so many memories that, very quickly, the pieces began to overlap as they neared the flame, and one ignited the next and then the next. Within seconds, the entire room was filled with a blazing swirl, an inferno of crackling thoughts and ideas. Iole was not only untouched and unafraid; she began to laugh with delight and abandon.

Beside Mnemosyne, they all saw Iole stop choking and writhing. Underneath the oozing gray foam, a smile crept over Iole's face.

Iole threw her hands up into the fire. The whirlwind was beginning to thin out as the mass of memory ashes flooded into the funnel. At last, there were only a dozen or so bits of flaming paper spiraling downward; Iole reached for the silver goblet as the final drops drained out. To her surprise, there was only a tiny amount of liquid in the bottom, barely a swallow. Keeping her eyes on the candle flame, she drank quickly; the taste was sweet, then bitter, then sweet again. Suddenly, the candle blew out, the smoke swirling as it rose on the soft, dying current of the whirlwind. Yet the room was light now and brightening with each passing moment.

Iole dropped the cup and ran to the doorway of the room. Instead of the gaping gray maw, she saw a reddish-orange glow in the distance spreading out and engulfing the darkness. Then appeared a white spot in the center of the glow, growing larger as the murkiness faded on all sides, underneath and above her. The next instant, she was pulled by an unseen force, lifted off the floor and out of the room. She was flying though space, leaving the abyss behind and heading joyfully toward the light. She turned and saw the tiny room receding at such a tremendous speed that, for a moment, she couldn't contemplate what force it was exactly that had ahold of her. Immediately, she answered her own question. It was her mind, igniting back to consciousness as swiftly as the bits of parchment had themselves been ignited. As the whiteness grew in scope and intensity, she began to hear familiar voices. Alcie was shouting the word "explode." Pandy was crying, and there was a rustling of fabric, which, even though unseen, she knew to be Homer's robes moving as he struggled against something; something that was holding him in a tight grip. She was almost into the white light as she heard another voice, authoritative but feminine.

"Wait for it."

Then, as the white light grew so intense she was forced to shut her eyes, Iole caught the faint scent of lavender and roses . . .

. . . and blacked out.

Iole opened her eyes. Her mouth was filled with a foamy, sticky substance that was alternately bitter and sweet as she swallowed what she couldn't cough out. She felt no pain in her body, but her head ached with a pain she'd never known before. She was lying on the ground; Pandy's face was directly above her, upside down, and Alcie and Homer were staring at her from only a meter away. Somewhere behind her, she heard whispers from a group of women—she was sure they were women. She remembered seeing them, or thought she remembered. Then the pain in her head was gone. She looked clearly at her friends, seeing the abject terror in their faces, seeing Alcie's cheeks wet with tears, seeing Homer's knuckles whiten as he gripped the fabric of his cloak.

"Gods!" Pandy whispered suddenly. "Look!"

"Her skin," Alcie gasped. "It's . . . the color of . . . skin!"

Iole raised her hand and saw that her flesh was, indeed, the color of flesh. But she had no idea there was any significance.

"Iole?" Pandy said.

Iole looked into Pandy's upside-down face.

"Yes?"

"Uh . . . how are you?"

"How am I? Well, for some reason unknown to me, I'm lying in the dirt."

She wiped from her mouth the last of the foam, looking at the grayish mess on her fingers. "And I surmise that I've been consuming chalk, but other than that, I'm fine. Why are you shiny?"

Alcie grabbed Iole's hand and tried to speak calmly.

"Okay. What's the square root of . . . of . . . six thousand and eighty-four?"

Iole raised her head and shoulders to shoot Alcie an incredulous glare, then with a sigh she lay back down.

"Well, Alcie, you happen to have actually chosen a real number; *real* being one that may be thought of as a point along an infinitely long line. By definition, every real number has two square roots, a positive and a negative. However the principal square root of a real number is its nonnegative square root. So for simplicity's sake and because I am absolutely flummoxed as to why you would be asking me such a question when I am lying on the ground and something has, quite obviously, *happened* to me, I'll just say seventy-eight."

"Right-o!" cried Alcie—who then started crying again.

"You *knew* the answer, Alce?" asked Homer.

"Oh Homie, I didn't even know the question!"

"May I get up now?" Iole said, sitting slowly.

Pandy helped Iole to her feet, while Homer held Alcie as she wept for joy. Then, after making certain that Iole was steady, Pandy threw her arms around Persephone. Alcie broke free from Homer's arms and ran to embrace them both. Then Homer hugged all three of them.

"Sometimes I surprise myself." Persephone giggled.

"I love you," said Pandy, burying her face in the goddess's gown.

"Who doesn't!" cried Persephone.

"So I'll just stand here until someone tells me—" Iole began.

"Oh, Iole. I'm so glad you're you!" Pandy interrupted as she grabbed Iole and hugged her so hard, Iole thought her ribs would crack.

"Gaaaack. What do you mean . . . umpffff! Gods, what's on your skin?"

"I'll tell you in a minute. What do you remember?"

Pandy finally loosened her grasp and Iole looked at everyone.

"I . . . I . . . remember being in the middle of the Styx. And then I was . . . someplace very dark. I was lost. And alone. And I could hear you but you couldn't hear me. And then . . . there were these little bits of . . ."

Iole began to vomit violently. Instead of bile, however, hundreds of lead chips came pouring out of her mouth. It came upon her so fast that Alcie and Homer were frozen where they stood, horrified; Dido was whimpering, his paws covering his head. Pandy held Iole as she wretched, doubled over, until she spit out the last few bits. Then Iole stood up abruptly and looked around as if she'd never felt better in her life.

"Well, that was unexpected," Persephone said flatly.

"You okay?" asked Pandy

"I'm . . . I'm fine, actually. Wow, that happened fast. But, Gods, what have I been *eating*?"

Without a word, Persephone waved her hand over the pile of chips, forming them into a small shield emblazoned with the aegis of a cerebellum.

"That's for you," she said to Iole, who picked up the shield and found it to be lighter than she expected. "The lead that coated your brain will now protect your body."

"*What*? The lead that coated my *brain*?" Iole said to Pandy.

"It happened when we crossed the Styx," Pandy began. "Your head went under for a sec. We all have an outer coating of metal, but it got inside you."

"Hey!" Alcie exclaimed. "My head went under too . . . but it didn't affect *my* brain!"

No one said a word for a long moment.

"I think I'm restored enough to know that I'm not gonna touch that," said Iole.

"You can talk while you walk," Persephone cautioned. "I don't need to remind you that, while time means almost nothing here, your days are numbered topside, where it counts."

"Do you know how many days we have left?" Pandy asked quickly.

"Yep. Can't tell you. Have to . . ."

". . . kill us, I know," said Pandy.

"I *know*!" Persephone laughed.

"We'll tell you everything, Iole. Everything that's happened since the Styx, that is," Pandy said. "But we gotta keep moving."

At that moment, a giant flaming wheel at least three meters in diameter went rolling past Mnemosyne, startling everyone. It crossed the main road and flew past Lethe, showering those waiting at the front of the long line with sparks before disappearing into the dimness of Erebus. That was incredible in itself, but even more so was the man on top of the wheel, rolling and steering it with his legs and laughing madly as he went by.

"Ixion?" murmured Iole.

"Oh, Zeus's fingernails!" Persephone said, throwing

her hands up. "He's supposed to be in torment, not having the time of his life! Yet something *else* I have to deal with. All right, I think you're good to go from here. Just follow the main road though Erebus to the palace. Try not to get lost."

With that, Persephone kissed Pandy, Alcie, and Homer on their foreheads. Then she bent down to Iole.

"Welcome back, genius." She smiled. Then she turned to the priestesses. "Ladies, thanks for the drink. It's all yours."

Then she hiked up the hem of her gown and took off at a tear after the giant wheel.

CHAPTER EIGHT
Tantalized

"Who is Ixion? Besides a guy who can balance on a wheel," asked Alcie when they all got back onto the main road. They were no longer jogging—the necessity for hyper-speed was gone—but walking briskly. "And why do I feel like I never paid attention to *anything* in school?"

"First of all, you didn't," answered Iole. "And second, Master Epeus covered Ixion last term. You were staring out into the olive groves and Pandy was staring at Tiresias the Younger. I was staring at both of you trying to make you listen, because it's so gruesomely grand. Ixion was an ancient king who was one of the very few mortals to be invited to a feast on Mount Olympus. He fell in love with Hera over the soup."

"That's just wrong on so many levels," Pandy said.

"Astounding, I know, but he did. He started flirting with her in front of Zeus. Zeus not only struck him with a thunderbolt, but he also bound him to a giant flaming wheel that revolves forever. Only it's not supposed to be rolling across the underworld. Okay, now that *that*'s explained, would someone tell me what's been going on?"

Pandy, Alcie, and Homer told Iole of her emergence from the Styx and how much it altered her. As Persephone's bright idea, they walked farther into the dimness of Erebus. Pandy noticed that the short, grassy terrain was giving way on either side of the road to stubby bushes and stunted, leafless trees. A little farther on, the trees were taller, more leafy, and covered the hills that had sprung up a short distance away. Over Alcie's chatter—

"And then I practically had to grab the oatie cake out of your hands to give to that three-headed beast . . ."

—Pandy heard muffled sounds—someone breathing hard and snuffling, snorting, and chewing. Loud chewing.

"Stop it, Alce," Pandy cut in, her head turned toward a grove of tall, mature trees and a light flickering through the branches. "Iole, it was all your idea. We just gave you a nudge, that's all. Guys, quiet. *Quiet*. Do you hear that?"

"Someone's . . . eating?" Alcie said after a moment.

Then the slurping and munching was peppered with several *plops* that sounded as if things had dropped or been dropped from a great height into liquid. Suddenly, a scream pierced the eternal dusk and plunged right into Pandy's heart, nearly stopping it. It was a man's voice and he'd screamed as if he'd been scared out of his wits. Pandy took off at a run toward the sounds, thinking only that they may have stumbled, purely by accident, on the seventh and final Evil. As she ran flat out, though, her reason took over; there was no way in Hades that finding Fear would have been this simple. And it might even be a trap, set by Hera. The man screaming might not have been the thing eating. In fact the thing eating might be eating the man screaming, which is why he'd be . . . screaming.

She slowed down, causing Alcie, Iole, and Homer to crash into her and each other. She gave a hand signal to be very quiet. They picked their way around tree trunks, low branches, and shrubs, always keeping the light ahead of them. The trees finally thinned out, and Pandy emerged onto a very small patch of fresh green grass nearly surrounded by beautiful, leafy trees of every type. The largest of these had low, long branches, which had been hung with many lamps so that the small clearing was nearly as bright as day. And this tree, far from being only green, seemed multicolored— covered from bottom to top with so many different types of fruit that Pandy instantly remembered the

Garden of the Jinn in ancient Persia, with its trees bearing jeweled oranges, apples, pears, and so on.

"This looks weirdly familiar," Alcie said. "Reminds me of the cherry tree I got stuck in."

"Except in that garden, not all the fruit was on one tree," Iole whispered.

As the group moved closer, they saw that the heavily laden branches of the enormous tree hung over a large pool with a stone pillar rising up in the middle of the water. On this pillar were two rings linked by chains to two open manacles.

"Uh-oh," said Homer, looking at the rings. "This is bad."

"Why, why?" Alcie clamored.

There was a rustling in the large tree, and a peach pit fell from some higher branch and splashed into the pool. It bobbed for a moment on the surface before sinking. They heard a cackling overhead, then a few grunts as something made its way down the tree, shaking the branches hard as it leapt from one to the next. A figure came into view standing on a thick branch perhaps five meters off the ground. It was a man with shaggy graying hair and a chin full of stubble. One hand was clutching at some twigs higher up to steady himself; the other was wrapped around a half-eaten pomegranate. His toga was stained and damp with fruit juice and spittle. He grinned at the group, then threw his head back and laughed like a child being tickled, pomegranate seeds dribbling out of his mouth. He was so histrionic that he began to choke and, forced to beat his chest, dropped the pomegranate from his fingers. Watching the remainder of the delicious fruit plummet downward and land in the pool, the man screamed so loudly and with such agony that everyone hit the ground. Homer instinctively tried to throw himself over them all. The screaming continued, one long breath, until it suddenly stopped. Looking up, Pandy and the rest saw that the man had simply grabbed the nearest piece of fruit—a tangerine—and was shoving it into his mouth, rind and all.

"Is that who I think it is?" Pandy asked of no one in particular.

"Fruit. Pond. Chains," Alcie said softly. "Even I know this one."

"Greetings!" the man called out, spitting seeds with every syllable. "My name is Tantalus and I bid you welcome to my home. It's just my pond and my tree, really, but I call it home."

"Greetings," Homer said, stepping forward. Clearly the man was mad, but more importantly, he was free when he shouldn't have been. He *should* have been, Homer knew, chained to the pillar in the middle of the pond. There was no telling what might happen if he decided to climb down out of the tree—insanity can often trump brute strength, and Homer knew this also. He made the introductions as quickly and as politely as possible. When Alcie was introduced she took a step forward and accidentally smacked her head on a low-hanging pear. When she reached up to bat it away, Tantalus began shouting at her to back away, not to touch anything. No one was to touch anything.

"I'd offer you some fruit," Tantalus went on, "if I were more hospitable, but I'm not, so I won't. Please don't think me rude, it's just that it's been eons since I've drank or eaten anything so, mine . . . all mine! Of course it's not as good as the ambrosia and nectar my daddy, Zeus, let me eat, but it's mine, mine, mine."

"We understand, sir," said Pandy, knowing full well the story behind the man's hunger and thirst. "We won't disturb your meal."

"You, Alcestis," Tantalus said, grabbing a nearby peach. "You're shiny. You shine. Why is that?"

Pandy looked at Alcie's copper hair and tinted skin reflecting the light ripples off the pool.

"Pandora, you and the youth shine as well, but not so much. Why do I have shiny people at my little watering hole?"

The honest answer that sprung to Pandy's lips was going to be far too long, so she quickly replaced it with another that was far more clever.

"We're members of a theatre troupe," she said.

"Summoned by Hades for a command performance, and we've lost our way. We're wearing makeup for our various roles. I am a bronze statue, Homer is an . . . an . . . anvil. And Alcie, I mean Alcestis, is a . . . uh . . ."

"Copper pot," Alcie cut in. "We're performing '*The Tale of the Wicked Blacksmith*.'"

"Why doesn't the short maiden wear any makeup?" Tantalus asked, looking at Iole.

"I'm the director."

Pandy's curiosity bubbled up to the surface.

"Might I ask, sir, how you came to be released from the pool?"

"Ah," Tantalus replied, beaming with no small sense of pride. "You know about me then?"

"Of course," she said. "Chained forever in a pool, fruit above your head that pulls back when you try to reach for it, water that recedes when you try to drink."

"Give the lady a hand! Very good, maiden. Well, it was no easy thing to capture me and get me in that pond in the first place, I can assure you. Daddy couldn't do it the honorable way, like a *man*, you know. He had to use his immortal powers. But I always knew I'd get out someday. The gods are really quite stupid after all."

"Whoa," said Alcie. She'd never heard anyone say anything like that about one god, let alone all of them at once.

"Do you know any gods? Have you ever met one?" Tantalus asked Pandora.

"I have, sir. All of them," Pandy answered.

Tantalus stopped in the middle of plucking a nectarine and gazed at her.

"So then you *know* how ridiculous they are! I'm sure they couldn't wait to tell you their side of the story, could they? Well, I'll give it to you straight. Yes, I invited all of them down to my house for a feast. Yes, I killed my son, Pelops, and served him up as the main course. Yes, they all recoiled in horror and left without so much as tasting the dessert. But I didn't *roast* Pelops, which is the way I know everyone tells it. I *boiled* him. Big, *big* difference. And he wasn't alive, the way some are saying; I *did* dismember him first. For Olympus's sake, he looked fine on the platter, like an oddly shaped calf. And what better way to honor the immortals than by offering up your own son! And Demeter actually took a bite! Ate his shoulder, the stupid cannibal!"

Out of the corner of her eye Pandy saw a shape moving through the trees, but somehow she knew to keep her gaze on Tantalus.

"Yes, sir, but how did you get free?" she called up.

"Hera," Tantalus said matter-of-factly. "She came through my clearing—waddling, actually, her bottom is in a bandage—and she knelt by my pool. Said she deeply felt my suffering, for which I was grateful, and my fear, which I didn't quite understand. In fact she kept asking me if I was afraid. I kept telling her no, not particularly, just really hungry and thirsty."

Pandy tensed. Hera had been at this exact spot asking questions about the very evil she sought.

"Then she asked me if I was afraid of fire. I told her I didn't really think much about it since I was neck-deep in water. She laughed; she was a bit of a nutso, truth be told, but I wasn't gonna say that to her. Then the gracious Queen of Heaven, that bountiful beauty in blue, fully acknowledged the extent of my eternal punishment: fruit hanging above my head that moves away when I reach for it, fresh water up to my neck that recedes every time I bend to drink. Forever hungry and thirsty. And just because I wanted to have something a little 'different' for evening meal. Well, she snapped her fingers, and my hands just slipped out of the manacles. Oh, that first drink . . . I nearly drained the whole pool. And all this fruit; I'll never be able to eat it all, but I'm going to have fun trying, so don't touch."

"When did this happen?" Pandy asked. "When was Hera here?"

"Only a short time before you arrived," Tantalus said, picking a wad of apricot skin out of the back of his teeth. "I knew she liked me. At my house, at the feast, after Zeus had used his powers to bind me and was about to send me down here, she came up to me and whispered in my ear that she thought I was terribly inventive in my choice of cuisine. Or was that inventively terrible. Either way, the lady knows talent. And thanks to her, I'll never be sunk up to my neck again. A few more juicy bits and then it's exit, Erebus left!"

A glint of white, close by, caught everyone's attention.

"Not so fast," said a young man stepping up beside Pandy. His silver-tipped bow was taut and not one but two arrows were set, ready to fly. He was only fifteen at the most, Pandy thought, but had the grace and bearing of someone much older.

"You?" yelled Tantalus. "You're dead! I cut you up myself!"

"That you did," said the youth. "And you have my word, no one's ever going to award you Father of the Year. But the gods took pity on me and restored me to life. I lived out my allotted span of years quite well, no thanks to you. And when I finally died, they rewarded me with the gift of eternal vigor and bloom."

"What's that thing on your shoulder, Pelops?" asked Tantalus.

"It's my *shoulder*, you idiot. The gods gave me a new shoulder of ivory to replace what Demeter ate."

"Oh, yeah. That's right," Pandy whispered to Alcie.

"You—you speak that way to your *father* . . . !" Tantalus choked out.

"That's it. Enough talk, crazy man. Hades asked me

if I would kindly leave the Elysian Fields and get you back into your pond. So here I am. Now are you going to get back into your chains like a good homicidal maniac or do I let fly?"

"Do your worst, you son of a dog . . . oh, wait, you're my son," Tantalus began.

Pelops plucked his bow and sent his arrows whizzing through the air. They both struck their mark, one in Tantalus's upper thigh, the other in his chest, with such force that he was falling headlong out of the tree and into the pool before he could take another breath.

"You," Pelops called to Homer even before his father hit the water, "help me!"

Pelops dove into the pool with Homer jumping in after. Quickly they bound the semiconscious murderer back to the pillar, cuffing his hands securely into the manacles.

"Are you sure he won't be able to escape again?" Iole asked Pelops as soon as he and Homer were standing, dripping wet, beside her.

"Absolutely," Pelops answered. "Immortal magic imprisoned him, freed him, and imprisoned him a second time. Hades himself enchanted the bow. I'm no archer."

"Well, you look like one to me," Pandy said.

"Never picked up a bow in my life," Pelops said. "Or afterlife, as it were. It was all Hades' enchantment. His kingdom is in chaos. He knew my father would be out of his pool so he asked me to help. I was only too happy, believe me."

Tantalus was slowly regaining consciousness. Realizing he was back in his pool of forever ebbing water, overhung with never-to-be-eaten fruit, he began wailing and gnashing his teeth, hurling the most horrible insults at the group on the bank. His words caused even Alcie to blush deeply.

"And now, I must be off," Pelops said over his father's expletives. "My work here is done and I have a long walk back to the Elysian Fields. Good fortune befall you."

He was gone as swiftly as he arrived.

"Should we follow?" Alcie asked.

"Persephone said to stay on the main road," Pandy said after a moment. "I don't know this place and even you don't know the terrain, Alce, only the palace."

"I hear you," Alcie replied. "Main road it is. Besides, ivory-boy walks too fast. We'd never keep up."

"What do you think Hera meant when she asked Tantalus if he was afraid of fire?" Iole posed, picking an apple—at which Tantalus called her a name even her huge brain couldn't comprehend.

"I think it was a clue," Pandy said, after a moment. "She knows we're here. She knows we're after Fear. There are only four main regions in Hades, right?"

"The Fields of Asphodel," Iole began.

"No fire there," Alcie cut in.

"Erebus, where we are now, and the Elysian Fields," Pandy continued.

"No fire," said Homer.

"That only leaves one place," Pandy finished. "But Persephone told us . . ."

"To continue on the main road," Alcie said. "To the palace. And I'm fine with that. Hera's out to kill us anyway, why would we go wherever she'd lead us, right? Am I right? Show of hands? Who thinks I'm right? I'm picking fruit."

As they all loaded up on fresh nectarines, pears, apples, and oranges—Tantalus cursing them so harshly that Homer threw a pomegranate hard at Tantalus's head, knocking him out cold once again—no one said a word.

It was on everyone's mind, however . . . Hera's clue. The fourth region of the underworld. The name they casually joked about and used with blithe abandon because none of them ever actually thought they'd have to go there. The place where the fires were so hot, your skin was said to bubble merely by standing at the gates. Where the eyeballs of the imprisoned spirits popped over and over again. Where even your teeth turned to ash.

Tartarus.

CHAPTER NINE

Hygiene

They had only been back on the main road a short time before a large building loomed in front of them.

"So, the road just *ends* here?" Alcie said, staring at the strange temple-like structure that clearly blocked their path.

"Is this Hades' palace?" Pandy asked, taking in the crumbling exterior plaster awash in hues of apricot and light green. She saw the strange vines that covered most of the front columns and hoped their journey to find the lord of the underworld might have just been cut very short.

"No way," Alcie said, shaking her head.

"The road continues on the other side," Iole said, pointing off to a line of dirt curving away from the far side of the building and off into the distance.

"Then let's cut around," Homer said, already leading Alcie a few steps into the grass and scrub.

"No," said Pandy. "C'mon, you guys. Nothing just *happens* here. Nothing just happens wherever we go. Not to us. We were meant to hear that clue from Tantalus, as dopey as it might have been. Now we have this. The building sits on the road, we go inside the building. Besides, now I *have* to see what's inside, so we explore every room if we have to."

With Pandy leading the way, the group headed through an open archway and saw that it was, after all, only one room, but it was enormous. There was another open archway directly across from the first, and the road did indeed continue on, but that wasn't the most surprising feature.

"Whoa," whispered Homer.

"This is like . . . I've never seen anything like this," Pandy murmured.

"Iole, I don't think we're in Hades anymore," Alcie said.

"Oh, but we are. We are," Iole countered, knowing at one glance full well where they were.

To Pandy's mind, it was the most beautiful interior space she'd ever seen, far surpassing the grandeur of Zeus's hall on Mount Olympus, the Garden of the Jinn, or even the wedding-decorated hall of King Peleus. There were so many rich carpets on the floor that they overlapped, creating little hills of softness as four or five topped each other, all displaying the most intricate of designs in pure silk. The walls, too, were hung with silk tapestries, each one depicting two people, Pandy was certain. They were set in some kind of scene, although she couldn't quite tell in the dim light what the people were actually doing. But the tapestries, what she could see of them, weren't what fascinated her most. Her view was also obstructed by the same vines as those covering the outside columns—thick, leafy, and vibrant mottled green—which were literally crawling as she watched, down from the four upper corners of the room. They slithered before her eyes, finding crevices and tiny outcroppings in the rock walls as if they had minds of their own—like serpents with huge red, orange, and purple flowers instead of heads, and large yellow protrusions for fangs. As she watched, one or two of the flowers would suddenly blacken, wither, and die. Then, just as quickly, another bloom or two would burst forth along another vine somewhere else. There was a constant motion of slithering, withering, and bursts of color.

"Those are pure gold," Pandy said, pointing to the two oil lamps hanging from the ceiling, each three times the size of a chariot wheel.

"How can you tell?" Alcie asked.

"Because I'm bronze and you're copper, and they shine a whole lot brighter than we do."

There was also a large opening in the ceiling from

which light, muted but still stronger than any they'd seen in Erebus thus far, shone down into the center of the room. There, illuminated in a shaft as if weak sunlight was breaking through a cloud, stood a water basin one meter high and perhaps two meters long. It was bone dry.

All at once, they heard a cough off to one side, and then a snore followed by a soft but stern voice telling someone to be quiet. Pandy took two steps toward the nearest wall and peered into the shadows.

"We're not alone," she said softly.

"No kidding," Alcie said, gazing intently into the darkness on the other side.

There were dozens and dozens of people—women, Pandy realized because of their dress and hair—sitting, leaning, lying on the ground, lying on each other, or lying on vines. Each one had a large urn at her side or on her lap. Several were trying to use their urns as pillows with little success. Most were asleep, but some held quiet monosyllabic conversations of which Pandy only heard snippets. Every once in a while, one of the women would stretch like a cat and find a new position, or a flower would pop to life under someone's leg or arm, causing a bit of a startle. But these women were nearly insensible to everything around them.

"Look," said Iole, nodding toward the basin.

A woman they hadn't noticed before was now

walking toward the basin. Only then did Pandy hear the trickle of water. In the same shaft of dim light, she saw a fountain on the back wall, the water streaming into a small pool. The woman was carrying an urn, like the ones on the floor around the perimeter of the room, and she was trying to bring water from the fountain to the basin. But, Pandy and the others saw, her urn was leaking badly and as she reached the basin, holding the urn up and over to empty its contents, there was not a single drop left. As the woman held it high, the light from the ceiling shone through hundreds of small holes that perforated the bottom. Sadly, the woman, who hadn't even noticed there were strangers present, began her walk back to the fountain.

"I know this," Pandy said to herself, taking in the entire scene. "This is familiar. But it's all wrong."

"Everything in Hades has been wrong thus far," Iole said. As Pandy and Alcie looked at her, she shrugged just a little. "That is to say, everything that I've seen when I didn't have a brain coated with lead. This one is easy . . ."

But Pandy had turned away, not realizing that Iole was about to tell her exactly what was wrong with the scene. She needed answers, but the woman at the fountain seemed so dejected, so lost in her drudgery that Pandy didn't want to disturb her; she instead approached the woman seated nearest to her along the walls.

The first thing that hit her was the stench.

When Pandy had been standing in the middle of the cavernous hall, the smell had somehow been masked, but as she got closer, it nearly knocked her over. Rotten food, body odor pushing its way through caked-on grime and dirt, putrid breath, human waste—all of these combining into the pure scent of filth. It poured off the women slouching, slacking, lying, and leaning against the walls and one another. It rolled off in great waves that hit Pandy and made her gasp. She brought the hem of her cloak up to her nose to block the stink, but it didn't work in the least; she didn't know if she could get any closer. She was close enough, however, to see that not only were these women covered in filth, but they also had insects, worms, maggots, slugs, snails, and leeches crawling all over their skin, hair, and clothes. Suppressing the urge to vomit, she called to the woman nearest—one who was leaning her back against the wall, her dirty, blackened legs stretched out.

"Excuse me, but could you tell me . . . ?"

"Not talking now," the woman said without even bothering to open her eyes. "Relaxing now."

Pandy moved farther down the row of bodies.

"Pardon me . . . ?"

"Don't bother me."

"Excuse me . . . ?"

"Can you get the caterpillar out of my nose?"

"Uh . . ."

"I'm too tired; talk to my sister."

"Which one is your sister?" Pandy asked, perking up slightly, thinking that there might possibly be a ray of hope if there was one woman with some answers, but mostly again feeling the urge to retch.

"All of them."

She scanned the women closest to her, then walked back to Alcie, Iole, and Homer.

"I probably should have asked everyone around the entire room," she said. "But I saw a leech stuck to one woman's eyelid and that was it for me. I know I've seen this before. Well, not seen exactly, but heard . . . maybe."

"I can tell you exactly what the problem—" Iole began.

"Who are you?" came a voice from near the fountain. They all turned to see the woman with the punctured urn move through the light toward the basin, staring at them. Her voice was light, but her tone was one of utter exhaustion. "Have you come to help?"

There was a snicker from a corner of the room.

"Good luck," said someone.

"I'd like to see anyone get me up off this floor," said another.

Pandy went to the woman and introduced herself, Alcie, Iole, and Homer.

"I'm sorry," said the woman, "but if you're here to help, please do it quickly."

"We'd like to help," Pandy said. "But we don't know what the trouble is."

"First of all, if you want to talk you'll have to walk with me. I'm afraid I'm unable to stop moving. Part of the curse, you know."

"You're cursed?" Alcie asked.

"Not me exactly," said the woman, dipping her urn into the fountain. "They are. My sisters that you see sprawled around you. Or at least they're supposed to be. But something's happened. My name is Hypermnestra and . . ."

"I know you," Pandy interrupted. "Wait, I know this one. Iole, you know this one!"

"I've been trying to tell you," Iole said.

"Well, *somebody* tell me," Alcie sighed.

"It all began . . . ," Iole started.

"No, let me," Pandy said as they all moved with Hypermnestra back and forth from the fountain to the basin. "I know you so well because my mother used your story to get me to take a bath when I was little. Okay, not you so much, but your sisters. Wait! You're the only one who shouldn't be working!"

"I know," Hypermnestra sighed.

"Story, if you don't mind," said Alcie.

"Oh, right. Well, when I was really little, I hated

taking baths. Sabina, our house slave, couldn't even get me into the water—and I'd do practically anything for her. Anyway, finally my mother had had enough and she told me your tale. Guys, guys, these are the Danaids! Fifty sisters who were forced to marry the fifty sons of their uncle."

"Cousins. Creepy," said Alcie.

"But, your father—right, Hypermnestra?—didn't want any of you to marry your cousins!"

"He only agreed to it after our uncle came with all his sons to fight for our hands. There was going to be terrible bloodshed in the town that had sworn to protect us, so father finally said yes."

"But, on the night of your big wedding he gave each of you a dagger and told you to kill your new husbands after the ceremony."

"Father. He meant well, but he was always a little shortsighted."

"And each of your sisters did it," Pandy continued. "You were the only one who spared your husband's life."

"What can I say?" Hypermnestra shrugged. "I liked him."

"And for that, you were excluded from the curse. But your sisters—and this is where my mother really got me—when each of your sisters died, she was brought here, given a pitcher full of holes and told to carry water to fill up a basin. The first one to do it would be able to take a bath, but until that time they would be covered in grime, dirt, and . . . and . . . icky stuff. She described the worms and the bugs, the dirt under their toenails. She even tried to describe the smell. Gods, did she fail that one! My mother said that if I ever missed another bath, worms were going to start eating me and snails were going to crawl into my mouth. And . . . other stuff."

"Never really liked your mother," Alcie said under her breath. The she looked around the room. "So—we're surrounded by forty-nine murderesses?"

"I'm afraid so," Hypermnestra said. "They're not really bad, you know. They simply didn't want their husbands chosen for them, so they took the first piece of advice they were given and went a little off course. Now, they have a never-ending task."

"Except you're the one executing it," said Iole. "Why is that?"

"I don't know," said Hypermnestra. "Not long ago, I was in the Elysian Fields with my husband, Lynceus, and Hercules and his wife, Deianeira, playing a game of possum lawn bowling. Because I refused to participate in my sisters' shame, and my husband and I lived noble lives, we were allowed to visit the Fields when we died. Anyway, we were all having a fine time when suddenly Hera appeared, and the next thing I knew, I found myself here in my sisters' prison. As soon as

I materialized, one of them shoved her urn into my hands and stepped out of this shaft of light. Then all the others followed. Completely against my will, I have been forced to perform their punishment for—I don't know how long now."

"Why can't you just walk away?" Alcie asked.

"I tried once, believe me. It was not my punishment, I thought. Hades would not want me to carry out their task, and so I left the light. It was then that I discovered Hades has devised a most convincing way to keep my sisters at their chore. Someone must always be in the light."

"What? Why?" said Pandy.

"I could show you," Hypermnestra said. "But it might kill you. None of you are already dead, correct?"

"Yes. We're only here to capture the evil of Fear," Pandy said, watching Hypermnestra try to fill her urn for the tenth time. "It's a very long story."

"Well, I don't want to be the cause of your death, in any event," the woman said. Pandy saw the gentleness and dignity with which this woman carried herself, as exhausted as she must have been.

"I don't understand," said Iole. "If you've replaced only one of your sisters, why are they *all* able to relax? Why aren't the other forty-eight working along with you? Or if only one is needed, why don't they take turns?"

"They are tied together as a group," Hypermnestra replied. "Because they committed the same act at the same time, each has been forced to perform the exact same task for eternity as punishment. It is only logical that, if something were to ever go wrong— which it most definitely has—they should, as a group, slack off."

Pandy flashed on the moments when she herself was forced to move against her will, flopping backward and forward like a dying fish, in the Chamber of Despair. Like Pandy, Hypermnestra couldn't stop for even a moment.

"We have to help you," Pandy said finally.

"I appreciate that, but it sounds like you have more pressing matters to attend to," Hypermnestra said with a sad smile. "Besides, Hades will right the havoc that Hera has created soon enough, I'm certain."

Suddenly, a vine sprung up from the earth right where Dido was standing. He'd given up walking back and forth with his mistress and was waiting patiently by the basin. The vine immediately issued two huge red flowers underneath Dido's stomach, which caused the frightened dog to leap to one side. This caused Homer, walking next to Dido at that moment, to stumble out of the way . . . directly into the shaft of light. His right arm flailed out and knocked Hypermnestra backward into the shadows.

Immediately, Homer began to scream in agony. He beat at his face and arms, whirling in circles until he fell to the ground. As he rolled around, shrieking, everyone saw his bluish-black iron skin begin to redden then glow, as if he had been thrown into an intensely hot oven. Smoke rose up off his flesh, but somehow his garments didn't char at all. Stunned, Alcie couldn't even find words and could only moan. She poised herself to dive into the light to save him and was only held back by untapped reserves of Pandy's and Iole's strength. With a grunt, Iole shoved Alcie onto the ground and held her there with that same force that Alcie had used against the Maenads.

"You can't *do* anything!" Iole yelled in her face.

"I'm gonna kill you!" Alcie spat.

"Guys! GUYS!" Pandy began shouting, loud enough to be heard over Homer's wails and the hoots and titters of the other sisters. Iole diverted her attention, and that was all Alcie needed to throw Iole off. But they were both dumbstruck by what they saw.

Homer, his skin glowing like a hot coal, was enveloped in a whirlwind of bluish-black dust. He'd managed to get to his knees and was slump-shouldered, groaning as the dust grew thicker and thicker, nearly blocking him from view. As they all watched, Homer struggled to his feet, then tripped over his cloak. He hit the ground with a thud, unconscious now, but one hand—the color of normal flesh—landed out of the light. Together, Pandy, Alcie, and Iole pulled with all their might and dragged Homer out of the shaft and into the darkness.

At once, the walls of the room burst into flame. Overhead, the oil lamps exploded, sending oily smoke billowing downward, and the water in the fountain began to steam. The floor began to glow with heat and Pandy felt the leather of her sandals beginning to shrivel and crack. The vines were withering and sizzling against the fire, creating more smoke, which drove the murdering forty-nine from their resting places. Then the flames began to creep across the floor. Pandy knew instantly that this was Hades' coercion; the reason someone always had to be in the shaft of light: the beautiful garden room would become an inferno so hot as to rival Tartarus, she was sure. A few moments more and Pandy's sandals would be charred; *she* could battle the heat with her own internal power over fire, but what about Alcie, Iole, and Homer—they were going to roast like meat on a frying stone!

"Help me!" she called to Alcie and Iole.

Together with Dido, they ran to the closest sister and grabbed her by the arms. Alcie and Iole were disgusted by the worms and spiders, the moldy food and grime that covered the woman head to toe, but they dragged, pushed, and pummeled her back into the shaft. Instantly, the flames began to die back. The floor began to cool, but not enough that the pads of Dido's feet weren't beginning to blister. Hypermnestra grabbed a sister running past her and shoved her into the light. Three, four, five sisters, fighting, kicking, and clawing, were forced back into the dim shaft, where they stood, helpless and huddled, watching the chaos around them.

As each woman was tossed into the shaft, the flames grew smaller until they were confined to only patches on the walls. Small patches of the floor were dark and cool once again; it was on one of these that Dido finally stopped and refused to move, licking his burned paws. Thirteen, fourteen, fifteen women were now crowded around the basin. Hypermnestra tried to help as best she could, but the third time she'd gone to corral one sister back into the light, she'd been knocked aside and had fallen in a heap. Pandy felt her strength leaving her, and with the eighteenth attempt, the sister was able to break free and run a short distance away, but not before delivering a sharp blow to Pandy's left cheek, which sent Pandy crashing to the ground. Iole sunk to her knees, Alcie was doubled over and gasping for air, and Dido, even if he would venture off his cool spot, couldn't drag any of them by himself. The sisters in the light were becoming quite verbal; they were beginning to think twice about their re-imprisonment, especially since their free sisters were calling to them to step away. Pandy was lying on the ground, her hand on her sore cheek, weak as a kitten. She'd lost this battle; the sisters were meant to be together as a group—wherever they were—and once the sisters stepped out of the light, the room would once again be engulfed in flames, cooking them all.

At that precise moment, Pandy heard, "No, *no*, NO!" Then there was a grunt and a shriek and a woman went sailing over Pandy's head, dropping slugs and rotten scraps of meat as she flew through the air, landing with a crash against the basin itself. As she turned her head to look, two more women went flying *into* the basin. And then three.

Homer was moving around the room, picking up anyone covered in filth and casually sending them flying. It was completely effortless. Sounds of exhaustion or pain were coming only from the women as they were flung with such ease it was as if Homer were tossing away the parchment wrapping off a midday meal from a fast-falafel stand. He moved with a force even Pandy had never seen from the strong youth, yet with such grace and bearing, it seemed as if Homer had done this all before and was making light of it. As if he were dancing. As if he'd lost some of his awkwardness and had grown up a bit.

"They need their urns," he said nonchalantly over his shoulder as he half hoisted, half dragged one woman by her feet, her arms being covered in maggots.

Pandy, Alcie, and Iole raced around the room, collecting all the urns and tossing them to Hypermnestra, who then lobbed them one by one, not *to* but *at* her sisters. The vines grew back to life and began trekking across the walls and floor, their red and orange flowers blooming, and the fountain began flowing once again. Pandy looked up and saw the oil lamps hanging solemnly, not even a hint of motion, as if the inferno and the explosions had never happened. The room was returned to its original darkened beauty.

As Hypermnestra tossed the last urn, the one that she herself had been using, Alcie grabbed Pandy's arm. Through the last remaining wisps of smoke and the dying firelight, Homer was rounding the far end of the basin, out of the shaft of light; his face was confident, his shoulders squared, his blond curls bouncing, and his skin completely normal. Alcie gasped and Pandy looked at her, feeling as if she was watching her friend fall in love all over again.

"He's not metal . . . ish," Pandy said.

"Has he gotten taller?" Alcie asked rather breathlessly.

Homer did, in fact, seem larger all around—as if, in

the last few moments of fire, terror, and bugs, he'd actually had a growth spurt.

"Uh . . . ," Pandy began.

As he strode up to them, he smiled and—for an instant, for one one-millionth of a second—his teeth sparkled. Then he turned his head and addressed the befuddled sisters, all of them leaning on, crying on, and picking bugs off each other.

"Move!" he called out, forcefully.

The Danaids started in fright, each one quickly taking up the urn closest to her. One by one, they began their futile walk, back and forth, never ending, from the fountain to the basin. They muttered, cursed, and wailed, throwing hateful dagger glances at Pandy, Alcie, Iole, Homer, and Hypermnestra.

"All right, maidens—and Danaid," he said, extending his arms to Alcie and Hypermnestra. "I believe our work here is done, and we should be moving on. May we escort you, Hypermnestra, to the Elysian Fields?"

"Thank you," Hypermnestra said as Pandy and Alcie gaped in wonder at Homer's newfound charisma and bearing. "But I would only slow you down. And I'd like to watch my sisters for just a bit longer. Make certain that their punishment is in full effect, no one slacks off, that sort of thing. Really, I just want to hide in the shadows and listen. See if any of them has any remorse or conception of their wrongdoing. If any of them has had a change of heart, I'll try to intercede on their behalf with Hades, because I can tell you from experience, this is a wretched existence and my pity goes out to all of them."

"Even after what they did to you?" Alcie said, as the group, with Dido padding behind, moved toward the opening that led to the continuing road.

"Of course," she replied. "They're my sisters."

They all turned around for one last look at the Danaids. In the light, Pandy could see that their torment was even worse than she'd originally thought; some women had live rats tangled in their hair. Some were losing their hair in great chunks and patches, obviously diseased with rashes and scabs. Now, though, all the sisters were weeping.

"They're remembering what it felt like to rest for a moment," Pandy said.

"The shaft of light fully illuminates their sin," Hypermnestra said, sorrowfully. "It is a light of truth. It reveals fully what they look like on the inside."

Good-byes were exchanged and Homer led Pandy, Alcie, and Iole out into the fresher air of the open underworld. Walking away from the strange prison, Alcie suddenly slowed with a look of bewilderment on her face.

"What?" asked Pandy.

"Okay, if the shaft of light illuminates a person's true insides, then why didn't we see creepy things crawling all over Hypermnestra?"

"That's precisely why not," answered Iole. "She not only didn't commit the murder as requested all those ages ago, but now she's hoping for the redemption of her sisters. She has a pure heart."

"Oh. Yeah," Alcie said after a bit. "I knew that."

Iole smiled at her friend.

"Of course you did, Alce."

CHAPTER TEN
Truth

"Then what about Homie?" Alcie asked when they had gotten farther down the road. Erebus was exactly the same in all directions: expanses of colorless, flat grasses and scrub.

"What about Homie—sorry, Homer—what?" Pandy replied, scanning the horizon for the next surprise, twist, or tormented spirit.

"Why didn't we see Homie's innards with all of his bugs and stuff?"

"I'm going to suggest," said Iole, "that we stop for just a moment and take a drink of water and have a piece of flatbread or a dried fig while we discuss Homer's . . . internal workings."

"Excellent idea, maiden," Homer said, leading the girls to the side of the road and spreading his cloak out on the ground, indicating that everyone sit.

"And what's with that . . . this . . . *that*?" Alcie said,

not to Homer, but to Pandy and Iole, as if Homer had become an object to be wondered at. "What's with his speech all of a sudden?"

"I think the shaft of light affected Homer the way it did because Homer's still alive," Pandy said. "Perhaps the shaft of light only brings out whatever that person's problems—flaws—were when they were alive. Like, it lumps every bad thing about a person together. Iole?"

"I have a different theory," she answered. "You're both forgetting that Homer's skin has been completely restored. And he's behaving much more—mature."

"That's it!" Alcie said. "He's gotten older!"

"Not older," Iole went on, "just more mature. Don't forget what Hypermnestra said; that light was a light of truth. We were all affected by the waters of the Styx. We took on a metal coating. I think if the great warrior Achilles had spent so much time in the river, instead of being held by his heel and simply dipped for a second, he would have had some metal coating as well. But I digress. Not only was Homer's affliction reversed by the light shaft, but Homer's only sixteen . . ."

"Going on seventeen," Homer quickly put in.

". . . uh-huh . . . and you haven't had time to do a great many horrible things and think so many horrible thoughts. There was nothing negative to illuminate, so the powers of the light concentrated on burning off the metal and, through that fire, forging a new *man*. In doing so, they revealed that the truth about you, Homer, is that your qualities inside are just as honorable and wonderful as you are on the outside."

"Thank you," Homer said.

There was a long silence as Alcie and Pandy stared at Iole.

"I try so hard to understand you, Iole. I really do. I just can't," Alcie finally said.

Iole smiled a small smile and looked at her friend. In that instant, Pandy saw something she'd never seen before from Iole regarding Alcie—or vice versa: complete acceptance. Iole, in that one smile, accepted Alcie and her flaws, faults, and shortcomings with nothing but perfect love.

"But what about you?" Alcie went on, not seeing the transformation. "When you drank the water out of that memory lake . . ."

"Mnemosyne," Iole said.

"Right. When you took a drink, you got your brain back but you didn't get more mature, did you? You didn't turn into a new maiden, right? I mean, you didn't get any smarter?"

"Of course not," Iole said.

"Well, there, you see . . . ," Alcie said, throwing her hands up.

"I couldn't become any smarter."

Alcie's mouth hung open, mid-sentence.

"But what I have acquired, I am coming to realize, is a fuller appreciation of my mental capacities and the understanding that I can be the smartest person in the room, *not* be afraid of it or the opinions of others, and accept it without arrogance or bluster. Not that I was terribly blustery in the first place, but to be at peace with myself, whether others are or not."

Again, Alcie and Pandy were struck mute.

At last Alcie turned to Pandy and popped a dried fig into her mouth.

"When this is all over," she said, "if I'm still alive, I want some of that memory water."

CHAPTER ELEVEN
The Puppet Show

The landscape had changed slowly from flat plains to gray rocky hills, but there had been no sign saying they were entering another realm, so Pandy and the rest felt they were still in endless—*endless*—Erebus.

Pandy had begun to worry about the day counter, knowing that even though there was no such thing as time or its constraints in the underworld, the days were passing on Earth. That meant that the days were also passing on Mount Olympus. Zeus, she was sure, would of course know when the final moment occurred and he'd be watching and waiting, especially now that there were so few actual days left to her quest. How many had been on the counter the last time she looked? Twenty, maybe? And then, of course, they'd taken nine days to walk the path down into Hades. So, eleven. But she knew that more time had passed as they'd journeyed through the Fields of Asphodel and Erebus. With a loud, involuntary gasp she realized that the deadline may have already come and gone and Fear was still free, hiding somewhere in the dim shadows—or someplace worse—in the underworld.

"What?" cried Alcie, startled.

"Are you all right, Pandora?" Homer asked.

"Uh, yes," she replied, instantly realizing that worrying her friends over events they couldn't control would produce no positive effect whatsoever. "I . . . just . . . remembered that I haven't talked with my wolf-skin diary for a long time. And I became a little concerned that I would forget everything that's happened in the last few . . . little bit. Um. Of time. Like, Tantalus and the Danaids. I want to remember to tell it about Iole and her memories, and Homer and his truth."

"We promise not to let you forget," Homer said, striding on.

"Great. Great. And Homer . . . it's 'Pandy,' okay? Always has been, always will be."

"Okay," he said with a smile.

"I didn't think it was possible to adore him any more than I already did," Alcie whispered. "I was totally wrong."

At that moment, Homer, who was a few strides ahead, also looking for danger or trouble, stopped short. The road forked; to the right, a large, black, beautiful palace was only a short distance away, rising out of a mist. But the way through was barred by an iron gate in a low wall.

"Aaaaaaand . . . we're here!" Alcie yelped. "Hades' palace! Dove hearts and snail custard, here I come!"

To the left they saw an identical iron gate also set in a wall, this one high enough that they couldn't see to the other side—but the skies beyond were a dull orange.

"Tartarus," Pandy whispered to herself.

"Ahem," came a cough from the one direction no one had bothered to look: directly in front of them.

Three men stood in front of a tall tree, all clad in the same deep, dark red robes. Their snow-white hair fell in almost exactly the same thin ringlets and their bright white eyes were fixed and unblinking on the group. The man in the center motioned for everyone to step forward.

"Alcie, did you meet these guys when you were here before?" Pandy asked quietly out of the side of her mouth.

"Nope," Alcie whispered back.

"Not surprising," Iole said. "You're not dead. These are the judges of all the spirits who enter the underworld. Aeacus, who judges the souls of the westerners; Rhadamanthus, who judges the souls of the easterners; and his brother Minos, who has the deciding vote if he doesn't agree with the others."

"These are the guys who send souls to either the

Fields of Asphodel, Erebus, Tartarus, or the Elysian Fields?" asked Alcie.

"That's them," Iole responded. "They're all sons of Zeus by—somebody and somebody else."

"Impudent maiden!" shouted one of the judges. "To speak of our mothers in such flippant and disrespectful terms!"

"Apologies, oh wise one," Iole said, immediately bowing low. "It is simply that I cannot remember the names."

"Liar," Alcie mumbled.

"You want me to also say that their mothers weren't really *worth* remembering?" Iole mumbled back.

"Approach as we have bidden you," said another judge. "Do not keep us waiting."

"I mean no disrespect," Pandy said, taking a step forward. "But we are not spirits here to be judged. We are very much alive and have come to the underworld on a quest. My name is . . ."

"Silence!" bellowed the third judge in a voice that Pandy thought was almost exactly like one of the others.' In fact, all three voices sounded slightly off—as if each man had a cold or a sore throat. She also noticed that the movements of the judges' arms and legs were stiff and slightly jerky.

"We care not what your excuse might be, spirit," said the first who had spoken. "We care not for your names, only your *crimes*."

Suddenly, ignoring the odd voices, Pandy was struck with panic; these men weren't listening to her and had no *intention* of listening to her. She knew enough to be certain that their word was final and, even though the underworld was in chaos, they could end her quest right here and now.

"You are westerners all," the judge went on, unblinking. "And therefore I, Aeacus, shall decide your fate."

"And if it is not harsh enough, I shall devise a punishment twice as horrible," said the judge who was obviously Minos.

"I only wish I could have a hand in this decision," said Rhadamanthus, grinning evilly.

"Wait!" said Iole. "Not only are you all in error, but you seem to have decided that we are criminals without truly knowing anything about us."

"Unless," Pandy said, turning to Iole, flashing on the worst-case scenario, "the deadline for the quest has come and gone and Fear remains loose in the world. I'd have to get punished for that. But not you all."

She turned back to the judges.

"Not them! Alcie, Iole, and Homer deserve nothing but the Elysian Fields."

"Pandy," Alcie cried, "we're not dead *yet*."

"Be silent!" screamed Minos. "We are not without mercy. We shall send each to his respective and deserved fate. If you each wish to make your case, I welcome your . . ."

In a swift motion, Aeacus hit Minos in the stomach with his arm—as if Minos had spoken foolishly and needed to be shut up. And that was the moment that registered with Pandy that the scene was not just odd but, once again, terribly wrong. As Aeacus lowered his arm after hitting Minos, who had only acknowledged the blow by closing his mouth, Pandy saw a fine string lifting up the sleeve of Aeacus's robe. She realized that Aeacus's hand hadn't moved, his fingers hadn't clenched in anger. She followed the string upward with her eyes until it finally disappeared into the branches of the enormous tree. Then she saw that fine strings were attached to the sleeves and ears of all three men and that there were even finer strings attached to the corners of each man's mouth. Someone or something was controlling the movements of the judges—as if they were crude festival puppets! Then Pandy took a good look at the eyes of the judges; their eyelids had been roughly *sewn* closed, and fake eyes, far too bright to be real, had been painted on top. Pandy and the others then heard heated whispering from the branches overhead. Looking up they could see nothing, but Dido began to whimper and gave a short bark. Pandy, Alcie, Iole, and Homer all glanced at each other.

"Uh, yes. My fellow judge has spoken too hastily," said Aeacus. "We are not interested in hearing your pleas. And now for your judgments . . ."

"Excuse me," Pandy said boldly in an effort to buy a little time and discover the secret of the strings and those dreadful eyes. "But can you tell me, if someone is bad, where do they go?"

"Idiotic mortal," said Rhadamanthus. "Did you truly learn nothing at the Athena Maiden Middle School? A bad life warrants an eternity in Tartarus."

"Yeah, I get that," Pandy said, with a glance to Alcie. "But if they're really, *really* bad, then what?"

"Uh," said Minos as Pandy watched the grotesque movement of the corners of his mouth. "Uh. Then they go into the *hottest* fires of Tartarus, silly!"

"Wrong!" said Alcie. "The *really* bad souls go to the little rooms in the palace to be locked away with their mothers. I've been there, I've seen it. You should have known that."

"They would have," Iole said quietly, now seeing the strings, "if they were really who they say they are."

She glanced upward and the others followed her gaze. Pandy and Alcie had to move slightly, but they finally saw the wide behind of Hera, wrapped in heavy padding, resting on a high, thick branch. A flash of orange and yellow autumn leaves in the otherwise grayish-green tree told them that Demeter was also high over their heads.

"Our decision has been made," said Aeacus. "It's Tartarus for all four of you! And since you are not dead, I cannot imagine the unending torment of fire consuming live flesh—for eternity!"

Minos's arm began to raise and motion in the direction of the gate to the left.

"Don't let him point!" Iole cried. "Actual judge or not, if he points and the gate opens, we have to go!"

"Dido, JUMP!" commanded Pandy, and the snow-white dog leapt forward, his strong forelegs knocking Minos and Rhadamanthus square in their chests. The two men toppled to the ground as if they were made of paper, the strings on their sleeves pulling taut and causing their mouths to gape open unnaturally, horrifyingly wide. Pandy heard a scream overhead as both Hera and Demeter, each holding many strings, were jerked from their perch and plummeted downward—smacking into several branches as they fell. Demeter landed on her side, but Hera hit directly on her bottom, causing her to bray in agony. Moments later, a golden tub—about the size Sabina had used to wash her mother's delicate undergarments, Pandy thought—fell out of the tree and landed with a thud, sending glistening gray matter flying in every direction, much of it splattering on Pandy and Alcie.

As the goddesses rolled in pain, Pandy and the others took in the scene. Aeacus had pitched forward as he'd fallen and now lay on his stomach at Homer's feet. The collar of his red robe had been torn off his shoulders, and there was a huge gray gash from the back of his head to—far, far down, Pandy surmised. Pandy instantly recognized the glittering gray substance from the tub as brains, hearts, tongues, and various other internal organs. Hera and Demeter had murdered the spirits of the judges; something that astounded even Iole and her vast knowledge. No one had conceived that such a thing could be done, but the proof was lying on the ground before them. The judges had each been separated from their insides to make them truly mute, enabling the goddesses to speak through them.

Demeter was on her feet and thrusting her shoulders back in indignation, preparing to pounce on Pandy.

"Helloooo?" Hera called to her, trying to roll over on her side.

"Oh, honey," Demeter said with a backward glance. "Can't you get up?"

"No. And you'd better help me if you know what's best for you!"

"Here, let me . . ."

"Iole," Pandy said quietly, as Demeter tried to get Hera on her feet, only to end up tumbling head over heels herself, "take hold of Aeacus's right arm."

Iole understood at once and propped up the judge's empty shell as it was finally about to collapse.

Hera was on her feet at last, batting Demeter out of the way as she straightened her robes neatly over her backside. Subtly, Pandy grabbed a mass of gray goo as it slid down her hip. In the last second before Hera focused on her, she made eye contact with Alcie; Alcie saw what was in Pandy's hand and nodded her head, reaching up and taking hold of a gray mass on her shoulder.

"Some time ago, brat," Hera hissed, "you made reference to the fact that I talk a great deal, but my—what shall we call it?—follow through, is a little weak. I'm going to amend that once and for all. Yes, I could strike you here and now, but I'm going to pass the sentence that's been ordered. You all, including that four-legged flea-bag, are going to spend the rest of your natural and unnatural mortal lives in . . ."

"The Elysian Fields," Pandy screamed. "Iole, POINT! Dido . . . Demeter! Knock her down! GO!"

She flung the gray blob, which she realized was a kidney, at Hera, catching her in the throat. Alcie threw a piece of lung and walloped Hera right between the eyes. Iole lifted Aeacus's spiritless arm and pointed in the direction of Hades' palace and the Elysian Fields, which lay beyond. At the motion of the judge's arm, the black gate swung open, and Pandy and the rest were rushed by an unseen force toward the wall. At Pandy's call,

Dido had sprung at Demeter, who'd thrown her arms up to protect herself only to find Dido's fangs sunk into her right hand. Dido chomped down hard, then was also made to follow after his mistress, taking an immortal pinky in his teeth. They'd all been propelled at such a speed that everything blurred around them until they were safely through the gate, with Hera and Demeter screaming in fury and pain on the other side. With no time to waste, everyone took off at a run toward the palace, not knowing if Hera would follow or if someone, somewhere, would know that these four could never be assigned to the Elysian Fields—not yet, anyway.

"My little finger!" Demeter was howling. "The dog *ate* my little finger. And I even tried to help him when you had him cornered in your apartments on Olympus!"

"Shut up," Hera snapped. "Shut up about your stupid finger. Grow another one, you fool. Oh, my husband's toenails! I had that beastly mutt in my possession and should have murdered it when I had the chance. I'm just too sensitive and kindhearted, that's the problem. That's always been my downfall. And the brat is right: I talk too much. But something about gloating is so delicious."

"Yes," Demeter said casually but with a slight exasperation, wrapping one of the puppet strings around her stump to staunch the blood flow. "But look where gloating gets you: you simply have no control. Not over the girl. Not over her dog. And certainly not over your mouth."

Hera turned with an icy glare to her friend, whose hair was now growing the dried grasses of summer.

"Really?"

"Mm-hmm," Demeter said, tying off the string with her mouth.

The next moment, Demeter had become a small apricot poodle whose tail sprouted dried grass, then autumn leaves, then winter icicles, and so on.

"You can't be serious," Demeter said. "A *dog*?"

"Until I decide otherwise. Whaddya gonna do about it, Demetie? Bite my finger?"

"What if I said I was sorry?"

"Save it," Hera said.

Hera twirled her hand in the air, materializing a long, emerald-studded leash. Fastening it to Demeter's emerald-studded collar, Hera patted the top of her head.

"I'll show you just how much control I can have over a dog," Hera smirked. "Now, what to do—what to do?"

"You ungrateful wretch," Demeter yapped. "When I think of the risks I've taken for you!"

Hera kicked the spiritless, gutted body of Rhadamanthus out of her way and led Demeter toward the dull orange glow, then she turned in the direction of the palace.

"The question is, do I head over to the palace now and be there to greet Pandora when she arrives and kill her then?" Hera pondered, glancing down at Demeter.

"And I will. I swear by all my priestesses, the next time I meet the brat I will not let my sensitive, generous nature get the better of me and I will kill her. Or do I go to Tartarus and make certain that Hades is still confined to the fire pit? It was easy enough to trick and capture him, but have his bonds held? It would have saved some time if Pandora and her friends had taken the bait and let themselves be sent into the flames, ending their pathetic lives and assuring that Fear remained loose. But now that I think of it, she really only has one path to trudge and this way, going by way of the palace, she might take so long that she'll run out of days, fail in her quest—and *that* would enrage my husband and provide delightful entertainment. I really must look into why I am so magnanimous where this girl is concerned, why my benevolence is such that I have yet failed to kill her or her friends. Why I have such a big, fat heart. Ah, well. We'll get ourselves warm, shall we, doggy? We'll go to Tartarus. I don't know where Fear is, but I know once Pandora discovers that Hades is my prisoner, she'll race to help him—and help herself—I'm sure. We'll meet again, not-so-pretty maiden!"

Hera felt something warm and wet on her foot. She looked down and gazed into Demeter's little poodle face, saw her hind leg lifted and a wide poodle grin on her face.

"Control this, Queenie!"

CHAPTER TWELVE
The Palace:
Garden... and Ovens

Hades' palace, which had seemed so close from the other side of the gate, now appeared to be quite a distance away and getting farther with every step—as if with each footfall, the immense black-and-gray building receded back into the surrounding mist. They'd been running flat out for a while, all of them afraid to turn around for fear of what might be right behind them. Finally, Pandy had to slow down, completely out of breath.

"Homer," she panted. "Homer, stop. I can't go on without a break."

Homer turned immediately.

"Would you like me to carry you?" he asked, without a trace of arrogance or weariness. "I could carry all of you. Although with Dido, it might get a little tricky."

Dido barked, indignant that anyone would ever think he needed to be carried. But he did flop down on his side in the gray grasses that bordered the road, his chest heaving.

"Where's Iole?" Homer asked.

"Huh?" Pandy said, looking around.

There was nothing past Alcie, who was hunched over on her knees, taking in gulps of air—except a tiny speck far, far back. Homer took off at a sprint and soon returned with Iole slung over his shoulders. Gently, he set her down on the ground.

"Thank you, Homer," said Iole, then looked at Pandy. "He's had to carry me on this quest far too many times for my liking."

"What happened?" Pandy asked.

"I just stopped for a moment and turned to observe if we were being followed and when I turned back to keep running, my legs refused. I had this mental image of my legs laughing at me—my kneecaps turning into smiling faces. Then I passed out and the next thing I knew I was upside down on Homer's back."

"Feel better now?" Alcie asked.

"Much, thank you," Iole said, squirting some water from her water-skin into her mouth.

"And are we?" Alcie went on.

"Are we what? Oh . . . being followed? I don't think so."

"That's just weird," Alcie replied. "Just plain weird. I know—she's a goddess and goddesses are strange, but come on!'

"All the immortals are unpredictable," Pandy agreed. "It's as if they have no filter in their brains."

"They don't need filters," Iole said. "There are basically no consequences for anything they do."

"Hera could have killed us all five times over by now," said Pandy. "She hasn't. But it's not because she doesn't want to. And she could have followed us just now, but it's almost as if she gets distracted by something and heads in another direction. She put a lot of effort into the puppet show, then she just drops it without really putting up much of a fight."

"Until the next time she just pops up," Alcie added.

"As if the overall focus of killing you loses importance when she sees a bright, shiny object," Iole observed. "Figuratively speaking, of course."

"She's a big fat baby, is what she is," Alcie said, definitively. "I'm glad Zeus spanked her. And she's still wearing the bandage; that must have been some thrashing."

"So," Pandy said, changing the topic and getting to her feet. "I see the palace, a little more of a hike than I originally thought—that's okay, no biggie. But isn't the whole thing supposed to be surrounded by the Elysian Fields? Where the green?"

Iole opened her mouth to answer, but Alcie cut her off.

"The Elysian Fields, at least the ones that I saw, are only on one side of the palace. I'm guessing the far side."

"But you didn't actually *see* them," Iole reminded her.

"Well, if you're going to get specific about it, no, I didn't lay my eyes on them. I saw only flashes of green through the windows before the shrubbery grew over and blocked my view. But believe me, if they were anywhere close by, we'd know it. That's a color you can't miss."

"I'm only suggesting that, when you were in the palace, you didn't know exactly which direction you were facing and you might have—"

"What? Gotten confused? You know, just because you have a brain the size of Athens does not mean the rest of us can't think."

"Guys! Come on, knock it off!" Pandy cried. As Iole and Alcie both turned to face her, each about to protest bitterly that the other didn't know what she was talking about, their jaws dropped and their eyes widened. Looking up, Homer gasped and Dido whined, then hid behind Pandy's legs.

Less than five steps away, the outer palace wall rose above them to a height well beyond Pandy's ability to see or calculate. The single black stones that formed the wall, of which there were thousands upon thousands, were each the size of Zeus's throne on Mount Olympus; no human could have set them into place. The mortar was black and coarse with bits of white bone mixed in. And the entire wall was covered in the same blackish-red substance that she'd seen on the mammoth gates leading into the underworld. So close now, she could swear that it was, indeed, blood. The whole building was steaming as if the blood coating were baking in the sun—except that there was no sun.

And, of course, the palace hadn't been there ten seconds before.

"Great!" Pandy said when she recovered from her initial shock. "That saves us a little time. C'mon."

"I don't have a good feeling about this," Alcie said, following Pandy along the wall toward one side of the palace.

"Alce, I haven't had a good feeling about pretty much anything since I walked out of our courtyard over five moons ago," Pandy replied, rounding a corner.

❧

Over four hours later, Pandy finally stopped in front of a crude wooden door on a rusty hinge.

"This is it?" Alcie asked incredulously. "No way. Where are the doors? A place this big has to have a big door!"

Homer grabbed a fistful of his cloak and aimed to a spot on the wall off to the side of the door. Carefully, he wiped away eons of dirt and gooey blood to reveal a small bronze plaque.

SERVANTS' ENTRANCE

"Well, we didn't see any other way in." Pandy sighed.

"Alcie, do you remember a door when you were here last?" Iole asked.

"No. I just sorta materialized into one of the rooms, but when Persephone took me on a tour . . . ," Alcie answered, thinking back to her time in the underworld. "No. Nothing. Wait! Yes, there was! There was a little door leading out of the food-preparation room. I think there was some sort of garden with dead vines on the walls and rows of brown things. It's where they grew the snails and let things like the liver and entrails spoil and rot. Gods, now I'm hungry. I'll bet this gets us there."

Two quick yanks from Homer on the handle of the door and they entered the garden, laid out just as Alcie had described it, and saw the small door leading back into the palace. But it was not overgrown with rotting foods and crawling with slimy, legless creatures. Instead, they were greeted with bursts of brilliant color as they came upon row after row of enormous strawberries, blueberries, squashes, and heads of lettuce. Greenbeans the size of small branches and huge crimson tomatoes hung from vines draping the inside walls. There were bright pink radishes and artichokes the size of Homer's head, some blossoming into royal purple flowers. Plump white and black grapes clustered in arbors, and bees were busy storing honey in massive honeycomb hives nestled in two tall trees.

"No wonder you loved the food here," Pandy said.

"Yes," Iole said, popping a blueberry the size of a walnut into her mouth. "I'm also understanding why you gained a little weight when you were supposed to be so depressed about being dead."

"No. *No!* This isn't right," Alcie cried, marching through the garden toward another small door set into an inside palace wall. "Where are the wilting field greens? Where's my liver pudding on flatbread? Where're my lamb entrails with minced kidney? This stuff is fresh and ripe and healthy—and—completely inedible! And I did not gain any weight!"

"Alcie, stop!" Pandy called. "Wait. Think for a moment. If everything else in the underworld is backward, upside down, in chaos, then it makes sense that nothing here would be as it should be, right?"

"Right," Alcie said, coming to a halt.

"Which means that there's probably a lot going on inside there and we have to be careful."

"I see your point."

"Okay, so just take it easy," Pandy said, moving past Alcie and entering the food-preparation rooms in the palace of Hades.

"Yeah, I'll take it easy. But I want some cream-of-tripe soup, I'll tell you that."

The cavernous food-preparation rooms were completely empty of spirits. The rooms were cold and still. Alcie went straight for the storage cupboards.

"Don't touch anything!" Pandy cautioned.

"Too late!"

Alcie opened a cooling box, meant to keep cold items from spoiling—or, in the case of these strange rooms, to keep mold and spoilage fresh—and received instead a blast of hot air.

"Backward," she muttered. "Everything is backward. Oooh, what do we have here?"

She reached for something small, black, and hard on the counter in front of a large oven and eagerly tossed it in her mouth. "Huh. No idea what *that* was."

Then she casually flipped open the oven door—and screamed.

Inside, three spirits were crammed like ill-fitting pieces of a wooden puzzle.

"Oh, Alcie. I knew I recognized your voice," came a familiar voice as two eyes peered out from underneath another spirit's armpit. "I was certain that was you."

"*Cookie*? I mean . . . uh . . . Cyrene?"

"Yes. Help an old spirit out of an oven, won't you?"

Quickly, Pandy, Alcie, and Iole got Cyrene and the two others onto the ground. Pandy felt a cold chill as she closed the oven door; she and Alcie glanced inside and saw that it had been packed with ice. Alcie introduced Pandy, Iole, and Homer to the wizened woman, who was still hunched over.

"Thank you, my dear," Cyrene said, straightening her crooked back with many loud cracks and snaps of her aged spine.

"Wow!" Alcie blurted out. Then, as everyone glanced at her, she flushed. "I just keep forgetting that you all are just like us except you're dead. I mean, you have bones—is what I'm trying to say. I mean—I mean, oh Ares' eyeballs, why don't I keep my mouth shut!"

"Not to worry," said Cyrene. "But, yes, in many ways, just like the living."

"Don't sweat it, Alce," said Pandy. "None of us really realized it until we saw that Hera and Demeter had murdered those three judges."

"What?" cried Cyrene. "Rhadamanthus, Aeacus, and Minos? Something's happened to them?"

Pandy gave a brief account not only of the massacre of the three spirits at Hera's and Demeter's hands, but of the other strange and frightening sights they'd seen since coming to Hades. Cyrene put her bony hand over her mouth in grief.

"The judges were my favorites," she said, her spirit eyes working hard to well up tears. "Especially that Minos—such a scamp. After a hard day of judging souls, they would come to my table, right over there, to sit and eat. We'd laugh and they would tell me stories of souls who thought they would surely be going to the Elysian Fields only to find out they were spending eternity in boring Asphodel. One woman who had led a rebellion of female slaves for better working conditions thought for certain she was going to Tartarus. Minos tried to describe the look on the woman's face when they sent her to Elysium. I can't believe they're gone."

Then Cyrene quickly sent the other two spirits out into the garden.

"Hide!" she urged them. "But keep your eyes on the door and I'll let you know when it's safe to come back inside." Then she turned back to Pandy and the others. "Hera has raised the stakes, I see. She's added a great deal of pepper to the soup, to use my language. Well, I can't say I'm surprised; she's always been the worst guest, had the filthiest eating habits and the manners of a gorgon. It was a nightmare whenever she ate at Hades' table. She'd literally walk back here from the main dining hall and throw food at me if something came out of this room that wasn't to her liking. My slugs are better behaved than she is."

"Has Hera been in the palace recently?" Pandy asked.

"Has she . . . ?" Cyrene looked at Pandy as if she were foolish to even ask. "Only days—or maybe it was hours ago—she stormed through here like she had a burr under her robes. The master had heard of some trouble with the hecatonchires. Apparently, they'd gotten loose. Although I have no idea why they would want to leave; they have a much better health plan than any of the rest of—"

"Yes, we know about them," Pandy said, now trying to hurry the woman along, but not wanting to appear rude.

"Well, Hades hadn't been gone but a short time when Persephone got word that other things were going awry in the kingdom, so she left to try to put as much right as she could. And that's when Hera blew in through the front doors like a storm."

"What front doors?" Alcie cried. "We didn't see any front doors!"

"Well, of course there are front doors, child," Cyrene chided. "What self-respecting palace has no front doors? Anyway, I heard the commotion way down at this end and I knew something was horribly wrong. So I got everyone out into the garden and out the servants' entrance. Then I snuck—well, I tried to sneak—into the main halls without being noticed, but it's been so long since I'd left the food-preparation rooms that I'm ashamed to say I got lost. I wandered about for ages, it seemed. I heard noises behind closed doors, but couldn't find another soul. Finally, I . . . I came upon the main hall . . ."

Cyrene's eyes grew quite large and there were actual tears. Her voice trembled as she became a little panicked. Pandy took hold of her hand to steady the frail spirit.

". . . I knew it right away, because of the two great thrones. This is where the great Dark Lord of the underworld sits with his beautiful queen. This is the room where they received Orpheus when he ventured down here to beg for his wife's return. This is where they hold an enormous party every year for Hades' birthday. And . . . and . . . what I saw!"

Cyrene stopped cold, reliving an awful memory.

"What?" Alcie asked. "What did you see?"

"Everyone, all the spirits, it seemed—chained together. Hands and feet. Some hanging from . . . and they were—oh, merciful Zeus! And the queen! Oh, my poor queen. So I ran—as fast as these legs would carry me, right back here. I found two other shades. I tripped on them as they cowered behind a large planter in one of the corridors. We didn't know what else to do, so we jumped into the oven. It seemed the safest and the coolest place to hide. Oh, please, don't make me go back there!"

"We won't," Iole said. "We promise."

Cyrene clutched at Alcie's and Pandy's arms.

"But Alcie, you—and *you*, Pandora—why, all Alcie did when she was here was talk about you and how courageous and cunning you are. And she ate a lot, I do remember that. You all must help the queen! And those poor other souls. Say you will."

"We will, Cyrene," Pandy said. "We'll do everything we can."

"The gods be praised. Go now," Cyrene said, using what little strength she could muster to shove them out into an immense hallway. "If you can help my poor queen, Alcie, there's a batch of dove hearts in it for you."

"You don't need to ask me twice." Alcie grinned. "Point the way, Cookie!"

Cyrene gestured in one direction down the long dark hall. Faintly, even from what was an incredibly long way away, came the sounds of moaning and weeping. Then, someone screamed.

"Fire up those ovens," Alcie said, adjusting her carrying pouch and grabbing Homer's hand, "or at least get the ice out of them. We're on it."

Walking away, Iole pulled Pandy close.

"Dove hearts?" Iole whispered. "She doesn't even know what we're getting into and she's doing it for the dove hearts? Seriously?"

"I had a few in Rome," Pandy replied out of the side of her mouth. "Totally worth it."

CHAPTER THIRTEEN
Preparations

A good distance from the food-preparation rooms, the hallway branched into several directions.

"Which way?" Alcie asked.

"I think if we follow the wailing sounds," Pandy said with a shudder.

"I hear it down here," said Homer.

"But it's also coming from this direction," Iole said, staring off down the second corridor.

"Nope, I hear it loudest over this way," Alcie claimed. "Do you think we should split up? I know my way around . . ."

"Alce, we're not splitting up," Pandy said. "I have a feeling this place is worse than the labyrinth of Crete."

"Before my dad moved us all from Crete to Athens," Iole said, "we used to go to the Labyrinth Land—it was an amusement park—all the time. I could find my way through the maze in under thirty minutes. I could take Homer and we could . . ."

"Everyone, stop!" Pandy said. "We're not splitting up for the simple reason that if Hera found any of you alone, she wouldn't hesitate to slay you on the spot. But she likes to chatter with me and that extra time might give us our best means of escape. But that's a brilliant idea, Iole."

"Of course," Iole said. Then, "What?"

Pandy pulled the magic rope out of her carrying pouch.

"Rope," she said, her voice low and serious. "The thickness of a thread and the strength of iron. Fade into the color of the walls. Length . . . uh . . . I don't know yet. Just don't run out."

She looked down one hallway and made a decision.

"Oh, *that* idea." Iole grinned.

"We're gonna pull a 'Theseus,' " said Pandy, heading off into the dimly lit unknown. "This way."

Unspooling the thread of rope as they walked, Pandy, in the lead, turned the first corner at an intersection of two new hallways and immediately shoved everyone back around the way they'd come. No one made a sound. They watched from the shadows as a small group of spirits, bound and shackled together, was roughly shoved down the corridor. They were led by two other spirits with nothing to distinguish them besides small swords. Some of the bound spirits were crying softly. Sticking her head out to watch, Pandy saw that the entire group was herded into a room only a short distance away. After waiting only a few moments, Pandy and the others tiptoed down the hall and, by arranging themselves just right, managed to get all four of their heads in a vertical position enabling them to peep into the room—through the legs of one of the huge, unsuspecting guards at the door.

The slaves, still shackled but able to move about, were polishing large mirrors and scrubbing the floors. Lamps, unused for centuries if ever, were being dusted and filled with oil. Carpets were being laid out and tapestries hung in the blackened windows. And two spirits were beginning to paint the room a shade of blue.

One spirit, taking a moment from beating eons of dust from a rug, was poked sharply in her backside with the business end of a sword.

"No slacking!" barked a guard.

Pandy moved herself back into the corridor and the others followed. Quietly, they tiptoed back to the intersection and followed the thread back to the first junction of hallways.

"Redecorating?" Alcie asked. "At a time like this?"

"No." Pandy shook her head. "There's something more to it. Why would Hades want to paint a room? C'mon."

Again, following the sounds of spirits in despair, she chose another hallway. This time, they met with no groups of shades on the move up close, although they did see two groups crossing at intersections far, far down the corridor. Pandy stopped and everyone flattened themselves against the walls, but they were all fairly certain that they were simply too far away to be noticed.

The first room they came to had a privacy curtain drawn across the entryway. Alcie moved past it, indicating that she'd look through, and gingerly separated the curtain from the wall. She gasped. This was a room she'd seen before when Persephone had given her a tour of the palace. Floor-to-impossibly-high-ceiling shelves held bottles and jars filled with potions and oils, which were now being smashed to bits by sobbing spirits, spreading musky, fetid, and medicinal odors all over the room. Upright stands filled with precious and ancient scrolls were turned over and emptied; charts of the human body were being ripped from where they'd hung on the walls since the creation of Hades' home. The only things that were being set, gently, on a table in the center of the room were several odd and dangerous looking devices (meant for practice of the healing arts, Alcie was certain, but used for Hades-only-knew-what). The guards were talking conspiratorially and gleefully about these rather sinister contraptions, picking them up and indicating how *they*'d use them if they had the chance.

As Alcie watched, other enslaved spirits swept up the shards of oily glass and parchment, while still others placed shiny new bottles and vials on the shelves. Without warning, a small bottle slipped out of the hand of a spirit who'd had her hands too full, trying to do too much too quickly and avoid being poked with a sword. As the bottle shattered, another scent wafted into the air: a perfume unlike any other. One that Alcie had smelled before.

She pulled her head out quickly, but not before catching sight of the window on the far wall. She remembered that she'd been able to glimpse, during her first visit to Hades, the most astonishing color of green through the windows in almost every room. Persephone had told her the Elysian Fields were right outside. Now, through this window, she saw only a whitish gray.

She tried to breathe in clear air as quietly as possible.

"Take a whiff," she said to Pandy.

Pandy put her nose to the opening in the privacy curtain and inhaled. Her brow furrowed as she looked at Alcie and then Iole, who was also catching the scent. Only Homer was completely clueless as to the various intricacies of this particular perfume, although he'd smelled it himself on a number of occasions. Pandy led them farther down the hallway.

"But why?" Pandy asked.

"And why here?" Iole furthered.

"Why what?" Homer asked. "What did you get from that noxious fragrance, which, by the way, Alcie, I will implore you never to wear when we're married."

"Oh, Homer. You're such a guy," Alcie smiled. "And don't worry. I won't wear it. I wouldn't be able to find it even if I wanted to. That scent belongs to one person only . . ."

The name was on the tip of her tongue when at that moment a tremendous crash echoed off the walls from a room just a little farther down. They raced as noiselessly as they could to the entryway; Homer swept everyone aside with his arm and took a look inside.

Weapons of all kinds were strewn on the floor; only a few were still hanging from their hooks on the walls. The tapestries had been pulled from the windows, and a table and chairs had been overturned and sent flying into the walls, shards of wood lying among the spears, swords, and shields. At the far end of the room, three spirits sat on the floor, their backs against the wall. Homer recognized them at once: Hector, Odysseus, and Achilles. Standing over them were four guards, their swords pointed at the heroes' necks. All around them, enslaved spirits piled the weapons near the door of the room as others hung floral curtains, polished a large standing looking glass, set up a reclining couch in the shape of a peacock, and added other feminine touches.

Homer withdrew into the hallway, his face grave.

"They should never have been caught unawares like that," he murmured.

"Huh?" Pandy said.

"Let's move," Homer said, picking up the iron thread and respooling it. "I'll tell you as we walk."

Making their way back to the main intersection, Homer sighed heavily, more than once. When they were a safe distance away from the room, he slowed.

"I'm thinking that was the armory," he began. "Or as close as Hades would get to having an armory. I saw Hector and Achilles . . ."

"I saw them too," Alcie said. "When I was here before. Very hunky. Uh . . . yes, go on, dearest."

"I think Odysseus was there. Anyway, there were three of them, completely overpowered by four swords. They must have been surprised—caught off guard. That's all I can think of. No true warrior would ever let himself be caught like that, with his defenses down."

"Did you see anything else?" Pandy inquired.

"The room was being redone, just like the first room

we all saw. Only worse. I mean more so. There were flowered curtains and a large looking glass."

"As if someone other than Hades was making the palace their home?" Pandy asked, somewhat rhetorically.

"Yes, exactly. I mean, I don't think Hades, or Persephone for that matter, would ever be interested in a couch the shape of a peacock."

"Gods," Alcie yipped. "And that was *her* perfume!"

"I think we can, in all logic, safely agree that it's official," Iole said. "Hera's moving in."

CHAPTER FOURTEEN
The Throne Room (and an Unexpected Encounter)

After three more failed attempts to find the correct hallway, which included peering into four more rooms being hideously redecorated and dodging groups of enslaved spirits, at last Pandy spotted what she was certain was the throne room. When she saw two huge, intricately carved doors blown completely off their hinges, she motioned for everyone to slow down, then drop to their knees. Just outside the entrance, she stopped, got as low as she could, and carefully craned her neck and head and peered into the room. At first, she was stunned by the sheer size of the room: while not as wide and deep as Zeus's grand hall on Mount Olympus, it appeared to be much taller. In fact, as Pandy glanced up high, she realized there was no ceiling at all that she could see; the room just went up and up and up. It was so high that there even appeared to be some sort of large bird circling and swooping with plenty of room.

Then, as she was glancing at the walls and the beautiful murals on each—especially on one at the back of the room, done in the most vibrant shades of orange and yellow—her ears once again registered the moaning. That's when she noticed the bodies. Bodies everywhere.

While they couldn't see her face, Alcie, Iole, and Homer saw Pandy's own body stiffen, her hand clenched in shock. Just as she was about to turn back, she had the oddest sense that she'd played this entire scene out before. But when? Then she remembered all of them being in these same positions in the hallway of the ship the *Peacock* as she watched the bizarre events inside the captain's quarters. That situation eventually turned out well; she only hoped the gods were still looking favorably on her.

"It's a sea of spirits," she said, turning back to her friends. "If I didn't know better, I'd say every inhabitant of the underworld is in there. But they're all chained. All of them. They're on top of each other, piled like floor pillows. And they're hanging from the walls and in midair over the entire room. Guys—they're *hanging* from the walls—like prisoners. And there's something happening at the back of the room that I couldn't see clearly. It's where the thrones are, and Persephone's there. But she's tied up, I think."

"You think?" asked Alcie.

"I could only see flashes of pink where her throne was."

"Hades?" asked Iole.

"Didn't see him."

"Hera?" Homer said.

"Nope," Pandy said, shaking her head. "But this is her work. We have to get to Persephone. Alcie, come on. Homer, Iole, follow my signals. Go when we go. And stay low and tight to the wall. Dido, guard the entrance, boy. Let us know if anything happens out here."

Pandy and Alcie scooted across the doorway, leaving Iole and Homer on the first side. Pandy motioned with her fingers that she and Alcie were going in and both groups should keep their eyes on each other.

Quickly they worked their way around the entryway and were stopped cold. There were so many spirits crammed together on the floor that both pairs could only go over the spirit bodies. Without thinking, Pandy and Alcie scrambled up and onto the crush of shades, crawling around the perimeter of the room, as Iole and Homer did the same. Suddenly, Pandy felt her knees and hands sinking into the bodies as she tried to work her way through the mass.

"Pandy!" Alcie nearly shrieked behind her.

Pandy turned and saw Alcie's arm buried to her shoulder in the stomach of an elderly man-spirit.

"Do you mind, maiden?" said the spirit, his neck, ankles, and wrists shackled together. "Or is this but another aspect of our enslavement?"

"I'm so sorry," Alcie said.

She just as quickly retrieved her arm, but they were all sinking fast whenever they made contact with a spirit, as if they were trying to crawl on a huge bowl of creamed oats.

"Try just using their heads," Pandy said, coming up with no other answer.

"I'm not gonna step on a dead person's head," Alcie said flatly.

"Well then . . . try crawling on just their clothes."

Across the other side of the room, Pandy saw Iole's head nearly go under. Homer helped her up and out, then he sank like a stone. She turned back to Alcie and saw a flash of copper hair below her. Sinking herself, Pandy felt Alcie thrashing close by as if she were drowning again, then Pandy's bottom hit the floor. Her eyes were closed as if she were underwater. She felt a whoosh close to one side. Carefully opening her eyes, she saw all around her an ocean of gray, opaque bodies and body parts; she could just barely make out lungs expanding and contracting, tongues swallowing, and spirit hearts beating. Then these views would be obstructed by bits of clothing. Just when she began to panic that she'd run out of air, she saw two small, white columns moving in front of her nose: Alcie's legs. The next moment, she felt herself yanked to her feet by the collar of her cloak, and the next, she was standing beside Alcie.

"Guess what?" Alcie said, with a self-satisfied smirk. "We can stand. And we can walk through 'em. As long as we don't stay in one place too long, no body seems to notice or mind too much. Careful of the clothes, though. Don't want to get tripped up. And watch the chain, P. The way I figure it, they're all linked together on one long chain."

As Pandy got her bearings, standing literally in a sea of souls, Alcie called out to Homer—whose head was just above the surface—as quietly as she could, and told him to get to his feet.

"Meet us at the thrones. At the back," she mouthed.

"Why are we whispering?" Homer called out, trying to keep his voice low.

"Duh!" Alcie cried softly after a moment, as if that one word in that one moment said everything that needed saying.

After several minutes of walking carefully and delicately—and apologizing—both groups were now halfway down the length of the grand hall.

"Well, I think—excuse me—I think—pardon us—I think this is borderline rude," Pandy whispered.

"Hi, sorry, was that your foot? Sorry. I think—oops, my bad—while it's not the most comfortable I've ever been—excuse me—it's kinda like wading against the current in the Aegean. If I'm ever able to do it again, Pandy, I swear to Aphrodite I won't take it for granted."

"*Pandy?*" came a voice nearby. "Pandora Atheneus Andromaeche Helena? Daughter of Prometheus?"

Pandy froze and her blood turned to ice water. Without even having to look, Pandy knew *exactly* who was speaking. She and Alcie turned and gasped. There, on the nearby wall, hung their teacher, Master Epeus.

"Oh, hi there . . . sir."

"Young maiden, you will march yourself over here right now. I'd like a word or two with you."

The courage that had been built up over the past five moons, the self-reliance and wisdom that she'd accrued from all the experiences and adventures she'd lived through—any one of which was more of an education that anything Master Epeus could have taught her—they all went right out the window. Or would have, had there been a window in the throne room. Her shoulders hunched over and she bit her lip just as she used to do whenever he called on her in class. She would have sworn she could feel a blemish erupting on her chin as she slunk her way through several spirits to her teacher.

"Greetings, Master . . ."

"Be quiet," he said dryly, gazing at her up and down. "Mm-hmm. *You're* still alive, I see. Well, isn't that just perfect? The dimmest, dullest child in my class, the least successful in every assignment *and* the least prolific. Of course. Of course, *you* haven't been touched by any of this. As Aristotle might say in the third definition of his reflections on the word 'perfection': this is that which has attained its purpose. I always knew you and your friends were trying to send me to an early grave, so bravo, Pandora. Well done! This is all your fault, you know. You brought that box to school and the next thing I knew, the Athena Maiden Middle school was in ashes around my feet. The board of elders called me in to see if I had anything to do with it. Me? Me! We tried holding classes out in the olive groves—well, where else could we go? You'd destroyed everything, you selfish girl. After my third breakdown, the board decided that I needed a rest, so they sent me to a nice little sanitarium on Mykonos. Only my ship went down in the middle of a storm and now I'm here. All thanks to you."

"I'm sorry, Master—"

"Silence! You have not been given permission to speak! Oh, if only I were free, I'd strike at you with all my fury. Fury I've buried deep inside ever since you slouched into my classroom. You, demigoddess and daughter of the great Prometheus! Such potential and all you liked to do was daydream your hours away. You and those two silly, good-for-nothing friends. Oh, how I would strike you."

As he railed on, Pandy turned her head away and closed her eyes. When she opened them, she saw Alcie, her head bowed and a single tear running down her cheek. Pandy knew that she wasn't on some great quest to find herself, she wasn't trying to search deep within to find some hidden meaning or purpose to her life. It wasn't as profound as all that: she was just trying to save the world. That was *it*. But she'd begun to feel as if maybe she and her closest friends had come to have a little more insight into themselves throughout all the struggles and trials they'd weathered. Now, she saw that Alcie could not only *not* come to *her* defense, she couldn't even defend *herself* against the tirade from this horrible, despicable spirit.

And then, like yet another frying stone hitting her square in the face—did the gods and the universe, she wondered, have a whole stack of imaginary frying stones just to whack her with whenever she realized something huge?—she got mad. Madder than she'd ever been at anyone or anything—except when Hera killed Alcie. He could blather on all he wanted to about her . . . but now he was talking trash about her friends. Her noble, courageous, loyal friends who had taken up her cause and put their lives on the line every day for the last umpteen weeks!

"Shut up!" she spat.

"Whaaaaaaaaa . . . ? How dare you!"

"I said shut up," Pandy bellowed. "I revoke *your* permission to speak, you—you—bully! That's right, you're a bully. You were never a teacher in the proper sense of the word. You were always a sad, pathetic little creature who played favorites and picked his toenails. You were a joke! You never inspired anyone to great heights, you just beat us all down—everyone in your class—until we were cowering sheep. We looked up to you; we trusted you, and you broke that trust. You were angry with me because I didn't live up to my *potential*? I was a girl growing into a maiden. We all were and we had a lot of . . . issues! You had no concept. You had no idea of our true potential. Not Alcie, Iole, me, or any other girl in school. You were always afraid of Iole because she was and is smarter than you could ever hope to be. It's obvious that you were jealous of a little girl who could have taught circles around you. And you hated Alcie for the same reason that everybody hated Alcie . . ."

"Heyyyyy!"

". . . because she's bigger than life. She's fun and

bright and has the whole world in the palm of her hand. She's a natural attractor for all those people who aren't jealous and insecure and small minded and stupid. I could tell you things about Alcie and Iole that would have your teeth on the floor, you'd be so impressed. So don't you ever say another word about Alcie and Iole. Not even down here, not even when you think I won't be around. Not for eternity!"

Master Epeus's nearly transparent face bulged with rage, and Pandy knew that if he'd actually been alive, it would have been bright beet red.

"Instead of trying to understand us, you just kept hitting us over the head, verbally, emotionally, and sometimes with your fat fist because you're so tied up in knots yourself, you sniveling worm. And now, you'd like to strike me? How? Like this?"

Pandy flicked her finger at—into—Master Epeus's opaque spirit nose.

"Like this? Huh? Or this? Or maybe this? Or would you strike me with your open palm? Well, guess what? You can't. You have no power here. And, oh wow, I just realized: you're dead! Fantastic. This means you won't be able to criticize and name-call and make fun of any more children the way you did to all of us. No wonder you always liked the two most horrible girls in school the best; you were exactly like Helen and

Hippia: a first-class bully. Only you were an adult, so you were supposed to know better. And you were a man who behaved like a mean girl . . . which is just creepy."

"I . . . I . . . was a fine instruct—"

"Ah, ah, ah," Pandy said, reaching into her carrying pouch. "Pandy didn't say speak. Someone isn't paying attention. Now what was it you used to do to us when we would innocently talk out of turn? Oh, yes, that's right: you'd shove an entire apple in someone's mouth and make her sit in the corner. And if it fell out, you'd roll it in the dirt and put it back in again. Well, guess who I just caught talking when he shouldn't have been, and guess what I have here?"

She reached into her pouch, expecting to only find a handful of dried fruit pieces. Instead, her hands closed around a whole . . . something. Surprised, but trying not to show it, she pulled out of her pouch the shiniest, most perfect apple she'd ever seen. A little small, she thought, but whoever saw fit to put it in there at that precise moment had added a nice touch: two ends of a fat worm sticking out as it wiggled its way through the center.

"An apple for the teacher," she exulted. "And a worm for the worm."

She shoved the apple deep inside Master Epeus's mouth, instantly understanding why the apple was small: the whole fruit, and the worm, sat nestled nicely between his tongue, his teeth, and the roof of his mouth. There was no possible way to choke or spit it out. It was destined to remain there as long as the terrible teacher was chained to the wall.

"And now, if you'll excuse me," Pandy said. "We gotta go capture another Evil. Later!"

Alcie moved past her and faced their teacher.

"It's rumored my aunt Medusa's head is somewhere down here. They keep it locked in a box because, even though she's dead and you're dead, it still has the power to turn spirits to stone. How about I arrange a little look-see? Whaddya say?"

Pandy turned away with a grin. Suddenly she heard a grunt, then a thud, then a different grunt.

Pandy stopped and let Alcie catch up.

"I kicked him."

"Oh, Alce . . . it was all handled."

"I know. It was just something I needed to do. Don't worry. It backfired. I connected with the wall. Lotta pain. Let's go."

CHAPTER FIFTEEN

Persephone

Quickly, Pandy realized why she couldn't clearly see the thrones or Persephone against the back wall; there was an entire wall of shades, at least four spirits thick in some places, blocking the view. These hapless souls were thrown on top of one another as if they were the stuffed-skin dolls her brother Xander carelessly tossed about his room back home. Only the occasional flashes of pink, fuchsia, and magenta told Pandy that the goddess of springtime was behind the filmy, grayish blur.

"Do you have any idea what kinda heroes we'd be if some of the maidens back at the Academy could Master E-*pee*-us right now?" Alcie said, picking her way through a tangle of twisted spirit legs and arms. "How many of our other friends would sell their parents to the Turks to have been able to stick an apple in his mouth!"

"Alce," Pandy said, trying to focus on the rosy fabric of Persephone's robes, which kept popping in and out of view, "we didn't have any other friends back at the academy, remember?"

"Well," Alcie chuffed, "I don't know about you, but I was becoming quite popular in certain circles. Very well liked, I must say."

"What circles?" Pandy asked, watching as Homer and Iole scouted the best route around the spirit wall from their side of the room.

"Megara and I were very close."

"The woman who swept the walkways and washed out the lavatoriums?"

"She was a wealth of knowledge. Came from a little town called Minoa, where they make flavored butters and those bone tips for the ends of sandal laces," Alcie said defiantly. Then, lowering her voice, "And she used to let me keep her company when you and brainiac were busy and I didn't want to go home after school."

" 'Cause your parents were fighting again?" Pandy asked.

Alcie didn't say anything for a bit.

"I also used to have midday meal with Orthia and Orithyia at least once a week," she declared at last.

"The transfer students from the island of Cynthos? The twins?"

"The very same. It wasn't all about you and Iole, you know. I was branching out."

"Alcie, they ate their hair!"

"They were delightful."

"Well, it's great that you have these deep relationships waiting for you at home," Pandy snuffed. "C'mon, cut it out. We have to get on the other side of this wall."

"I don't see any easy way around," Alcie said. "We have to go in."

Carefully, she and Pandy waded in the sea of spirits until they came within a few centimeters of the wall. Pandy gazed up at the bodies, each shackled at the wrists and ankles, and at the single chain by which each soul in the hall was bound. She took Alcie's hand.

"I lied," Alcie said, before she took in a huge breath. "I never ate with the hair girls."

"I know," Pandy said, and filled her lungs.

They moved in to the wall. Pandy ducked as the first object at face level was someone's stomach, still half full. She straightened up and into three faces, a man and two women, crammed together. She nearly cried out and would have lost all her air, but she kept her wits and moved on. She and Alcie were bobbing under togas and robes, stepping over the chain, weaving around cloak pins and hair combs. They ignored the intestines, kidneys, and bladders that brushed their arms, necks, and faces. The fuchsia and pink flashes ahead were becoming steadier and brighter and just when Pandy felt the last bit of air leave her body and her chest begin to tighten and ache, she felt a tug on her arm as Alcie pulled her out of the wall and back into a low-level sea of spirits.

Then she gasped again and almost blew out her deflated lungs.

Persephone was indeed on her throne of cold, black marble. And she was bound so securely that she couldn't move a single immortal muscle.

Only she was bound upside down.

Her back rested on the seat, her legs rose up the back of the throne, and her feet dangled off the top while her head hung where her legs should have been. Her beautiful robes were gathered tightly about her as the chain, which now linked her to every other soul in the room, wound its way around and around her perfect form including holding a gag of golden-colored silk cloth in her mouth. But, Pandy observed the chain was ultimately not so thick that the goddess couldn't have broken it easily if Persephone had chosen to be free. Then Pandy saw the glint, the dull color that was not quite silver, not quite bronze or copper. Pandy knew this metal only too well; after all, she had a net made of exactly the same substance: adamantine.

Quickly, Pandy sped through the small span of shades that divided her and Alcie—and now Homer and Iole, who'd joined them—from Persephone. The goddess seemed to be sleeping; her breathing was even and she didn't appear panicked. Sensing Pandy's approach,

Persephone opened her eyes. Seeing Pandy and the others, she squinted and tried to smile. Then she wriggled in disgust and frustration.

"We have to get her upright," Pandy commanded.

"Impossible," Homer said. "The chain not only wraps around her, it binds her to the throne."

"We have to get the gag out," Alcie insisted.

"May I try, goddess?" Pandy asked.

"Uhhhh cuhhh yuhhh cuuh twwah," Persephone choked out.

Pandy and Alcie both tried to work the chain off the golden cloth with no success.

"Might I suggest burning it?" Iole ventured.

Persephone's eyes went wide.

"A controlled burn," Iole pressed on. "Pandy, you can just smolder the fabric until it can be pulled it out."

"I promise not to hurt you, Persephone," Pandy said resolutely, not having the faintest idea whether the immortal would be affected or not. She remembered what Hera looked like after she'd set the Queen of Heaven on fire, but this would be small and—simple. "Besides, you saved my life. I owe you this at least. So . . . can I?"

Persephone looked at Pandy for a moment.

"Uhkaaaahhy."

Immediately, Pandy focused her fire-power on the cloth, and the edges began to blacken and singe. Alcie began to pull the charred silk away from the chain, trying to get every scrap and ash before the goddess could swallow any. At one point, Alcie had to work her fingers underneath the chain and almost into Persephone's mouth. Persephone tensed just a touch and inadvertently and accidentally bit lightly on Alcie's fingers. Alcie yelped and fell back, nearly crashing into the sea of spirits. Persephone, even though she was bound and still gagged, managed a small shrug and a weak smile.

"Yes, yes!" Alcie said, as if talking to a mischievous toddler. "Yes, funny goddess. Funny, funny immortal."

Finally, enough of the silk had been singed and pried away that nothing remained but several links of adamantine chain, which Pandy gently pulled from Persephone's mouth and down onto her chin.

"Well, that was brilliant, I must say," Persephone said, trying in vain to twist her head into a more upright position. "I can see, Iole, that your brain has regained all its power!"

"And then some," Alcie said.

Iole just smiled.

"I don't need to ask who did this to you," Pandy said. "We already know."

"I know!" Persephone said, smiling sadly, which of course, since she was upside down, looked like a frown; Pandy decided that either expression would have worked in the moment.

"I left you all and went after Ixion," Persephone started. "I materialized both him and his wheel back into the proper spot in Hades, got him nice and tied up, set the wheel spinning and set it on fire. Then I rushed back to the palace to see if Buster had returned. I walked in here, took a look at the far wall, screamed and fell splat into the 'carpet of shades' that Hera had created. The next thing I know, that she-dog has me trussed up like a goat for a sacrifice. I was unconscious for a moment and when I woke, she was hovering overhead—at least I think it was overhead, my perspective is a little squirrelly—anyway, she was laughing like a Maenad and prattling on about how she had enslaved everybody with one turn of a key; how everyone was doing her bidding and I wouldn't even recognize this palace when she was through with it. How, when she ruled the earth and skies, this would be her underworld base of operations. Blah-bitty-blah. That was I don't know how many days ago."

Pandy looked toward the ceiling, suddenly noticing that the chain that wound over, under, and around all the souls in the room, connecting the thousands of shackles on one long length of adamantine—the same chain that now held Persephone fast—ascended from the goddess's throne and finished off in a single, final shackle binding together the taloned feet of the bird she'd seen earlier—a giant eagle spinning in lazy circles high above the room—and closed with an enormous lock. And out of that lock protruded a golden key.

"An eagle?" Pandy whispered to herself. "Where would Hera get an eagle *that* size . . . ?"

In that same instant, she knew: this was the same eagle that had tormented her father for so many centuries ages ago. This was the bird that had, day after day, eaten away at Prometheus's liver until Zeus had finally ended her father's punishment.

"*And*, she turned my mother into a dog!" Persephone was saying. "A tiny little dog like you'd put on your lap!"

"Kinda fits," Alcie mumbled.

"I *heard* that!" Persephone squealed. "But you're right. Mother's been doing Hera's bidding for so long now, she should probably stay like that; pooping out autumn leaves and snowflakes and little springtime flowers."

"I'm sorry," Iole said, trying to keep a straight face, "but I need a moment to get that image out of my head."

"How do you know your mother's a dog?" Pandy asked.

"Same way I know what Buster's been going through. I've been watching the wall, what I could of it. And I've been getting reports from those spirits closest to it. That's the reason I screamed when I first came in here . . . that's when Hera caught me by surprise."

"Persephone," Pandy said, her mind leaping ahead, not really processing the goddess's answer in trying to come to the point, "we have to speak to Hades. I must find the lord of the underworld. I think he alone may know where Fear is hiding or what form it may have taken. We've come across nothing else and it's the only thing I can think of—wait, why did you scream when you looked at a wall?"

"Well, look for yourself, honey; the story is right there."

"I just see some nice murals," Alcie said, gazing around.

"Really?" Persephone chided, as if Alcie had gone blind.

Pandy stared around the room from one wall to the next. One was a nice, if somewhat dark, bland pastoral scene—very familiar. One wall was unusually grayish-white. The third wall seemed similar to the first. Until she saw them: the figures moving in the third picture, the tree leaves bending ever so slightly, the water rippling softly in a pool. A pool she'd seen before: Lethe.

"Gods," Iole said softly.

Each wall of Hades' throne room gave a perfect view of one region of the underworld and whatever happened to be going on at that precise moment. Erebus, bland and flat. The Fields of Asphodel and the pool of Lethe, only Hera had ensconced two gorgons to prevent anyone from taking a drink of the forgetful waters and now the line of spirits, still with all the memories of their ended lives, wailing and weeping and unable to drink, stretched back and out of sight. To the gates of Hades, Pandy was certain. She looked at the whitish wall and had no idea what region that could be. Then she looked at the wall closest to her—the back wall. The wall that mattered most to Persephone, and the one that she could barely see.

The pretty orange, yellow, and white splashes were the flames of the fire pits of Tartarus growing brighter and hotter with every second. The inferno was so fierce and blinding that Pandy was surprised she couldn't feel the heat coming from the view. Smack in the middle of the wall burned the deepest pit, and in the middle of it Hades was bound, completely, to a huge glowing iron chair. He was not screaming in agony from the flames; in fact, he only appeared slightly inconvenienced by the searing heat, but utterly furious at his bondage.

Hera stood off to the side, tossing bits of wood and charcoal into the fire. She was saying something to Hades, sneering and taunting him by the looks of it. Every once in a while she'd address the small dog at her feet who was huddling close to Hera's robes, trying to avoid its tail catching a spark.

"Buster's still in there, isn't he?" Persephone asked, two small tears rolling down onto her forehead and into her hair. "He's still in that horrible pit?"

Pandy sighed and nodded in resignation.

"Exactly where Hera's been trying to get me all along. I hate giving her what she wants, but now we have no choice."

She twisted her body so that, out of respect, she was at least trying to face Persephone.

"I'm sorry, but we have to go . . ."

"No! You can't! You can't leave yet!" Persephone wailed. "Pandora, listen to me. I don't matter and Hera knows it. I mean that she won't want to hurt me because . . . because . . . she won't gain anything by it. But if you leave without helping to free these spirits, almost all of whom have done nothing to warrant this kind of punishment—except one silly little man on the wall over there—used to be a teacher, I think. Horrid. Anyway . . . you cannot leave without trying to help them. If you're killed and Hera comes back here and uses this palace as her underworld home, this enslavement will continue forever. But if you can free them, then I'll also be freed and I can try to get them to a safe place."

"What safe place?" Alcie cried. "Where?"

"I haven't thought of that yet, Alcestis!"

"Sorry."

"It's as simple as turning the key," Persephone said, gazing straight up.

"But we don't have time," Pandy said, pacing back

and forth before the throne. "I don't even know how many days I have left before my time for the quest runs out!"

"Days?" Persephone said. "Days? You don't have days, honey. You've been down here a little over ten days—topside days, that is—already. Why do you think Hera is so excited? She's probably staring at Fear right now! She's not leaving Buster or the flame pits, because she wants to have Fear in her hands when your time runs out. You have . . . lemme think . . . ten minus the four, but then you have to add the . . . and divide by . . . Pandora, you have three hours left."

Pandy stood stock-still for only a second. Then, without any warning, she threw up.

"Nice," said a splattered spirit close by.

As Iole took her arm and helped her to straighten up, Pandy glanced at the view into Tartarus; Hera was throwing back her head, laughing as if she just played the funniest trick on everyone. She lit a stick from the flames and flung it onto Hades' robes. She picked up Demeter and tossed her high into the air. Behavior, even Pandy knew, she would never dream of were she not sure of impending and complete victory.

"Three hours or three minutes," Pandy said, wiping her mouth and standing straight, even though she felt like curling up into a ball. "We're at least gonna try . . ."

"No, no. Listen to me," Persephone said, her voice

urgent. "There's only one way to get to Tartarus if you're not initially sent there by the judges: through the Elysian Fields. And you, mortals and un-heroes, would never be allowed to enter from the palace. But there *is* a way. If you had an escort, you could go. Someone who rightfully belonged there. If you free everyone, you also free the heroes inside the palace. Oh, didn't Hera gloat over their bondage! Free them and you free Achilles, Ajax . . . you name it. I'll send one of them with you. Deal?"

Pandy didn't need to look at Iole and Homer and Alcie, although they were staring, trying to anticipate her next words. But already the answer was on the tip of her lips. The logic was simple—charge ahead and the allotted time would certainly run out and she'd fail. Take the time for a good cause and, perhaps, the way would be made easier. Months ago, she'd have fretted over this decision—talked to Iole and Alcie about it, weighing their instincts with hers. Now, she didn't need a conference on what to do.

"Deal."

CHAPTER SIXTEEN
The Lesser Evil of Slavery

With every second that passed of the full sixty she'd spent staring at the eagle circling overhead, Pandy felt the tension building.

"Pandy . . . ," Iole said.

"We have to bring it down," Pandy blurted, ignoring her friend. "That's Zeus's eagle. I know it is. He looks just the way my father used to describe it; gold beak, silver talons and tail feathers. Dad would wake up, chained to his slab, and see that bird's outline right before dawn—just waiting on a peak high above him. The first ray of sunlight would bounce off the eagle's beak and Dad knew it was gonna swoop down and start pecking at his liver. *This* is that bird, and we have to get him down here. That's all there is to it. Homer, you're at the bottom of the chain, then Alcie, then me, then Iole."

Pandy pointed to the chain floating up from the

back of Persephone's throne. "We're gonna pull that bird down out of the air and when it gets close enough, I'll turn the key, unlock the lock, and release the end of the chain. Easy as oatie cakes."

"Pandy?" Iole said again.

"What?"

"Did it ever occur to you that this might be a lesser evil?"

Pandy paused a moment.

"Uh . . . no, no it had *not* occurred to me. *What?* Lesser evils were in the box with the great Evils. Hera has enslaved all these spirits, but . . . but . . . she couldn't *create* the evil. Wow! Could she?"

"Don't forget," Iole answered. "The gods themselves were the ones who originally put all the evils, large and small, in the box in the first place. I wouldn't put it past Hera to know exactly where this one landed and use it for her own purposes. Or maybe she did fashion a new evil just for this reason."

"After all," Alcie said. "We have slaves back home and we've never thought it was wrong or anything. Temples have slaves. So why do we think this is so wrong? We do, right? I mean, it's wrong, right?"

"Of course," Pandy said. "This is horrible."

"Conquered warriors are sometimes brought home as slaves, but that was always considered one of the spoils of a victory. Neither side saw it as an evil," Homer put in.

"But let's not forget," Pandy continued. "This is not the first time we've encountered slavery and thought it wrong since the box was opened. My uncle Atlas enslaved men to do his job and hold up the heavens on Jbel Toubkal, but that effect there was broken when I put Laziness back in the box."

"But we never put this *particular* lesser evil back in," Alcie said.

"Hera might have fashioned this lesser evil . . . ," Pandy began.

"Or, specifically, our new perspective on it," Iole said.

". . . right. She might have taken whatever ripples were sent out when my uncle's slaves were freed and created this."

"Yeah," Alcie said, looking around at the sea of souls. 'Cause this is, like, out of control."

"So if this actually is a lesser evil and not just Zeus's eagle out for a nice spin in the underworld, we need to be on the lookout for anything odd or difficult when we try to capture it, okay?" Pandy said as everyone wrapped their hands around the chain. "Ready? PULL!"

The two results of that mighty pull happened almost simultaneously. The first was that, since Homer was behind everyone else on the very end of the chain, the strength of his tug sent Pandy, Alcie, and Iole tumbling to the floor with Iole's robes covering Persephone's face. The second was that the eagle, jolted out of its slow-circling stupor, gave a piercing shriek and dove like an arrow toward the the sea of spirits. As it neared, it opened its talons as wide as it could with the shackle still binding them together and lifted a hapless spirit into the air. With one peck the eagle tore out the man's gray, transparent liver and gobbled it down. Tossing the spirit back into the pile, it rose high into the air above the room, the ceiling of which was still too far up to discern.

"You mean odd like *that*?" Alcie asked.

"Okay," Persephone said, muffled until Iole pulled her robes off. "This is completely my fault. I forgot to tell you that while Hera was chaining everyone up, she used to tug on the chain to let the bird know when it could eat. I can't even begin to tell you how many shades out there are liver-less. Guess all of you combined have the strength of the Queen of Heaven. I heard you hatching your plan and knew there was something you needed to know; I just couldn't remember. But now you know!"

"Riiiiiight," Pandy exhaled, picking herself up off the floor. "Thanks for that. So what have we learned here, besides the fact that the hourglass is running out?"

"Any great weight or pressure on the chain and the eagle thinks it's feeding time," Iole said.

"Which means," Homer furthered, "that we cannot bring it down."

"Nope," Pandy said. "We have to go up. Actually, *I* have to go up."

"I'll do it," said Homer.

"Too heavy," Pandy countered, then, when she saw Iole about to speak, "And you're afraid of heights. And no, Alce, you can't do it. I was the best rock and tree climber of any of us. And this is the bird that tormented my dad; he's mine. And maybe I'll pluck a couple of tail feathers while I'm up there . . . bring 'em home. Show Dad."

She removed her leather carrying pouch and her water-skin and handed them to Alcie. Then she unlaced her sandals and kicked them off, climbing to stand on Homer's shoulders as he knelt. Wrapping the chain around one foot, she then stepped on that foot with her other foot and let the chain fall away. Rewrapping the chain on the second foot and repeating the process, she climbed ever so slowly, foot over foot and hand over hand.

Ten meters off the ground, she realized that all the tree and rock climbing hadn't even begun to prepare her for this. With the fourth step, she knew her feet couldn't possibly hold out; the chain was already beginning to cut into her flesh. Her palms were sweating, making each grasp a little less sure. At fifteen meters, she undid her cloak and, as subtly as she could, let it slide down the chain to the ground where Homer caught it. She refused to look down; not because she feared heights—any fear she'd once had had been lost after hanging over the impaling poles in the Chamber of Despair or when she'd been swung wide off the edge of Jbel Toubkal clinging to her uncle Atlas's overgrown nose hair. She didn't want to look down now because she didn't want the further frustration and disappointment of seeing just how far she hadn't climbed. She tried to think of other things. She forced herself to remember walking through the Agora back home and rummaging through the remnants box of the silk trader, trying to find any pretty scrap with which to tie up her plain brown hair. She thought of her favorite fast-falafel shop and how the first thing she was going to do when she got home was get one . . . no, *two* smeared with tahini paste. She thought of her little brother and how she was going to hug him so hard she'd probably make him cry.

Then her foot slipped and she grabbed the chain as tight as she could, hanging in midair. From far below, she heard someone—Alcie?—gasp.

Slowly she found the chain and wrapped it around

her foot again. The pain went through her almost as sharply as when Lucius Valerius had plunged his knife into her shoulder. Fifty meters above the floor, she realized that the entire hall had gone silent as a tomb. For the first time, she dared to look down: every head was turned toward her, eyes wide, mouths closed. Then she focused on the tops of her feet; the thin bronze coating curling and chipping away in tiny flecks. The flesh shredded—gone in some places. Maybe. She couldn't tell: there was too much blood.

There was also nothing she could do about it. She would, of course, if she lived, use this as lesson to *always keep the Eye of Horus around her neck and not in her carrying pouch where it wasn't doing any good!* But for now, she knew she couldn't climb solely hand over hand; this was the safest, the best—the only—way.

Her eyes went instinctively to the spots of color in an otherwise gray wash. The wall of orange flame, Persephone's pink robes, and Alcie's copper-red hair. Then, across the throne room, she saw a teensy speck of red—the apple still firmly ensconced in the mouth of Master Epeus.

Whatever fear she had of falling or failing vanished.

"You wanna see potential, you bully? I'll show you potential," she thought, and kept climbing.

Twenty meters higher—and two near slips off the chain—the four differing views of the underworld began to fade into the bleak, gray stone. The eagle was still oblivious to anything or anyone tampering with his long leash; Pandy's weight was obviously not enough to make any kind of a difference.

But, he was close now. Really close. Two meters at most. One meter. A half. The eagle's silver talons were almost within her arm's reach; all she needed to do was turn the key in the lock, unlock the chain, and the chain would fall away.

Pandy froze.

The chain would fall away.

The chain that connected her to the bird, the only thing holding her up and keeping her from plummeting to her death, was going to drop, with her on it, like a stone.

She paused for a moment to reflect on how none of them, neither her, nor Alcie, Homer, or Iole with her gigo-brain and all her new confidence, foresaw that this was going to happen. She had no way to get down!

As soon as the bird was released, she realized, it would sail high into the farthest unseen reaches of the throne room while she would land in a shallow sea of souls and crack her head on the tiles below.

And then, nearly seventy-five meters in the air, Pandy began to think. Methodically. If a, then b, then c . . . then, with any luck, d . . .

A, with one hand she reached for the shackle around

the eagle's feet. B, holding fast to it, she reached with her other hand for the golden key and turned it, opening the lock and slipping the key deep into a pocket in the folds of her toga. C, she pried the chain out of the lock while still holding fast to the end of the chain *and* the eagle's shackle.

"Timing, Pandy," she whispered to herself. "It's all in the . . ."

D, she let go of the chain with her hand while still keeping it wrapped around her feet.

"PULL!" she yelled down at the top of her lungs.

"What?" cried Alcie.

"She wants us to pull on the chain," said Homer, not even bothering to wait for Alcie and Iole. He gave a tremendous yank and instantly realized what was coming.

"Under my cloak!" he commanded, spreading the fabric wide as Alcie and Iole rushed underneath, all of them protecting Persephone's face and torso.

The chain was ripped away from Pandy's feet, and the pain was so shocking it was all she could do to keep from losing her grip on the shackle. But the force of the pull was enough to signal meal time to the eagle, and swiftly it began its downward descent.

"What's happening?" Alcie asked, clinging to Homer.

"She released the chain," Homer said. "I pulled and felt it give. It's heading down and I have no idea where it will land."

But after at least a full minute had passed with no feeling or sound of the chain hitting anywhere, Homer dared to poke his head out from underneath his cloak. There was no chain plummeting through the air; instead he saw bits of crumbling adamantine and metal dust where the chain should have been, the chain disintegrating link by link as it fell. Within moments the chain had started crumbling around Persephone's throne, eating itself into nothingness.

"Gods!" cried Alcie, now out from underneath Homer's cloak and pointing across the room.

The eagle was still a good fifty meters high, but swooping toward the front of the room. With all her might, Pandy swung herself up and plucked the first silver tail feather that she grabbed. The eagle screamed hideously and, thinking it was being attacked from behind, instantly changed direction and headed for the back wall.

Directly over the wall of souls.

"Good girl!" Iole said, understanding instantly.

But the eagle, seeing no attacker, began to turn away.

"Here!" screamed Iole, jumping up and down "Here! Take my liver!"

Alcie had no idea why Iole had gone insane, only that it must have had something to do with Pandy—and that was good enough for her.

"Over here! My liver's great . . . and it's alive!"

"Here, you overgrown chicken!" yelled Homer, waving his arms furiously.

The eagle spotted the three living bodies and swung back around, flying in low.

"Think fast," Pandy said to herself.

"Calculate, calculate," Iole prayed.

"Concentrate," Pandy murmured, beginning to lose her grip on the shackle.

"Now!" screamed Iole at the exact moment Pandy let go of the shackle and dropped into the wall of souls.

"DUCK!" yelled Homer, pushing Alcie and Iole down as the eagle, unable to pull up quickly, sailed over their heads and slammed into the back wall and the orange-and-yellow vision of Tartarus, rendering it completely unconscious.

Pandy hit hard; her speed and weight carrying her through the opaque bodies like she were a knife cutting into goat butter. She emerged out the other side, but she'd been slowed enough that she simply rolled down into the sea of spirits covering the floor at the foot of Persephone's throne. She lay there for a moment, her eyes closed, feeling cushioned, kinda warm, and extremely guilty that she might be smothering someone, all at the same time.

Suddenly, several pairs of hands were lifting her up, tugging gently on her arms and hands, pulling her into a standing position. Pandy opened her eyes and saw those shades closest to the throne now upright and dropping their shackles. A few spirits embraced her and thanked her for her courage. She looked up at Iole as Homer and Alcie were helping—delicately and slowly—the freed Persephone to stand. Iole pointed to the chain and Pandy watched it disintegrate, freeing spirit after spirit from bondage and enslavement.

The key!

Pandy fumbled in the pocket of her toga and sighed deeply when she wrapped her fingers around the golden key. She took one step toward Alcie and her own carrying pouch, then fell to her knees.

Like lightning, Alcie was by her side.

"What?" she said, then she saw Pandy's feet and tried to stifle a scream.

"The eye, Alce," Pandy moaned, her mind now allowing the full effect of the pain to register. "I need the eye."

"One eye, coming up," Alcie said, rifling through Pandy's bag until she found the Eye of Horus on its chain. She slipped the amulet over Pandy's head and watched as Pandy's whole body visibly unclenched. Homer, Iole, and Persephone hurried over, through the throng of spirits joyfully milling about, and Iole crouched down beside Pandy.

"What can we do?"

Pandy was watching the flesh on the tops of her feet

slowly knit itself back together, the blood drying and flaking away, the exposed bones disappearing, the bronze coating covering again—the pain receding.

"Pandy?"

"Huh? Oh. The box," Pandy said.

Alcie fished it out of Pandy's carrying pouch, then she handed the adamantine net to Iole.

"Ready?" Pandy asked.

Iole readied the net, just in case, as Alcie removed the hairpin from the lock, nodding.

"Now," Pandy said.

Alcie flipped the clasp and opened the lid. Pandy tossed the key inside and Alcie closed the lid, flipped the clasp, slid the hairpin back in the lock and put the box back in Pandy's bag.

"It's almost becoming too easy," Alcie said. "Is that horrible to say?"

Pandy looked around, confused, as she laced her up her sandals.

"I don't get it," she said, trying to keep her eyes on the chain and follow the progress of the disintegration. "I thought the *key* was the evil. Why was everyone being freed if the key wasn't in the box yet?"

"We've had slaves for years," Iole answered. "No one ever thought of it as evil—just normal, because most households treat their slaves fairly decently. Doesn't matter though. Hera needed something to bind the lesser evil which was—is—the key. We weren't going to be able to put the entire chain or all the dust in the box. The key represents everything: the bondage and the solution. We just have a new perception of it; after all, no one could look at what's been going on here and *not* think it's wrong."

"I'm gonna free our house slaves when I get home," Alcie said. "And Homie, when we're married, I'm gonna do all the housework myself!"

That stunned everyone into silence.

"You know you're gonna have to pay people just to hang up her robes, right?" Pandy said quietly to Homer.

"Way ahead of you," Homer answered softly.

"Heard it," Alcie said.

"Well, it's going to be up to us to spread the word, either way," Iole said.

"I'll have a talk with all the immortals about it," Persephone added. "Even though we don't have slaves down here, this has shaken me something awful."

"This will be a tough battle back home and we'll probably come up against a lot of resistance," Iole furthered.

"We won't be battling anything back home if we don't get going," Pandy said, rising to her feet and looking at Persephone. "Who do we get?"

"Huh?"

"The hero," Pandy said impatiently. "You said we could have a hero to guide us."

"Oh, right! Of course! Hero," Persephone said with a start. "C'mon, let's see who's available and not hacking up anyone at the moment, 'cause I have a feeling they're all pretty angry."

Many of the spirits in the throne room, almost all now standing, were trying to realign various organs and body parts that had shifted due to their prolonged cramped and odd positions, but as the goddess of springtime pressed forward through the throng, they parted instantly, providing a clear path to the doorway. Dido jumped on his mistress as soon as Pandy stepped back into the hallway, overjoyed that she hadn't been smashed into bits and wanting now to follow. But Pandy instinctively knew that what lay ahead, whatever it was, would be far too dangerous for her beloved dog.

"Dido—Dido, listen to me," she said, kneeling and taking his face in her hands. "Back to Cyrene, hear me? Go back to Cyrene and wait. Wait in the food-preparation room. I'll find you. Listen, boy, I'll *find* you. Now go."

Pandy and Dido both knew this might be the only lie she'd ever told him. It wasn't really a lie, she thought, kissing him on his nose; if she were alive at the end of all this, she *would* find him. With only one backward glance and a short yelp, he trotted away through the crowded corridor. As she watched him go, praying she would see him again, Pandy let her focus be drawn to several groups of once-enslaved spirits disarming, battling, and overpowering their spirit captors . . . those who had worked in alliance with Hera.

"Well," Persephone sighed, moving forward through the hallways at a brisk pace but glancing at the combatants. "I'm going to have to put out some fires, I see. Persephone Peacemaker, that's me. But later, am I right? First things first."

"I know," Pandy said.

"I *know*!"

CHAPTER SEVENTEEN
Achilles

"And may I just say, Pandy," Persephone went on as she expertly negotiated the labyrinth, "that was some seriously fancy-schmancy bravery I saw back there."

"Thanks," Pandy said, feeling the straps of her sandals scraping against the tops of her feet where the skin hadn't yet completely healed, and privately vowing to never again take off the *eye*. Ever.

"I'm only saying that I've seen full-grown men playing bladder toss in the Elysian Fields for doing far less. Armory . . . armory? Ah, here we are . . ."

But no sooner had she pulled aside the privacy curtain, than two of the spirits Homer had seen guarding the captive heroes earlier, two who'd been allied with Hera, came flying through the entryway and crashed into the opposite wall. Then the spirit of Hector, eldest son of the royal house of Troy and one of the greatest warriors of the Trojan War, strode out of the room. He picked up the two spirits by their hair and began dragging them down the hallway.

"Back to your mothers with you!" he bellowed.

The two struggling spirits screamed in agony, and Alcie looked at Persephone.

"Hera let all of *them* loose?" she asked.

"Of course," Persephone said.

" '*Them*' whom?" asked Pandy.

"Remember how I told you that if you were really, *really* bad in life, you didn't get sent to Tartarus when you died; you were sent here to the palace and locked in a little room with your mother nagging at you for eternity?" Alcie replied.

"Oh, right!" Pandy responded.

"Hera opened every single one of those doors, and they're the ones who've been doing her down-and-dirty work around here," Persephone sighed.

"Makes perfect sense, if you think about it," Iole said. "Hera probably promised them freedom, authority, you name it, if they helped her. And she knew they'd have no trouble abusing their fellow spirits."

"Persephone? Hero?" Pandy said, thinking she was once again feeling the passing of every remaining moment.

"I have just the man," Persephone said, ushering them all into the armory.

Which was now very tidy: chairs and tables upright, knives in their cases, larger weapons neatly stacked and hung. And it was also empty.

Or so it seemed.

"Achilles? Oh, please be here and not off impaling someone," Persephone called. "Achilles?"

"Be with you in just a second!" came a voice from behind them. An impossibly high-pitched voice. The voice of a child . . . or a woman. Before she turned around, Pandy had a wild thought that her little brother, Xander, had somehow been transported to Hades and was talking to her now. Then she turned and looked up. On a small ledge off the wall, Achilles—every inch the hero: tall, muscular, and handsome—was doing the last little bits of straightening on several shields that he'd recently re-hung.

"There! That should be perfect!" he said, leaning back just a little to admire his work. Then the second-most famous hero in all of Greece (Hercules would always retain the honor of being the best) jumped the three or so meters down to the floor and landed without so much as a wobble.

"I can't *bear* an untidy room," said Achilles, as Pandy felt her mouth open slightly. "Pain, starvation, war? Please, I'm fine. Blood gushing, broken bones, arms ripped from their sockets? That's a good day. But a messy room darn near gives me a panic attack!"

Alcie's mouth dropped a little.

"Achilles," Persephone said. "This is Pandora, Alcie, Iole, and Homer."

"Pleasure. Hi. Nice grip, youth. Oooh, love the copper hair . . . ," he said, shaking everyone's hand in turn.

"They need to get to Tartarus and fast," Persephone pressed on. "They know the rules, so you're their escort."

"Can I just straighten the gaming room first? Apparently, Hera was putting up chintz drapes and, even though I might lose my mind, I have to see for myself . . ."

"*No!*" Persephone cried in a tone no one had ever heard her use before.

"All right, serious mode. I'm on board. Sorry, boss," Achilles said, standing straight, then moving his hand down in front of his face and turning his smile into a frown.

"You will take them straight through the E-Fields, understand? You will not stop to toss a javelin. You will not stop to throw a discus. This is a matter of life and death!"

"Oooh! Well, it all *is* down here, isn't it!" Achilles joked, his smile back again, then his face fell when he saw no one was laughing. "Okay, sorry . . . didn't mean to be a heel! Get it? My heel? Achilles' heel?"

Pandy was on the verge of taking Persephone aside

and begging for someone else—anyone else—to guide them.

"Right," Achilles said, moving to the wall and removing the biggest sword anyone, including Homer, had ever seen.

"C'mon, honey," he said to the blade, tossing it in the air as if it were light as a feather. "We've got work to do."

Then he took his personal shield off the wall and turned to face everyone, shoulders back, mouth set in a firm line. Pandy gasped. *This* was the picture she'd always had in her mind of the great man; this was a man she could follow.

"Everyone ready?"

Alcie threw her arms around Persephone, who then hugged Iole and kissed Homer on the cheek. Bringing everyone close together in a small circle, Persephone touched Pandy lightly on the forehead.

"You all know I'm horrible at good-byes," said the goddess.

"I know," Alcie said.

"I know," Persephone went on. "So I'm not going to say it. I'll see you all again; I only hope it's in sixty or seventy of your years . . ."

"They'll be all wrinkly by then!" Achilles chirped, sticking his head into the circle.

"But," Persephone continued, pushing Achilles' head

back, "just know that I adore all of you and even if Hera turns you all into little cinder piles, there will always be a place for you here."

"Group hug!" cried Achilles as everyone bunched tightly together.

"Now go!" Persephone said, waving her fingers in front of her face as if to prevent her tears from falling. "Go before I make a fool of myself."

Running to keep up with Achilles' enormous strides, they were many hallways and many corners away from the armory when Pandy moved next to Alcie.

"Do you think that's really Achilles?" Alcie asked softly, running backward so as not to be heard and nodding her head toward the warrior.

"Of course it is," Pandy said, then her brow furrowed. "Why? Who do you think it is?"

"I have no idea," Alcie said, turning to run face forward again, only keeping her voice very low. "I'm just thinking he's not really warrior-like, y'know? His voice is more my-mom-like."

"I know!"

"I *know!*"

"Well, he can talk like your mom or Sabina or me for all I care, as long as he gets us through the fields. I'm more worried about Persephone's good-bye," Pandy huffed. "Cinders? Piles of cinders? Not quite the farewell I expected. Not really a rousing, cheering send-off."

"I'll say it again," Alcie said. "Persephone's great, but she's bonkers."

Ten minutes later, Homer was barely breaking a sweat. But the blood was pounding in Pandy's forehead, and she was starting to feel a searing in her lungs, as if each new step was bringing them closer to exploding.

"This place couldn't have been this big the last time I was here," Alcie was muttering, trying to keep up with Achilles as her footfalls became heavier and heavier. "They must have added on."

Iole, however, was resting comfortably on Achilles' shoulders, where she'd been for most of the long jaunt through the palace.

"May I ask a question of you, sir?" Iole said, not bouncing a bit because Achilles' gait was so smooth.

"Ask away," he replied.

"Do you like your name?"

"Wow," Achilles answered. "That goes right into the category of bizarro, but yes, I love it. Why do you ask?"

"Oh, I'd just heard a rumor that your mother was thinking of naming you something else," Iole said, recalling her time in the private chambers of Thetis just before Thetis's marriage to King Peleus—thirteen hundred years earlier—when they were all on the hunt for Lust. "Something like Carpus or Cleon."

"I'd heard that too! Crazy how stories get passed down, huh? Yes, I overheard Mother talking once about how she'd always liked those names, but some servant girl mentioned 'Achilles' and Mother went for it. Very glad she did—Cleon gives me the willies! And Carpus! Can you imagine doing something like that to a child!"

Iole's very self-satisfied grin lasted only a few more moments until Achilles rounded one final corner and almost everyone found themselves in a massive entry room lit by two hanging oil lamps in the shape of huge narcissus flowers, one of Hades' symbols. There, looming before them, were the front doors to Hades' palace.

"Hey," Pandy panted, slouching against the wall and looking at Alcie, far back down the corridor, now on her hands and knees. "Guess what we found?"

"Please tell me it's Fear . . . you've put it in the box . . . you don't need my help . . . and . . . I can just lie here for the next week," Alcie gasped as Homer ran back to lift her onto his shoulders, carrying her forward.

"Could have used this about five kilometers ago," she wheezed.

"Why didn't you let me know?" he said. "Of course, I would have carried you."

"Brains had her own personal chariot," Alcie said, looking at Iole and feeling her heart rate slowing at last. "If you'd carried me, that would have left P running solo. Couldn't do that to her. *Wow!* I knew this place had doors, but wow!"

The front doors were at least twenty meters high and ten meters across, and each door made a single flat-faced diamond. They reminded Pandy of Wang Chun Lo's magic crystals—only about twenty times larger. And these doors seemed to be sparkling far more than they should have been in the light of the lamps, accompanied by a crackling sound.

"Something's wrong," Achilles said, his hand on the hilt of his sword.

"Yeah," Alcie said, staring. "They're cracking up!"

"What?" Achilles started. "Oh, no, silly. That's not destruction you're hearing. That just means the population is expanding. You're hearing facets being cut."

"Well . . . sure," said Alcie.

"Every time a new soul enters the underworld, a new facet appears, magically cut into the doors. And since so many are always arriving, these doors are never silent. No, I'm talking about something else. This entryway is a rather dull shade of gray. There's no color coming through the doors from the other side."

"White is predominant," Iole said.

"And boring," Achilles said, poking her lightly in the ribs.

"But, what's wrong with that?" Pandy asked.

"The Elysian Fields are right outside those doors. Also, the only place where the underworld sun shines as brightly as yours does on Earth," Achilles answered. "This whole entrance should be awash in the most delicious shade of green."

"Then these are back doors! Maybe?" Alcie said. "Anyway, I was still right. Doors!"

"C'mon," Achilles said to Homer. "Usually there are four or five of us athletic, burly types to open the doors. But you're a hero in the making if ever I saw one. I'll need your help."

Homer shot a look to Alcie that, for one-tenth of a second, expressed pure pride and followed Achilles. They chose the door to the right and began to pull, their fingers finding easy holds in the many facets. At first, the enormous diamond wouldn't budge and once again, Pandy became aware of time slipping away. Then Achilles let out a tremendous yell as he redoubled his efforts. Wanting to prove himself to the great warrior, Homer joined in with a long, loud shout and a greater pull. At last, the heavy door began to swing inward, revealing to all that it was at least two meters thick.

Instantly, the white light glinting off the doors blinded everyone.

"Outside, all of you," Achilles said.

Shielding their eyes, Pandy, Alcie, and Iole brushed past Homer and Achilles and out onto a large terrace from which descended a long flight of stairs.

"Acclimate to the light before you fully open your eyes," Iole cautioned.

But Pandy had already been peeking through her fingers. She saw the top of the stairs, and then she looked down to the bottom steps. Steps that should have led into the green meadows and rolling hills of Elysium but instead led directly into . . .

Snow.

CHAPTER EIGHTEEN

Cold

"Okay, seriously?" Alcie said, opening her eyes slowly and taking in the vast expanse of white.

"That blue-robed bovine!" Achilles exclaimed. "Look what she's done to my playground! I have always hated her! Even though she sided with us during the Trojan War, there was just something nasty about that goddess."

Off in the not-too-great distance, all could see a faint orange glow on the horizon: Tartarus.

"So close and yet, so far," Iole murmured.

"Hera," Pandy said staring at the snow fields and the hills of solid ice, then she turned to Achilles. "We'll never make it. We'll freeze before we get there."

"Our feet!" Alcie cried.

But Homer was already unfastening his cloak. Taking out a knife from his carrying pouch, he split the fabric and ripped until he had one long strip, then he sliced that strip neatly in the middle and handed the two pieces to Alcie.

"Off with your sandals, Alce," he said. "Wrap your feet."

"Nice thinking, youth," Achilles said with a smile.

"Truly," Iole agreed.

Homer began to rip another long strip when Pandy stopped him.

"You can't go out there without a cloak."

"You have no idea what I endured at gladiator school, Pandy," he replied. "Especially when the instructors discovered that I wanted to drop out to become a poet."

"Poet. Nice," Achilles cut in.

"They put me in a box on the roof of the administration building for two weeks with no food or water. Blistering hot during the day and freezing at night. I can lose my cloak. I'll be fine."

"If I had a cloak, I'd cut it up for you, just so's ya know," Achilles said. "But living in a perfect paradise—normally—no need. Sorry."

After everyone had wrapped their legs to the knees and re-laced their sandals, leaving Homer with a tiny capelet around his shoulders, Achilles led the way out onto the snow. They hadn't gone but several meters when an enormous spike of ice burst through the ground, nearly cleaving Achilles in two. Another ice-spike erupted only centimeters away from Iole.

"Hera's spiked the field! We have to make a run for it!" Pandy yelled, breaking into a tear as Homer scooped up Iole onto his shoulders for the umpteenth time. "How far is it to the other side?"

"I can usually cross it in one rotation of your topside sundial—that would be sixty minutes of your time," Achilles replied, dodging a particularly jagged ice-spike. "But that's at leisurely pace. We may be able to do better if you all can keep up."

"Don't worry about us," Homer said, momentarily jerked backward as a spike shot out behind them, slitting Iole's cloak.

"Follow in my path!" Achilles cried. "If I get impaled, I'd suggest going around me."

They galloped, flat out, for the next quarter of an hour, Pandy consciously trying to forget that she'd just run like a hound through the long hallways of Hades' palace. She tried instead to find that "feeling" that she'd heard about—the one the marathon runners always talked of when they got to a point where there was no longer any pain, only a sensation of exhilaration, a sensation that they were running on air.

"Yeah," she thought to herself, dodging a spike. "Not really feeling it."

"Oh, my beautiful Elysium," Achilles moaned as he ran on, looking at icicles hanging from the trees surrounding the fields. "You're never going to come out of this unscathed. I'll be spending the next two hundred of your topside years just pruning and clipping. How's everybody doing?"

"Good," Pandy cried, slipping slightly on the slope created by an ice-spike exploding right next to her.

"Fine here," Homer yelled. "Alce?"

There was no answer.

"Oh, Mother's silver feet," Achilles said, looking back only a moment. "I forgot to warn you all about . . ."

"*Alcie!*" Homer barked, stopping to turn around.

". . . the well."

Alcie was gone.

"ALCIE!" screamed Homer, Pandy, and Iole together.

From about fifty meters back came a cry, too muffled to be intelligible. With Iole still on his shoulders, Homer immediately began to head toward the sound as Pandy and Achilles followed.

"Wait!" Pandy said, halting for only a moment, noticing a stillness surrounding them on the frozen field. "The spikes have stopped."

"Homer, keep going! I hypothesize that they're only triggered by forward motion," Iole said, scanning the field from her heightened position as Homer moved forward. "They're not springing up to either side of us. My assumption is that they're rigged to sense oncoming footfalls and, once sprung, that's it. Don't stray from our original path, Homer."

"ALCIE!" he bellowed.

"Here!" came her voice, bouncing off the protruding spikes and now seemingly all around them.

"Gods! You didn't think it might be smart to warn us that there's a *well*?" Pandy all but screamed at Achilles—the greatest warrior and second-greatest hero Greece had ever produced.

"Hercules' bad haircut," he huffed. "I certainly didn't see it! I just forgot, *okay*? Pardon me if I was just trying to get you all to the other side in the fastest possible time!"

"I don't know why you spirits have to have a well in the first place," Pandy went on, brushing past the demigod who now stood with his hands on his hips. "You're all dead! It's not like you get *that* thirsty."

"It's a delightful touch of home for most of us," he called after her. "I'll have you know *I* was in charge of the decoratives around this place!"

"Shut up and help us!" Pandy now really screamed back at him."

"Oh great, now I have to deal with attitude."

She ran over to where Homer and Iole, now on the ground, stood looking into a deep hole flanked on two sides by ice-spikes, one of which had snared Alcie's cloak as she fell.

"Alcie?" Pandy called down. In the darkness, she could just make out Alcie's form against a lighter background, perhaps twenty meters down.

"Here," Alcie said. "I'm right here."

"Are you all right?" asked Homer.

"Yeah, yeah. I guess when Hera started making it snow, it fell down in here as well. I landed in the stuff. My behind's a little sore, but I'm good. Ares' fingernails, it's cold. It's, like, twice as cold down here as up there."

"Oh, if only we had a rope!" Achilles said.

Pandy, Iole, and Homer did a slow look to Achilles.

"What?" he cried. "I was just saying. What's with the look?"

"Hang on, honey," Homer yelled down as Pandy fished the magic rope out of her carrying pouch.

"Help is on the way, Alce," Pandy said.

"Good. 'Cause it's really, really cold down here. And I don't feel so good. It's like something's pushing me from all sides. Yeesh!"

"Rope, original thickness," Pandy ordered. "One end stays here in my hand. Lengthen down to Alcie and tie yourself around her in a harness. Then wait for further instructions."

Achilles watched as the rope stretched itself and disappeared down into the darkness.

"Now *that's* just *faaab*-ulous!" he cried. "I could have won the Trojan War with that; wouldn't have had to lift my sword."

"Hey! Hey!" Alcie was suddenly protesting from the bottom of the well. "What's this? . . . I think this rope's trying to get fresh . . . What the? . . . Oh. Oh, okay. I get it."

"Are you secure?" Pandy asked.

"It's around my waist," Alcie called. "Wow, do I feel weird. Okay, good to go!"

"Rope, *pull!*" Pandy commanded.

The rope began its ascent.

"*What the . . . ?*" Alcie cried. "OW!"

"Alcie?" Pandy yelled.

"Ow! Whoa! OW! OW!"

"She's hurt!" Pandy said, nearly dropping her end of the rope. "She's hurt worse than we thought!"

"*Rope, stop!*" Iole screeched.

"*Alcie?*" Homer shrieked.

Silence.

"ALCIE!" he shrieked again.

"Alcie, talk to me!" Pandy called down. "Alcie?"

Nothing.

"Gods!" Homer wailed, then he grabbed the rope end from out of Pandy's hand. "Okay, rope, tie this end here around my waist and lower me down . . ."

The rope had just begun to obey when they heard a soft moaning from the depths of the well, then Alcie coughed and cleared her throat.

"No. No, Homie, you don't need to come down."

"Rope, stop," Pandy ordered.

Alcie's voice sounded weak and breathless, but there was also a tinge of calm that surprised everyone.

"I'm fine. Just a little tingly, that's all. Wow . . . that was wild. Pull it up first, then the rope can come back for me."

Everyone quickly looked at everyone else.

"Huh?" Pandy asked.

"Pull it up," Alcie replied. "And I'm gonna ask that you do it fast, because it's kinda freaking me out."

"Pull *what* up?" asked Homer.

"Oh, you'll see," Alcie said.

Pandy was so stunned that she just looked from Iole to Homer and back again, a large part of her now not wanting to ever know what was on the other end of the rope. She was silent so long that finally Iole issued the command.

"Rope, pull."

They all peered into the well as the rope obeyed. At first, their combined shadow obscured any clear outline or shape. Then as the rope continued lifting upward, Pandy was the first to see the glint off Alcie's red hair. And she could easily make out the white of Alcie's toga. But copper specks were swirling away from and around the form and there seemed to be something strange about the form—something was missing.

"I see her cloak," said Iole.

"And I'm seeing copper flickers," Pandy concurred.

"No mistaking those tresses," Achilles chimed in.

Then, as the rope brought its freight into sharp focus, Pandy gasped and stumbled backward. Iole clutched Homer's arm as Achilles grasped hers. The rope lifted Alcie's toga and cloak, torn and tattered, out into the bright sunlight, but no Alcie.

Only Alcie's copper skin.

The now transparent copper coating was still somewhat in the form of a person; the contours of the face were almost recognizable as Alcie's and the hair was, if possible, even thinner, but there were long rips along the backs of her legs, arms, and spine where the copper had split away from her body. The rope set the skin on the snow in a standing position where it promptly shattered into a billion little pieces.

Now, it was Homer's turn to throw up.

"Alcie!" Pandy screamed, when she thought that her friend might be skinless at the bottom of the well. She became so panicked as all the blood rushed to her face, that she thought the piece of golden teardrop shrapnel might just pop out from its resting place underneath her eye. "Are you bleeding?"

"No," came the reply.

"Are you *all right*?"

"Yeah," Alcie said. "You remember that mole I had on my left shoulder?"

"Uh . . . yes?" Pandy answered, not really remembering at all.

"Well, it's about half the size now, so that's a good thing, I suppose. Okay, so I'm kinda clothes-less down here; could someone toss me a spare toga?"

Quickly, the rope magically lowered itself down into the well a second time, carrying one of Alcie's spare togas (months ago, she'd had the foresight to pack two) and what little was left of Homer's cloak. Three minutes later, Alcie's physical form could be seen rising up out of the darkness.

"What happened?" Pandy asked, trying to keep her voice even.

"Hades if I know," Alcie said, climbing out of the well, holding her sandals and leg wrappings in one hand. "One moment I was freezing, but all in one piece. The next second the rope started pulling and I started coming apart."

"It was the cold," Iole said plainly. "Cold makes metal contract. It was so cold down in that well that your skin shrunk on you to the point that it was able to peel away when the rope pulled it. That was the pressure you felt; the copper contracting in on you. It's a good thing we pulled you out when we did, otherwise . . ."

"Otherwise?" Pandy yelped.

"Otherwise, I might be shorter, thinner, and deader," Alcie answered, turning to Iole. "Right?"

"I'm afraid right," Iole said.

Pandy noticed that Alcie's skin—her true skin—was positively glowing. If fact, Pandy realized, Alcie seemed to be glowing from both the outside and the inside. Was it possible that she'd become even prettier? Had Alcie also grown a centimeter down in that well? And why was she standing just a little straighter than she usually did? The next moment, and totally without warning, Pandy was pierced through the heart by feelings she'd felt often in her own life, but never—ever—about Alcie and Iole.

Ever.

She stood mute, watching Iole explain in slightly greater detail the laws of contraction and expansion as Homer sat next to Alcie in the snow, his arm draped protectively around her shoulder, as Alcie wrapped her feet and laced her sandals once again. This was something Alcie needed to do, Pandy mused; the still rational part of her brain knew Alcie wasn't dawdling, for Hermes' sake. Yet, Pandy suddenly felt as if she were an outsider, and one with a completely different agenda. She was watching these three people as if they were absolute strangers; as if they were all in on some tremendous secret and they were wasting *her* time talking about it while *she* was left in the dark. Alcie, for her part, was not making some flip remark or staring at Iole as if she were an unknown creature from a far-off land; she was actually listening and trying to comprehend. Pandy's hand brushed against her leather carrying pouch. She pictured the box in her mind. Jealousy was in it. So was Greed. And what she was feeling didn't really compare to either of these. It was—it was—

". . . so the basic principle is not that difficult to . . . ," Iole finished as Homer helped Alcie to stand.

"Hey!" Pandy cried, stamping her foot in the snow. "Here's a thought: while we've been standing around talking about hot and cold *metal* and how exciting that is, time may have already run out! Anyone think maybe *that* principle isn't so difficult to understand? Anyone feel like—oh, I dunno . . . coming with me to capture Fear, *if we're not too late*?"

Without waiting for an answer, Pandy spun on her heel and marched off onto the path of exploded icespikes, leaving Alcie, Iole, Homer—and even Achilles— stunned into silence.

CHAPTER NINETEEN
Fifty Heads and One Hundred Arms

"What in the . . . ?" said Alcie. "Where did *that* come from?"

"Rather uncalled for," Iole said, looking after Pandy.

"Is she always so touchy?" Achilles asked.

"I'm not sure why, but I think we need to let it go," Homer said thoughtfully.

They all watched as a spike burst through the ice, sending Pandy, now a good distance away, sprawling on her bottom.

"Well, we can let *it* go, but I can't let *her* go," Achilles stated. "Not alone, not now. Gotta do my job. Catch up when you can!"

He took off running, desperate to outpace Pandy and make certain that his footfalls were the ones that triggered the spikes.

"Ready?" Iole asked.

"More than ready," Alcie replied.

"That mole on your shoulder is smaller," Homer said, taking the lead back the way they'd come.

"Thank you for noticing." Alcie smiled.

"You're more beautiful than before you went down that well," he continued, trying to step in Achilles' footprints.

"Aw, Homie," Alcie said, as she and Iole followed. "That's so sweet. Yes, I guess you could say the underworld has been good to all of us in a weird way. You're more manly and mature. Iole's smarter, if that was possible, and not ashamed of it. I feel—well, I don't know that I'm prettier, but I just feel all-around different. Better. And Pandy . . ."

All three stopped short in the snow.

"Pandy," Iole said, understanding.

"Gods," Alcie whispered.

Not caring where their feet landed, they all broke into a run.

🍇

When Pandy realized that Achilles was racing to catch up with her, she began to sprint. She didn't want to be caught, she didn't want company, she didn't want to talk. After what had to be, she surmised, the midpoint of the field, the ice-spikes stopped erupting and she was left with a clear path to the gates of Tartarus—which, though still a good ten-minute brisk walk, were directly in her line of sight. The sky was beginning to fill with clouds, blotting out the underworld sun, in shades of black, gray, red, and orange. The snow had disappeared some meters back and now she was traversing pure, slippery ice; but her sandals were so worn, so beat up, that she found herself with plenty of traction and didn't miss a step. Achilles, when he saw she was in no further imminent danger, hung back to try to observe what he could about the strange mortal maiden with the large mood swings. Alcie, Iole, and Homer caught up with him and he stopped them from passing him by.

"Why aren't you leading the way for her?" Alcie asked.

"You see any spikes?"

"He's right, Alce," Iole said. "Hera must have never imagined that we'd get past the first half of the field."

"Well, Hades' hip replacement!" Alcie cried, beginning to run. "C'mon, then!"

"I think we should give her a little space," Homer interjected, grabbing Alcie's arm."

"No!" Alcie cried. "No space. She can feel whatever she wants, but I for one am not going to let her walk into Tartarus alone. She can hate me for the rest of her life, if she has one, but I'm going in there with her."

"Agreed!" shouted Iole, who took one step, slipped on the ice, and went spinning off on her bottom almost ten meters. Alcie tried to help her up, slipped herself, and took them another three meters off course. Homer slipped trying to get both of them up. Naturally, Achilles reached Pandy first.

"Hey, intrepid explorer," Achilles said when he'd caught up with her. "Mind if I take the point?"

"Point?" Pandy said.

"The lead? Go ahead of you? I see that the spikes are no more, but you never know what other delights that red-headed, blue-robed Kraken has planned."

"Fine," she answered brusquely. "Take the point. Whatever. Knock yourself out."

"All righty, then," Achilles said, facing forward.

Long moments passed in silence; Pandy could hear Alcie, Iole, and Homer gibbering as they struggled to catch up, but she never once turned around. The gates of Tartarus loomed large now. Pandy saw that they weren't really gates at all, just a gargantuan opening in the face of a sheer rock wall from which balls of red-hot lava and black ash would spew forth. She also saw three enormous creatures, each as large as her uncle Atlas and each with fifty heads and one hundred arms. One had heads with coal-black hair, cut to just above their eyes. A second had several patches of bright red hair sticking straight out from the sides of all fifty heads. The third was completely bald, not one strand of hair on any of his heads. Their clothes were dirty and tattered; all three creatures were lumbering back and forth, carrying rocks from a pile off to one side to the opening, where they were slowly sealing it up.

"Hide here," Achilles said, maneuvering Pandora into a crevice in some boulders on the edge of the Elysian Fields. "Let's wait for your friends to reach us."

"I'm not interested in waiting for my . . ."

"Very well, then, Miss Sass," he hissed, indicating that she should lower her voice. "But those are the hecatonchires."

"Cottus, Gyges, and Briareus. I know," Pandy said, rolling her eyes.

"So let's just take a moment to get a better idea of what we're dealing with here, all right?"

"Fine."

"*Fine.* Sheesh!"

They observed the creatures for only a moment before Pandy noticed something odd. There was some type of black pitch or tar over every mouth on the three huge monsters. Every mouth but one. Then, as one creature was passing another on his way to the entrance, he dropped a huge stone on the second creature's foot without realizing it. The second hecatonchire jumped up and down in pain for a moment, then spun the first to face him and smacked him on all fifty foreheads.

"Hey, Bri!" said the only open mouth. "What was that for?"

"That was for dropping a rock on my foot, you lead-brain!"

"I'm sorry, Bri."

"You oughta be."

"Where do you want me to drop it next time?"

"Why, you!"

Bri poked the other hecatonchire right in all his eyes.

"Ow!"

"Hey, Bri," said the third creature, "stop beatin' up on Cottus!"

"Quiet, you," said Briareus, "and get back to work."

Gyges stepped up to Briareus and puffed out his chest.

"I'll do it when I'm ready."

"Are you ready?"

Briareus stared Gyges down for a long moment. At last Gyges shrugged.

"Yeah, I'm ready."

"Hey, Bri," asked Cottus. "Why do you think Hera wants us to put all these rocks in front of the opening?"

"What do I look like, a scroll in a library? A know-it-all?" said Briareus. "Besides, you've got a hundred ears. You heard her just like I did. Something little is comin' in and she wants to make sure it doesn't get out again. And if we find it first we're to take it right to her."

"You mean little like a mouse?" said Cottus. "I love little mice!"

Gyges leaned in to Cottus.

"I like mice too!"

Briareus yanked Gyges back by his bright red hair.

"Spread out!"

"Ow!"

"Listen, you pea-brains," Briareus said. "I don't want you messin' this up. You think we got it good now; well, Hera could make things even better around here for us."

"Like the last time we did something for her?" asked Cottus.

"What did you do for her?"

"Nothin', what'd she ever do for me?"

Then Briareus smacked both of the others on all their foreheads.

Cottus did a goofy little wave in front of Briareus's noses. Then Briareus smacked his foreheads again. Cottus put all one hundred hands behind his head, waggled all of the fingers and barked like a dog. Briareus reached down and tickled Cottus, who jumped up and down.

"Woo woowoowoo woo!" he cried, a lopsided grin on his face. "Pardon me if I laugh."

Briareus smacked him again.

"Why, I oughta . . . !" said Cottus.

"What?"

"Nothin'."

"That's right!"

Pandy could hardly believe her ears or her eyes. These were the dreaded and fearful hecatonchires? Briareus was obviously the one in charge—and the bruiser—but he was just as silly as the other two. They looked like they would probably end up killing each other before they could harm anyone else.

"These guys are in top form today," Achilles whispered. "Sometimes, some of the other heroes and I come to the edge of the Fields and just watch and laugh for hours."

"Fascinating," Pandy said snidely. "But I don't have hours. I may not even have minutes."

"You know those are the hecatonchires, right?" Iole said, overhearing Pandy as she came up, following behind Alcie and Homer.

"Gods!" Pandy shouted, worming out of the crevice and out into the open, as far away from her friends as possible. "Yes, Iole, yes! I know that those creatures with the fifty heads and the one hundred arms are, indeed, the hecatonchires! Did you think that maybe I would think they were, oh, I don't know . . . winged horses? Are you *that* concerned that I'm *that* stupid? You know, I'm really glad that you're even smarter now and that you're not ashamed of it or afraid of it or whatever you were about it anymore, but that doesn't mean that no one else around you can think for themselves, okay? Yes, I know exactly what they are!"

She turned and gestured to the opening of Tartarus. But the hecatonchires were gone.

"Huh?" Pandy humphed.

Suddenly a net dropped over the crevice, trapping Achilles, Alcie, Homer, and Iole underneath. From behind the boulders, Briareus and Gyges stood up, towering over the crevice as Pandy watched, too stunned to move.

"Hey, Bri! Look what I found? Little mice!"

"Those aren't mice, ya maroon. Those are people. And I'll just bet they're the little things Hera's lookin' for!"

"Pandora, run!" shouted Achilles.

Without thinking, Pandora began to race toward the opening in the sheer rock wall. But she hadn't gone ten paces when a giant hand blocked her way. Another came down right behind her blocking the rear, and two more came down on either side. A fifth hand reached in and held her firmly as it lifted her high into the air. The next instant, she was staring at Cottus's hundred eyes as they all stared back.

"Hey, Bri," said his only open mouth as Briareus came up alongside. "Can I take this one to Hera?"

Briareus plucked a large coin from the folds of his shredded garment.

"We'll flip for it."

He tossed the coin into the air with one hand, caught it with another, and slapped it onto the back of a third.

"Zeus's head, I take 'em in; Zeus's backside, you don't."

"Sounds fair."

Briareus revealed the coin.

"Zeus's head. You lose."

"Shucks," Cottus said, his shoulders sagging as he gently dropped Pandy into one of Briareus's waiting hands. "I'm just a victim of *soi*-cumstance."

"Tell you what," said Briareus. "I'm feelin' generous, so you and Gyges take the net in while I carry this one."

"Gee, thanks, Bri."

"Don't mention it."

Fortunately Briareus, as ridiculous as he was, didn't squeeze Pandy too tightly as he held her. From the vast height, she was able to see the snowy Elysian Fields behind her and a narrow road off to her left, which she surmised led back to the place of judgment and the iron entry gate.

"Hey, Bri!" said Gyges, as he and Cottus approached the entrance into Tartarus, each one gingerly holding two corners of the net. "We made the hole too small for us to get through now!"

"Why you . . . you two have oatie cakes for brains,

y'know that!" Briareus grumbled. "Gyges, you take some rocks away and we'll just have to wait."

"Why can't Cottus help?"

"Don't make me come over there!"

"Okay, okay."

"Nnyahhh," said Cottus, sticking out his tongue and taking the net from Gyges. "Thank you!"

As Gyges worked to remove some of the stones blocking the entrance, Pandy tried to catch a glimpse of anyone in the net; tried to make eye contact with Alcie or Iole. But she couldn't see past the thick rope, and everyone seemed to be pretty tangled up inside. She could hear them whispering but couldn't make out any words clearly.

"Quiet, mice!" said Cottus. "There's a big blue cat waiting for you; one of you in partic'lar. Which one is it, huh?"

He started poking into the net.

"It's me!" Pandy cried. "I'm the one she wants. Leave them alone . . . lead-brain!"

"Okay."

Gyges hefted a final rock back onto the rock pile, then turned toward his brothers and again took up two corners of the net.

"It's all clear!"

He turned back toward the entrance and was instantly smacked in ten of his heads with a red-hot lava bomb. As the lava singed his scalp and fried his hair, he bowed low to Cottus.

"You first."

"Don't mind if I do," Cottus said moving ahead, then he paused. "Hey, what the . . . ?

"Get moving!" barked Briareus, shoving them both through the entrance.

And into the most dreaded part of the underworld.

CHAPTER TWENTY
Tartarus

Her ability to be stunned continually surprised her. Fortunately, at this moment Pandy was too stunned to be terrified.

Tartarus stretched into the endless distance ahead, to the left and to the right. Before them, thousands of pits—more than Pandy could count—of varying shapes and sizes had been dug into the earth, each one filled with fire, oil on fire, burning coals, lava, hot ash, molten metal, and a variety of other blazing torments Pandy couldn't even guess at. The heat was so intense that the ceiling—the underbelly of the mountain—glowed orange and red, steam rising from the pits collected on the rock overhead and dripped back down only to be instantly changed into steam again.

Then Pandy saw the spirits—those whose lives on earth had been so ill-spent that they'd been condemned to remain forever in this inferno. A few—comparatively—were merely chained against the wall, tormented only by the unbearable heat. Some were sitting, chained, on the edge of the pits, their feet positioned on top of yellow-hot coals or on what looked like a simple but enormous frying stone, cooking oil popping and sputtering between their toes. But all the others were actually *in* the pits, buried to varying degrees. A large number had their feet submerged in boiling oil or bubbling pitch. There were those standing up to their knees in something white-hot that smelled like sulfur. Some were waist high in molten metal, burning garbage, or pure fire. Not a few were actually chained next to a pit on their bellies, their arms sunk deep into coals or flaming tar. And lastly were those buried to their necks in never-cooling lava.

All of them, however, had signs around their necks (in the case of those up to their necks in lava, the signs were balanced on top of their heads) clearly stating why they'd been sent to the flame pits in the first place. Along the wall, most of the signs described things such as ABANDONED FAMILY or NEGLECTED SPOUSE. But those in the pits were guilty of more heinous crimes; almost all of those with buried hands had signs reading THIEF—WITH WEAPON or THIEF—REPETITIVE. Many, buried waist high in what had to be—from the scent—burning alcohol, had signs that read INTOXICATED IN PUBLIC. Others were charged with various abuses of the law, sacrilege against the gods, and ill treatment of their fellow men and women. Those sunk to their necks were charged with the most hideous crime: murder.

And just like the pits themselves, the number of shades seemed limitless.

For the second time in what she calculated to be less than three hours, Pandy threw up, splattering Briareus's hand—he didn't even notice. Her arms were bound at her sides in the monster's snug grip, so she wiped her mouth as best she could on the shoulder of her cloak. As she lifted her head again, she thought she saw something off in the middle distance, another creature, similar to Briareus—but it was too far away to be truly recognizable and the next moment, as Briareus took his first step, it was gone.

There were narrow walkways winding between the pits and it was along these that the hecatonchires began to move slowly forward. Without any warning, there was a splash into a lava pit far enough away that no subsequent splatter reached any of them. But to her right, only two pits away, there was a whoosh as hot coals dropped seemingly out of the air. Then, five pits beyond that, Pandy saw a small trapdoor open in the rock overhead and a stream of molten metal poured into the pit and onto the spirits below. To her left there was another lava splash and, as she was trying to find the source, she saw a shower of hot oil rain down from a tiny hole in the ceiling over another pit. Then, Pandy saw the machine: a catapult, ornate and beautifully detailed—and one of several Pandy saw—being loaded every few moments with lava bombs that moved ever forward on a long ramp that descended from the ceiling. On its own, the machine swiveled to launch its bombs into the right pits. The next bomb flew right through an ash rain, scattering ashes everywhere, including onto the net. Pandy thought her heart would crack in two as she listened to Alcie's and Iole's screams. Even Homer and the mighty Achilles were wailing as hot ash lit on their skin.

"Alcie!" Pandy called out.

"Quiet, you," Briareus said roughly, shaking her a little from side to side—which nearly caused a concussion.

There was no response; only a dying flurry of moans as the last of the hot ashes cooled, and Alcie and Iole tried to brush them away as best they could. But their cries were truly nothing compared to the lamentations of the spirits all around her, punished for eternity. How could neither she nor any of them not have heard the sounds of utter anguish from the Elysian Fields?

Briareus, Gyges, and Cottus were strangely quiet now; no goofing around or bullying. Pandy knew that, for all their simplicity, their cargo was precious and one false step would send them into the pits and bring the wrath of Hera down upon them. She realized she was sweating buckets and there was the barest hint of an odd tingling all over her body. A flicker of movement to her right caught her eye and, for the second time, she could have sworn she saw Briareus—and now herself, held high—in the distance. But the figure was gone almost as soon as she turned her head. Then she spied two creatures who looked like Gyges and Cottus plodding a parallel path, perhaps forty meters away; yet as soon as she looked at the real hecatonchires, their doubles vanished. Garbage rained from another trapdoor in the ceiling almost exactly overhead and she buried her face as deep as she could into her shoulder. Looking up again, she saw something that was no figment, no false vision. Ahead, a dark figure was seated in silhouette against the endless fiery, steamy background.

Hades.

As the hecatonchires drew near to the lord of the underworld, Hades looked up from where he was bound to an enormous superheated iron chair, and the faintest hint of a smile replaced the look of utter weary weakness. He sighed—relief or resignation, Pandy couldn't tell—upon seeing who Briareus held in one of his hands. Then his brow furrowed and he glanced around Tartarus.

"And where *is* Hera?" Pandy thought.

The Queen of Heaven was nowhere to be seen.

"Put her down," Hades commanded.

"You'll pardon me for sayin' so," Briareus replied, "but I don't answer to you no more . . . uh, anymore. I'm takin' my orders from Hera *di*-rect."

"If you don't put her down now, I shall see to it that you are placed in the hottest lava pit—on your head," Hades said quietly, lowering his head.

Briareus looked at his master only a second, then shrugged his shoulders.

"Okay."

Setting Pandy gently on the ground at Hades' feet, the god motioned that Gyges and Cottus should also set down the net. Hearing their brother's potential fate, they were especially gentle and placed Alcie, Iole, Homer, and Achilles in a large intersection of two pathways.

"Now, all of you, out!" Hades ordered.

"But . . . ," Briareus began.

The next moment, all anyone could see of the heca-tonchire were two legs sticking up out of the nearest lava pit. Three seconds later, he was back on the path-way, standing right side up, lava dripping down his head and onto his shoulders.

"Gotcha," he said with a nod to Hades. "All right, you maroons, move it!"

Gyges and Cottus left the net where they'd set it down, a good distance from Pandy and Hades, and the three monsters all but ran back the way they'd come.

"I may not be able to counteract the cow's enchantments," Hades said, with a wry gaze to Pandy, "but I still have a little power where it counts. Hello, Pandora. We've not officially met. The last time I saw you, you had a knife handle sticking out of your shoulder and there was certain talk of officially losing you to my realm. I believe my wife was instrumental in bringing you back among the living."

"Yes, she did. Uh, was," Pandy answered.

"And speaking of bringing someone back," Hades said, glancing at the net. "Is Alcestis with you?"

"She is, mighty Hades," Pandy answered, acutely aware of the minutes slipping away. "But I have so little time left and I have to find Fear and I don't know where it's hiding."

Pandora got up and began circling the glowing iron throne.

"We've looked everywhere in the underworld and we didn't see it. Persephone—uh, your wife—thought that if anyone would know . . ."

"What are you doing, maiden?" Hades asked, confused by Pandy's walking around and around the chair.

"Oh. I'm looking for a way to untie you."

"That's very kind of you," Hades said with a sad

smile. "That's something my wife would do. But Hera's binding will have no knots and you wouldn't be able to touch them anyway without burning yourself."

"You might be surprised," she answered. Then she felt the tingling sensation throughout her body growing slightly stronger. She came around to stand in front of Hades. "Anyway, we—I—thought you would know where it is. Fear, that is. Your wife thought you might."

Hades looked at her and slowly shook his head.

"Pandora, I have no idea," he said at last. "It's not here, that much I can tell you. I'm sorry."

Pandy stood silent for a moment, her mind racing. Ever since she'd begun this quest, there were so many occasions where she'd been sure she'd failed—that she'd run up against a wall she just couldn't get around, over or under. Always, in every instance, she'd been able to find a way out. Or Alcie had. Or Iole. Even Homer. Now, with seconds dropping away like grains of sand through an hourglass, to be thwarted by the lord of the underworld himself. To have gotten so close, only to be utterly denied . . . Her lower lip began to quiver.

"But it has to be!" she cried at last. "There's no place left. The map said 'Underworld' and that's where we went."

"It's not here. Look around. Do you see Fear?"

"You bet I do!" Pandy yelled. "I see it everywhere.

There's someone right over there with sizzling feet . . . she's screaming in fear!"

"No," Hades said. "That's not Fear. She's in a great deal of pain, to be sure. But she's looked within herself. She has to—every moment for the rest of eternity. . . ."

"But . . . but . . . we've done everything that's been asked of us!" she said, breaking into tears. "All of us. We've been pounded and pummeled and baked into stones. Our bones have been broken and Alcie was killed and we've been enslaved and been turned into dogs and gotten sick and bit by scorpions and been flooded in a sewer and Homer had to fight for his life and Iole was almost buried alive."

Hades stared hard at her.

"Pandora, are you *listening* to me? That woman over there, the one you pointed out. She has to look at herself every moment. She's looked within and has accepted her fate. Everyone here has to look at themselves forever. Their pain is only a *result* of their fear—their personal fear—but it is not the Fear you seek."

"We've—we've been good," she stammered, not noticing Hades' eyebrows arching up in that way her father's used to when he was trying to get his daughter to understand something. Usually something right in front of her face. "We fought for each other, we protected each other, we kept each other alive. That's got to count for a little bit!"

She was so intent on getting the story out, as choppy and brief as it was, that she didn't register Hades' eyes as they moved to focus on something that had appeared behind her.

"And we got them all back!" she railed on, her voice beginning to break in frustration. "All of them . . . except one. And this is where the map said it would be. So you can't tell me it's *not here*. Time is almost out, do you understand? Maybe it's already out and . . ."

She finally realized that Hades was no longer even listening. It was then, as her words slowed in their mad rush out of her mouth, that she heard Alcie and the others yelling. Something about turning around. Something about behind. Behind?

Slowly, Pandy turned.

Out of the lava pit directly in front of her, a huge figure was rising up, nearly halfway out of the molten pool. Pandy didn't need anyone, at this point, to tell her who was making such a dramatic entrance. As the lava fell away and the blue robes began to be revealed, Pandy felt the tingling increase as her knees went weak. She caught Alcie's voice over the pounding of her own heart and glanced at the net: Achilles was furiously trying to sever the netting with his sword, failing miserably. Nothing was going to cut through those ropes, Pandy thought; Hera would have seen to that.

The last of the lava dripped away and Hera, in all her

evil glory, was floating above the lava pit, her arms folded across her chest. Her hair was now fully restored from the moment in Aphrodite's temple when Pandy had set her on fire, and her bottom was no longer in its bandage from the spanking her husband had given her only a short time before. Hera was completely restored and intact and, Pandy had to admit, absolutely beautiful. Hera looked down at Pandy and smiled.

"Flattery will get you nowhere."

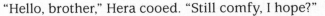

CHAPTER TWENTY-ONE
Fear

"Hello, brother," Hera cooed. "Still comfy, I hope?"

"Fine."

"Well, that's just wonderful. Although when this is all over and I'm on the big throne and you're on that chair for eternity, I'll make your bindings the kind that get a *lliiittle* bit tighter every ten topside years or so. I made your darling bride suffer, that's for darn-tootin'. But I don't really care about her."

"If you harmed . . ."

"Quiet!"

Hades' jaw slammed shut. Hera turned to Pandy.

"And speaking of things I don't care about—hello, brat. Did you like my entrance? Wasn't it just too dramatic for words? My husband has always said that my real calling was the stage. And not just the chorus, mind you. No, no, front and center; out there all alone. Hey, *you're* alone! Where are the other worm-buffets?"

At that moment, Achilles managed to sever a single piece of rope and open a tiny section of the net; Alcie gasped. Hera turned to see the blade of his sword poking through. With a flick of her finger, the net was instantly hoisted up to the ceiling where it hung directly over a pit of molten gold. Everyone screamed as they were crushed in on each other once again.

"Go ahead, cut through all the net you want, hero," Hera snarled to Achilles. "Be my guest. Maybe you can get a few more sections cut before the little door opens and liquid gold starts gushing all—over—you."

Pandy began to shake, her knees felt as if they were going to give way at any moment, and the tingling sensation was growing. Her entire body felt as if the blood were rushing furiously everywhere.

"Wow," Hera said, turning her gaze back to her nemesis. "Awwww. Just couldn't find it, eh? My little contribution of Fear? And you're right, you all were doing so well, despite my best efforts. But boo-hoo, boo-hoo. Yes, I heard you gnashing your teeth, wailing like a baby. Even through the lava, I heard you. You know, I think that's just about the worst thing I've ever heard. To get so close, to go through so much and then . . . to fail."

The Queen of Heaven began to laugh. At that moment, out of the corner of her eye, Pandy clearly saw a second Hera, fairly close this time. She turned her head slightly and the vision was gone. Then she moved her head back the other way—just a tick—and the second Hera was there. Lowering her head, trying to ignore the tingling, her eyes did a subtle sweep of Tartarus, all that she could see.

"Hey, you know what I'm going to do?" Hera went on. "After you're dead, I'm gonna take you and your palsy-walsys up there, dip you in gold—might not wait until you're dead for that—"

And there it was. A shimmer. A very slight flux. There were two women, identical, right next to each other, both suffering in a fire pit. Two men across the way, dressed identically, each with their feet in exactly the same position on a bed of coals. Only, it was an opposite position.

"Looking glass," Pandy thought. "This whole place is paneled with looking glass."

"—and then I'm going to stand you up in the agora back in Athens. I'm going to make you all minor deities. 'Pandora, Goddess of Failure.' I love it!"

She glanced at Hades, trying to make it seem as if she were turning away in despair from Hera's awful words. Hades, his jaw tense and unyielding, only stared at her knowingly. Suddenly, Pandy felt the tingling turn into a burning and she doubled over.

"Oooh, am I frightening you?" Hera sang out.

With all her might, Pandy tried using her own

power over fire, the power that had grown and been refined over the past months as she'd learned more about it. She focused her mind swiftly on cooling herself down. Nothing. In fact, it only seemed to make matters worse. Pandy glanced at Hades once more and saw his eyes move slightly to his left. Pandy tried to follow, but the fire inside her was growing in intensity—exponentially. Every second brought a new wave of searing heat. And it was nothing she'd ever felt; never once before had she been in any pain, but this was not a fire over which she had any control. Her organs were ablaze, her muscles, tendons, and sinews were being burned to crisps.

"Hey!" Hera screamed. "Pay attention!"

In the net, Alcie grabbed Iole.

"Say it again," Alcie whispered through tears. "When metal cools it contracts. And when it gets heated?"

Iole just looked at Alcie and tried to sob as quietly as she could.

Pandy's eyes felt as if they were going to pop out of their sockets. But it was her skin that was truly burning. She doubled over again and looked down at her feet.

She couldn't believe what she was seeing.

Small cracks were appearing in her bronze-covered skin, exposing blinding white-hot flesh underneath. She managed to get to her feet and focus her eyes to the left. Exactly where Hades had indicated. And there she was. Her—Pandy—in a shimmering, almost hidden looking glass. She stared at herself as Hera ranted on and on about her impending, torturous death.

"Maybe I'll flay you first and then just dip your skin in gold. By my husband's silky silver beard, to think a simple mortal maiden could have ever succeeded. It's a wonder you got this far."

She was thirteen years old, her hair and eyes were a dull brown, and she had a tiny overbite. Her skin was cracking and her life was at an end. She was now and had always been plain, ordinary, and really . . . nothing special. This was how she was going to die.

And that's when the pain in her body felt like nothing compared to the pain in her heart. She felt it: pure, unadulterated . . . *terror*.

"ALL RIGHT!" Pandy screamed as another wave of fire split the skin on her shins. "You WIN! You hear me, you WIN!"

Hera was startled into silence.

"That's right, we *didn't* succeed. We tried and we failed. But we did our best and that's all any mortal can ever do!"

Pandy flashed on Master Epeus.

"That's all we mortals have is potential and maybe we didn't live up to ours, but at least we stepped up and tried!" she cried, trying to make her words heard over the choking in her throat as her body burned and her deepest, darkest secret heart cracked open. "You think you're so clever, hiding Fear in a box. As if! You couldn't hide it at the bottom of the sea. We humans live with Fear every day! I've lived with Fear for as long as I can remember. I'm afraid of not being smart enough. Or pretty enough. I'm afraid of not being special enough or being too special and everyone will think I'm weird. I'm afraid of being weird!"

Behind Hera, unseen by her, Athena and Hermes began to emerge, slowly and silently, out of a large pit of smoldering sulfur. They stopped rising with only their upper halves exposed and gazed at Pandy as the horrible, awful truth poured out of her like water from an urn.

"I'm afraid of other people. I'm afraid of bullies. Of new kids at school. I'm afraid to just say hello because I'm more afraid of what they're gonna think of me. I'm afraid my mother thinks I'm nothing. That my father thinks I'm nothing. That I think I'm nothing and maybe I really *am* nothing. That I'll be nothing when I grow up. I'll be nothing special and my life will be just as miserable as it always was. Maybe that no one will love me just for me. I'm afraid I'm not really lovable. I'm afraid that my friends . . ."

Pandy broke into wracking sobs, burning alive as her expanding skin split up to her belly button.

". . . my best friends who have done more in the last six months than any twenty people could do in six years . . . are now just plain better than I am."

"We're not," Alcie muttered. "We're not."

Pandy looked up at the net, trying to bring Alcie and Iole into focus in spite of the pain, the torment, and the tears.

"I've just treated them so badly because I'm afraid that they're gonna start thinking I'm nothing!"

"Oh, honey." Iole wept softly.

"Boo-hoo," Hera spat.

"SHUT UP!" Pandora screamed, nearly ripping her vocal cords to pieces. "You, you—what did Zeus call you? A giant nesting water hen? A ripe but gargantuan grape? That's gotta make you feel great, huh? The Queen of Heaven, and your husband calls you that? Oh, but *you're* not afraid are you? Afraid that, like, maybe you're fading away, that the people don't love you like they should 'cause your husband sure doesn't so why should they? That you've become . . . become . . . Iole?"

"Obsolete!" Iole called from up high.

"Obsolete. You're so scared of that you had to chase down three girls for six months to keep them from finding out. But that's *nothing*, you rotting falafel patty! Nothing compared to me. This is one time where a mortal really does surpass the gods because I'm afraid of everything! *Everything!* And I have been for a while now and maybe I would have been for the rest of my life."

Pandy managed a glance at Athena, who smiled and nodded her head—not in agreement—but simply to urge her on.

"So you wanna kill me, you big blabbering fool. Go ahead. Because you wanna know what I fear most? I'm too afraid to tell anyone that I'm afraid. And I don't want to live that way anymore. You want to know where Fear is, you big, stupid, horrible Queen? IT'S RIGHT HERE!"

Pandy pounded on her chest as a final sob wracked her body. Her bronze skin tore apart and spiraled upward in a whirlwind. The pain shot through her as if she'd been hit by one of Zeus's lightning bolts and every muscle tensed like the string on a bow. She stood upright, straight as a rod, then crashed to the ground. Athena and Hermes, as if on cue, both blew softly in the direction of the bronze whirlwind, condensing it and sending it spinning downward toward Pandy as she lay in agony on the ground. Then Athena flicked some hot coals down the back of Hera's blue robes. Hera, caught off guard, immediately conjured up memories of being set on fire and whirled around, trying to reach down her back.

"Come on, girl," Alcie said, watching the scene below.

"Come on, honey," Hermes said softly to himself.

"You can do it," Athena murmured.

Pandy opened her eyes and saw the small cloud of bronze skin drifting toward her. Her skin, soaked through with fear, now blown apart. Her fear, which she realized was, in fact, *the* Fear. Not really believing that she was still alive, she reached for her leather carrying pouch—the smallest movements bringing searing pain—and slowly removed the box and the net. In a near stupor, she threw the net up into the air, but it sailed too far to the right and was about to miss its target. Still unable to open his mouth, Hades shook his mane of inky-black hair and created just the right breeze to settle the net neatly over the bronze cloud, which brought it down just within Pandy's reach.

Hera had pulled the coals out of her robes and turned to see who or what had done that to her.

Pandy removed the hairpin from the lock on the box.

Hera glared at Athena and raised her hands to deliver a hefty blow.

Homer unconsciously pulled on the rope net so hard that he broke several strands.

Pandy dragged the adamantine net over to the box.

The spirits closest to the scene ceased their wailing and began to softly chant, "Pandora, Pandora."

Hera registered that Athena wasn't even going to fight back; that her eyes were focused intently on something happening in front of her.

Pandy flipped the clasp and lifted the lid.

Alcie and Iole were clutching each other so hard that their nails drew blood. Neither of them noticed or would have cared.

Hera turned, Pandy in full view.

Pandy dropped Fear, the seventh and final Evil, into the box, closed the lid, flipped the clasp, and slid the hairpin back into place.

Hera let out a scream that shattered the spirit eardrums of those close by, but the whole of Tartarus erupted into cheers. Athena and Hermes smiled at each other as they sunk back into the sulfur pit. Hades, with Hera's enchantments now broken, immediately freed himself and brought the rope net down to a safe place in front of the iron chair. Untangling themselves, Alcie, Iole, Homer, Achilles, and Hades rushed to Pandy, flat out on the ground and almost insensible. Her flesh was cooling but her skin was still bright red and burned. There was no touching her.

"Hera?" Pandy asked weakly.

Everyone looked around.

"Gone," Iole said.

"Did we make it in time?" she asked, closing her eyes.

"You did," Hades replied. "With eleven . . ."

As if the moment weren't dramatic enough, he paused and let the word hang in the air.

". . . seconds to spare."

"Oh, P," Alcie sobbed, looking at Pandy's traumatized flesh.

"Just a scratch," Pandy joked, but she could feel herself slipping away; this time, she had a strong suspicion, it would be for good. The damage was just too great. She thought about the Elysian Fields—she hoped she might get to visit them once in a while. She opened her eyes and looked at Alcie, Iole, and, yes, Homer too: the best friends anyone ever had. Then she looked at Hades.

"Looking glasses?" she said. "Why?"

Hades smiled.

"Because, Pandora—you great and wonderful girl—you now know what the true secret of Tartarus is: looking at yourself, truly looking at yourself, is the hardest and the most frightening thing anyone can ever do."

It was Pandy's turn to smile. And with that, Pandora Atheneus Andromaeche Helena blacked out.

CHAPTER TWENTY-TWO

Olympus

The sensation was familiar, but with her eyes closed, she couldn't place it and she just wasn't ready to lift her lids. She was lying on something soft and billowy; it puffed up all around her and yet she floated securely on top. And then a second familiar sensation found its way into her sleep-laden brain. Pandy had the notion that everything that happened to her—and to Alcie and Iole—and to someone named Homer—had all been a terrible, wonderful, frightening dream or series of dreams; that she would wake up on her own sleeping pallet and it would be the day of the big project due at the Athena Maiden Middle School and that she would have nothing to show.

And Master Epeus would give her a delta, or worse: maybe kick her out of school for the rest of the year.

Pandy stretched out, expecting to feel nothing but a slight ache in her bones from such a restless sleep.

Instead, there was a tightening of her skin all over her body; she thought she could also *hear* her skin pulling taut against her muscles. It was hot and prickly but not entirely unpleasant.

She opened her eyes and trained her focus on her forearm; her skin was clear and white. Too white. Where was the browning that she gotten from years of running about Athens in sleeveless garments? She looked at her legs. White. It was as if her whole body had somehow been covered in brand-new skin. It was almost as white as the clouds she was lying on.

Clouds!

Clouds meant only one thing: Pandy leapt off her bed of clouds and onto the floor a good distance away just as the clouds disappeared, revealing that same terrifying expanse of a jagged, rocky mountaintop. The next instant the opening disappeared, replaced with the same pristine marble as the rest of the room. She was back on Mount Olympus. At the same moment that realization hit, the little pink mouths and tiny pairs of eyes appeared, hovering in midair, all staring once again at her.

"Hello," she paused, recollecting, "daughters of daughters of daughters of Zeus."

"You remembered!" said the tiny mouths in unison. "We are honored."

"Kinda hard to forget."

"We welcome you. You are . . ."

"Let me guess," Pandy said, a slight tremble in her voice; it was all very good, or it was very, very bad. "I've been summoned."

The mouths said nothing, but each one broke into a wide grin, the sight of which caused Pandy to start, then giggle. As she passed though the eyes and mouths, one vivid blue eyeball winked at her and a rosy pink mouth blew her a kiss. She couldn't tell if this was a saucy show of support or they were gleefully sending her off to her doom. As before, a door in the room was opening outward and a set of unseen hands was already pushing her into the same long, impossibly high white marble hallway. And, as before, the air was perfumed with lavender and honeysuckle. And then she realized something astonishing and marvelous: she was no longer afraid. Something was going to happen to her in the next few moments, in that enormous hall, and she was going to face it with every ounce of stamina and every centimeter of spine. Consequences, cheers, fire pits, ridicule, shame, a pat on the back, torment, hugs and kisses, exile; whatever lay beyond those doors, let it come. She took a deep breath and found her resolve.

"Guys, guys!" Pandy said, bucking up against the force of the hands. "I've got this. I do. I know where I'm going and I'm good. Really."

Instantly, the pressure on her back was gone. She straightened herself and began to walk forward, tilting her head upward to take in once again the beautiful oil lamps in the shape of great eagles on gold chains and the ridiculously high ceiling. She was heading toward the great hall of Zeus, passing by the fountains depicting the titans: Cronus, Rhea, Oceanus. Then she found herself approaching the stunning fountain depicting the titan Mnemosyne—"memory"—and she stumbled.

Without warning, it all came rushing into her mind, every event flooding every crevice of her brain in no chronological order whatsoever: Iole drinking from Mnemosyne, Persephone tied upside down to her throne, Lucius Valerius stabbing her in her shoulder, swinging from her uncle Atlas's nose hair, watching Wang Chun Lo move like water through his magic crystals, young Douban putting his hand over hers, lemon seeds pouring from the mouth of Mahfouza's brother, Hera's bald head after she'd set the Queen of Heaven on fire, Homer baked into the top of a column and forced to hold up the vault of the heavens, Iole nearly being roasted over the altar of Apollo's temple at Delphi, Hermes taking the emerald bracelet from Iole's wrist, Orpheus and his orchestra . . .

. . . Alcie, dancing blissfully about on a mountain top, right after Homer had asked her to be his . . . forever. *They had all happened*, every single moment, and now they hit her like chunks of stone crashing onto her head; it was all just too much.

With a wail she slumped forward, fully expecting to hit the hard, white marble floor. Instead, she was caught up gently in a hug, a pair of strong, safe arms around her. She looked up, the fountain of Mnemosyne in the distance, and found a joyful sight. Her father held her fast, his smiling face now only inches away from hers.

"Oh, Daddy!" she cried, burying her head in his neck, sobbing with everything she had.

"I know, honey," he whispered. "I know."

Far off, she heard the sound of a door opening, then she felt her father shake his head as if shooing someone away. Prometheus let her cry for a long while, rocking his daughter back and forth.

"Daddy, I . . . I . . ."

She tried to speak several times, but with every glance at her father, smelling the cedar oil in his hair, seeing the new touches of gray at his temples and in his beard and knowing she'd been the cause of all his worry and so much else, she just couldn't formulate any words. Then Prometheus looked at his girl.

"Big-time phileo, my daughter." He smiled.

"Me you more, Daddy."

Their special words of love; this father to this child and back again. Pandy dissolved into another flood of tears. So long, so loud that this time she didn't hear the door open again.

"Hey, pal," came a familiar voice from the entrance to the great hall. "Seriously, you've been out here, like, a full rotation on the sundial. *Someone*'s getting a little impatient."

"Okay, okay," Prometheus said. "Keep your helmet on. We're coming."

Hermes ducked back into the great hall as Prometheus slowly got Pandy to her feet. He raised her red eyes to meet his and wiped away the tears from her cheeks. He held up one finger and looked at the droplet glistening at the tip.

"Guess we don't need to save any more of these, do we?" He grinned.

Pandy shook her head and smiled back.

"You ready?"

"Uh-huh," she answered.

But for the second time, she couldn't remember those last few moments in Hades; whether she'd managed to capture Fear or whether she'd somehow bungled it and was heading toward Zeus's judgment of an eternity in the fire pits. She'd find out soon enough, but she checked in with herself and her emotions: nope, still unafraid.

They passed by the last fountain in the hallway: Prometheus; in full battle armor, his sword raised high as he helped Zeus and the other Olympians to victory. Suddenly, Pandy understood every moment of her father's struggle, his courage and determination. She hoped that, no matter what lay waiting in the hall, she'd measured up in some small amount to her father and hadn't thoroughly disgraced the great House of Prometheus.

"Dad?" she said, as they neared the golden doors.

"Yes, honey?"

"I'm proud of you," she said definitively, walking boldly into the enormous hall.

"Uh . . . okay," said Prometheus, following her, a surprised smile on his face.

But instead of being led to the great teardrop table and the gods sitting in judgment upon her (she had now thoroughly convinced herself that she'd messed up and would soon be on her way back to Hades), Hermes quickly ushered her and her father across the length of the hall, creating a corridor through a packed throng of people, and out onto a large terrace overlooking, as far as Pandy could tell, all of Greece. It was only during the last few moments of traversing that gauntlet that Pandy realized everyone was smiling and laughing. At one point everyone began to clap—for *her*—and several people congratulated Prometheus and a few even patted her on the back.

She headed straight for the railing of the terrace, her mind spinning, and she allowed herself to find a tiny ray of hope in the adulation from all of those strangers. Maybe things weren't so bad and maybe—wait—was it possible that she'd *recognized* one or two of those faces in the crowd? No—that was ludicrous. What would Balbina, chief cook and head of house slaves of Lucius Valerius, and Cleopatra, future Queen of Egypt be doing in the great hall on Mount Olympus?

She turned toward the entrance back into the room, her curiosity rising, and just at that moment out of the corner of her eye she saw three figures flying at breakneck speed down the length of the terrace.

Alcie, Iole, and Homer threw themselves onto Pandy with such force that Prometheus and Hermes had to catch them all to keep them from tumbling onto the tiles in a heap.

"We thought you'd never wake up!" Iole said, hugging Pandy tight about her waist.

"Zeus let you sleep as long as you wanted," Alcie said. "At least that's the rumor, lucky. We didn't get such royal treatment."

"Did you sleep here?" Pandy asked. "How long have you been up?"

"Well, we've had morning meal and midday meal . . . ," Homer began.

"Homer's also had midmorning meal and pre-midday meal." Iole laughed.

"They've set up a feast table in the far corner of the

terrace, Pandy, just for us," Alcie said, jumping up and down a little. "You just have to think of what you want and it appears, *and* Aphrodite says we can eat everything and nothing will make us fat—for today only. It was only you coming out here that made Homer budge away from it."

"The three of us slept most of the day before yesterday, the entire day yesterday, and all of last night," Iole said. "You, just a little longer. But then, after what you did, I'm not surprised in the least."

"How 'bout those clouds, huh?" Alcie grinned.

"Guys, wait! Wait," Pandy said, holding her hands up for silence. "The end in Hades is a little fuzzy for me, but I'm guessing we did it . . . right?"

"Are you kidding me?" Alcie said, her jaw dropping. "You're kidding right?"

"Pandy . . . ," Iole said, her face becoming very serious. "Yes, we were all there and yes, we helped, but in final analysis, you—*you*—were magnificent."

"Duh!" cried Alcie, who instantly furrowed her brow and regained her composure, trying to be a little more mature. Then she shrugged her shoulders and just giggled at herself.

Pandy looked at Homer, who caught her in hug and whirled her around in the air.

"Sorry," he said sheepishly, setting her down on the ground. "Not terribly adult of me."

"Homer," Pandy said, the wonderful realization that she was probably not going back to the fire pits of Hades anytime soon settling over her like a silk scarf, "you can do that all you like."

"Until he and Alcie get married, at any rate," Iole said.

A horn sounded from somewhere deep in the great hall.

"I think that means it's showtime!" Alcie chirped.

"Why are we out here?" Pandy asked.

"They sent all of us out here as soon as we awoke," Homer replied. "Apparently, it's quite a to-do in there."

A sharp movement—Hermes raising his hand to his ear—caught Pandy's attention, and she looked to see him listening intently, nodding slightly as if something was being said to him by a tiny or invisible person. Then Pandy spotted a shell, nearly identical to the one she'd been carrying for the last six months only much smaller, embedded in Hermes' ear. She saw a second shell fastened to a gold cuff around Hermes' wrist. Hermes nodded, then brought the cuff up to his mouth and spoke into the shell.

"Acknowledged, Sky-command. We are on the move," he said. "Repeat, 'Travelers' are on the move. Hermes out."

Hermes and Prometheus, who had separated themselves from Pandy and her friends to give them just a little privacy for their reunion, now approached as if they were on some type of secretive mission.

"This way, Pandora—Alcie, Iole," Hermes was saying, pretending to be stern and somber now as he corralled them all toward an open door farther down the terrace. "Homer, this way, please."

Prometheus chuckled at his friend.

"Goof."

"Hey," Hermes said, a mock serious look on his perfect face. "I'm on Sky-Lord business. Big doings. This way, please. Pandy? Cohorts? This way."

As Hermes led them down the terrace to another entryway, he called out to the few lesser immortals and demigods manning the feast table or drinking nectar and enjoying the view.

"Everyone, we're beginning. Inside, please. Come on, let's go—don't make me smite you."

Those around them nodded and bowed low as Pandy and her friends passed by. Drawing aside heavy purple curtains, Hermes ushered them all into the great hall. Immediately, the applause began, accompanied by much bowing. Again, Hermes went before them, magically but gently parting the crowd. Now more than a little confident that she'd not doomed the world and had actually been successful in her quest (oh—who was she kidding?—*their* quest: this had been a four-person operation pretty much the entire time), she gratefully accepted the adulation and smiles—at least, she assumed people were smiling. She tried to focus on some of the faces around her, but it was impossible: everyone was bowing so deeply at the group's passing that she couldn't identify anyone. But with everyone nearly down on the ground, Pandy could see just how far back the crowd stretched; the entire hall was jammed wall to wall, and Hermes was heading toward a huge dais—the teardrop table was nowhere to be seen—on which were seated, on large jeweled chairs, most of the great Olympians. Athena caught Pandy's eye and gave her a wink. Aphrodite smiled so big and bright, all four friends felt a white-hot glow in their stomachs and nearly dropped with joy. Ares, his helmet still on and his yellow eyes glinting, drew a big smile with his fingers right where his mouth would be just to let them know that, underneath, he actually was . . . smiling. Even Hades was there—not smiling, exactly—but a look of admiration and amusement on his face. Persephone stood next to his chair, nearly beside herself with glee.

Zeus sat in the center of the greatest immortals on his enormous throne with Dido at his feet. On seeing his mistress, Dido bolted up but Zeus held him back from running pell-mell into the mob. Pandy's heart soared seeing her beloved dog and she turned back to Alcie to grasp her hand.

Wait . . .

Did she spy a purple toga close to the back of the hall? Like the one Julius Caesar wore? And off to the left, was that the pointed blue headdress and light green skin of Osiris, God of the Egyptian Underworld? Then, close to the dais, an old woman raised her head for a moment.

"What did I tell you about peeking?" Zeus said. "Head down!"

"Listen, Mr. Sassy-Toga," screeched the woman. "I've had just about enough ordering from you . . ."

Zeus blinked once and the woman's head went down again.

"Sabina!" Pandy gasped, recognizing at once the voice of her house slave.

"Hi, honey," said Sabina, her voice muffled by her robes. "Good job!"

Then, of course, it was too late. Heads popped up all over the room and Pandy, Alcie, Iole, and Homer were jolted to a full stop.

"Mahfouza?" Pandy cried, seeing the beautiful dancer in the crowd and remembering the last time she'd seen Mahfouza's family in Baghdad.

Mahfouza waved, as did all of her brothers and sisters standing beside her.

"Hi, Homer!" cooed a voice right next to him.

Homer turned to see Rufina winking scandalously and nearly jumped back a full meter.

"I look a little better than the last time you saw me in Rome, don't I?"

"I'm gonna deck that cow if it's last thing I . . . ," Alcie muttered, balling up her fists.

"Stop it," Iole scolded, turning Alcie back toward the dais. "She's nothing. She's a . . . oh, what would you say? She's a plebe. You're his intended. Keep walking."

"Iole, look!" Alcie nearly shrieked as she moved forward. "It's the pirates! The ones who captured us and took us up Jbel Toubkal!"

"Hi there!" the pirates called.

"Yes, hello. Hello," Iole answered, thrilled to see that they were all in chains.

"Pandy! Pandy!" yelled Ismalil and Amri, jumping up and down at the back of the room, next to their mother and a man who was obviously their father.

"Oh, boys." Pandy gulped, so glad to see them and—even in the few weeks since they'd parted—how much they'd grown.

Everyone was there.

Wang Chun Lo's entire troupe of entertainers; the Persian barbers; the captain of the *Peacock*; the slaves of Cleopatra; the old man who sat at the golden door of the Garden of the Jinn; Achilles; all the Roman immortals except for Juno and Ceres; King Peleus and Thetis; the generous silver merchant from Baghdad; Echidna; Lucius Valerius and Varinia; Chiron; Charon; Prince

Camaralzaman and his evil grand vizier, momentarily restored, gagged, and looking much the worse for wear; and all the Vestal Virgins with Melania spreading her arms wide in respect; the Danaids; Pelops with his ivory shoulder; and so many more. There was even an enormous tank of water against the far wall in which swam the dolphins who had taken them up the Nile, balancing on their noses and waving their tails.

In addition to the entire pantheon of demigods and goddesses, nymphs, naiads, dryads, creatures and immortals of every stripe, *every* individual they had ever met on the course of their travels and adventures was there in the great hall of Olympus. Except, Pandy thought, there was something—someone—missing, she was sure of it; but she was too taken aback to be able to think clearly.

"And so much for the surprise." Zeus sighed. "Very well, you may all rise."

Only a few more steps and Pandy and her friends were all on the dais. Zeus beckoned them forward and Pandy walked in as stately a manner as she could, her heart beating so fast at the now thunderous applause. Hermes lined them up; Homer next to Iole next to Alcie next to Pandy. At this point, Dido was straining so that his veins were bulging on his hind legs.

"Go," Zeus said.

Dido shot like an arrow and actually knocked Pandy

down as another huge cheer went up from the crowd. Pandy let Dido lick her face for few seconds, burying her face in his fur. He was right there, as he'd been from the very start—except for the days that Hera had stolen him away. She flung her arms around his neck and hugged him tightly. He was the most real, true, and tangible thing about this moment. In a strange way, his hot doggy breath on her face was the only proof she needed that she was home—almost home—at last.

Hera!

Pandy moved Dido aside and got to her feet. Where was Hera? And Demeter? Her eyes frantically searched the hall and found nothing—except a huge, rather bulbous mass shoved into one corner and nearly knocking out the ceiling which, when she recognized her uncle Atlas, caused her jaw to drop. He was actually sitting cross-legged on the floor and he still had to scrunch over to keep from banging his head. He gave her a little wave and patted the side of his nose. She waved back as she turned to Zeus.

"Not to worry," said the Sky-Lord, reading her mind—as, she'd come to realize, all immortals were able to do. "I'm seeing to it that the heavens stay in place while he's here. I couldn't have him miss the festivities."

Zeus looked out over the crowd and raised his hand.

"All right, that will do. Quiet down. Everyone. Everyone . . . inside voices. Thank you. While I think the achievements of the past six moons speak for themselves, Gray-Eyes—you'll pardon me—my daughter Athena has prevailed upon me to say a few words about our returning wanderers and their adventures. But as I have tried to tell her upon many occasions and as most of you well know, I have absolutely no idea of anything that's happened since I sent Pandora out of this hall so long ago; and I'm sure neither do any of the Olympians seated here."

There was an uncomfortable silence that settled in the room. Ares sank deeper into his chair as Zeus paused.

"After all," he continued after taking a moment to gaze sternly around the room, "it was my express wish that Pandora receive no help of any kind, my order that she be left entirely to her own devices, that she sink or swim of her own accord. And we all know that each of the Olympians always obeys my every word."

He scowled for a moment, then broke into a wide grin and the entire room began to laugh; of course Zeus had known about everything.

"So, what to say regarding Athens's prodigal daughters and adopted son? Oh, that's quite nice—prodigal—I must remember that."

Zeus rose off his throne and began to walk between Athena, Ares, Aphrodite, Artemis, Apollo, and a sleeping Dionysus seated on their chairs, and the line of four friends; the confused and worried looks on Pandy's and Alcie's faces causing a ripple of laughter through the crowd. Zeus stopped directly behind Homer and although Homer towered over most people, Zeus now towered over him. Zeus paused again—not only for effect, but to allow Homer's father, Iole's parents, Alcie's parents, and Prometheus to emerge at once through the crowd and into the front row.

"Homer of Crisa," he said at last, his voice booming through the hall.

Homer stood straight, at full attention.

"Relax, youth. Just relax," said Zeus, as everyone began to laugh. "Homer of Crisa. You took on a task that was not yours. You shared no blame in the origination; you carried neither responsibility nor allegiance to this cause. Yet you have served this quest with more honor and dignity than We would be able to find in ten of the finest men in the known world."

Zeus glanced at Alcie, who was beaming at Homer.

"And you did this because, not only was your heart true, it was no longer truly your own. You had lost it and, to keep feeling its beat, you needed to stay close to the one who now possesses it; to keep her safe. Yet, We also know how your affection for Pandora and Iole has grown as well on this great journey, just as We know every incident of your courage and bravery. It was not merely love that made you stay but a broader perspective of a world potentially in peril and the sacrifices that must be made to put things to rights. A perspective shared, I believe, with an ancestor of yours . . . a poet, I think he was."

There was a twitter through the crowd; many nodded their heads and smiled. On cue, three young, identically dressed maidens stepped up onto the dais; one held something behind her back.

"We know your heart's desire—with whomever your heart happens to be—and We say yes. Calliope, Erato, and Euterpe, muses of all known poetic forms, at my request, have fashioned for you this small token of Our appreciation, infusing it with all of their inspiration and powers of creativity. Wear it well. Write well. Live and love well."

The maiden with the object stepped in front of Homer and floated off the floor to lay a golden laurel wreath on his head. Then she kissed Homer on the forehead and floated back to the ground.

"Thank you, Calliope," Zeus said as he moved to stand behind Iole.

"Iole. I have never said this before to or about anyone, but you might be smarter than me."

The crowd roared with laughter.

"Yes . . . well, it's not *that* funny," Zeus said scowling, at which the crowd nearly convulsed. "Uh-huh . . . yes. Who wants to be a goat?"

Instant silence.

"Right. So we have established that your brain, which started out the size of Athens and is now probably the size of Greece, is a mighty force. But, maiden, you have proven yourself to be much more than a collection of large words and a keen grasp of facts and figures. You are loyalty personified. You, too, did not have to accompany Pandora on this adventure and no one would have thought any worse. It was your intuition that urged you to go, and We know what you have gained from this adventure. Something that no philosopher has ever put into words and something that has, unfortunately, eluded the immortal mind for eons: a true comprehension of the human heart, most especially, your own. And so I present you with this . . ."

Two incredibly old men were shuffling onto the dais, one holding a golden wreath and the other assisting a third who looked twice as old. Iole gasped audibly; Pandy and Alcie looked questioningly at each other and just shrugged.

"You have one cycle of the moon to learn as much from these men as you can. At that point, Aristotle, Plato, and Socrates will be returned to the underworld and you will be given a one-year internship in the Athens senate and then either the position of curator of historical and philosophical documents at the Athens library or a professorship at the university of your choice . . . what?"

Zeus had noticed that Iole was looking at him, almost pleadingly.

"You'd prefer something else?"

Iole felt a twinge of fear at actually addressing the greatest being in the universe with anything less that full-blown gratitude, but then, certainty in her mind and newfound confidence coursing through her veins, she squared her shoulders.

"I have no words to express my true appreciation, Sky-Lord. But I would like to teach. Here. In Athens, at the Athena Maiden Middle School."

"Yes!" hissed Athena in glee from her chair, pumping the air with her fist.

"I believe that my abilities will be best served helping girls such as myself to recognize and utilize their own potential—and greatness."

A ripple ran through the crowd; not only had what Zeus proposed been nearly unheard of, a young woman teaching other young women was a fantasy. Then the crowd broke into applause. Zeus almost—almost—smiled.

"As I said," he murmured to himself. "Smarter than me."

He placed his hand on Iole's shoulder.

"Done."

Then one of the old men took the wreath and placed it on Iole's head.

"Thank you, Plato. Wear easy this golden wreath upon your brow, Iole. It has been infused with knowledge, understanding, and enlightenment. We know you will use these tools well."

He made a move toward Alcie, then—becoming quite the showman—bent down to Iole's ear.

"Oh, and there's also someone here to see you."

Iole looked at Zeus, startled, then gazed around the hall. The crowd was rustling halfway back and someone was walking toward the front. Iole's breath caught in her chest as she recognized the mane of black curls. Crispus, sixteen years old, walked out of the crowd and stopped, gazing up at her.

"Yes, stay right there, youth. You'll have time enough later on to explain—and I mean *much* later on," said Zeus, as the audience giggled again and he placed his hand lightly on top of Alcie's head.

"Alcestis."

Then Zeus seemed to stare straightaway into the middle distance, as if incapable of landing on the right word.

"What is there to say about the maiden with a loud mouth, raucous humor, witty but sometimes inappropriate insights, and a quick temper?"

Trying to keep the smile steady, Alcie's face was fast

becoming a mixture of shame and confusion. Pandy felt her stomach tighten. Suddenly, out of the crowd stepped Hercules, holding another wreath. He smiled broadly at Alcie as Zeus continued.

"Except to say that she is also the embodiment of courage. She did what, I dare say, no one else in this room would do; she gave of herself the ultimate sacrifice solely for the greater good. This girl's bravery is greater than any Olympian seated behind her—greater even than my own. In our battle with the titans, in our present lives, we knew we could not and cannot perish. Our courage has been stunted because we know and count on our immortal state. You have been a catalyst for all of us, Alcestis, as again and again we watched you place yourself between your friends and peril, both physical *and* emotional, by using your 'gifts': your loud mouth, your raucous humor, your witty insights, and your quick temper, all for a cause that wasn't really yours, a mission you didn't need to undertake. It is my hope that, in learning from you, we all may take a few more risks when it comes to doing the right thing. We also hope that, even though you have shed a few outer layers of your former self, you will always retain these 'gifts' and use them often, to their greatest good. Although We, personally, enjoy the fact that you've given up swearing . . . for the most part."

He gazed fondly down at Alcie, who gazed back and

began to open her mouth; Pandy saw the word forming on Alcie's lips and knew she couldn't stop Alcie any more than Alcie could stop herself.

"Duh!"

Alcie slapped her hand over her mouth and winced up at Zeus.

"Exactly!" laughed Zeus. "And so We have found someone equally courageous to present your wreath. Hercules?"

Hercules, clad in his Nemean lion skin, his mighty club in his other hand, stepped forward and bent low to place the golden circlet of leaves on Alcie's head, then kissed her forehead. Alcie's father let loose with a giant "whoop" and gave a thumbs-up signal to his daughter as other "whoops" and "wooos" peppered the air. Then Zeus turned to Pandy, and the room became so quiet you could hear a hairpin drop. He was silent for a long time, both of his powerful hands resting on her shoulders as she faced the crowd.

"If I did not already have the most perfect daughters in the universe," he began slowly, "I would wish for a daughter like you."

Pandy looked at her own father, who smiled softly and nodded. For an instant she choked and broke into tears, then she fought them back and stood erect.

"Let the tale be told from this day on of the maiden who said, time and time again, 'I can' and 'I will.' Who did not take on lightly the mantle of responsibility. Who, for the rising and setting of six moons, persevered and persisted until the job was done. Who experienced a gamut of emotions far too early and too intense for one so young and yet never said 'enough.' Who never took no for the final answer. Who explored, tested, and strengthened the bonds of friendship and in so doing discovered her own strengths and her decided lack of limitation. Whose mind became as sharp as her focus became keen. Pandora Atheneus Andromaeche Helena of the great house of Prometheus, who learned that, when you take responsibility for your personal actions, sometimes you get to have the adventure of a lifetime and, just perhaps, save the world."

Then the audience let out an enormous collective gasp as Zeus turned Pandy to face him . . . and knelt in front of her.

"For this, Pandy, I present you with a golden laurel wreath. Not only will it be a much safer item to take to school if you ever again need proof of the enduring presence of the gods in your daily life . . ."

A ripple of laughter went through the crowd at the mention of the school project that had started the whole mess.

". . . but it will be proof, should you or anyone close to you ever need reminding, that you learned this above all: it is both word and deed that determine not wealth, nor success, nor fame, but simply the quality of your character. It is all you have at the end of each day, all you have to truly call your own."

Out of thin air, a fourth golden wreath materialized in Zeus's hand and he moved to place it on Pandy's head.

"Uhhchhahemmmm," choked Athena.

"Huhhuh . . . metoo!" Hermes coughed.

"Oh, very well." Zeus sighed, rolling his eyes. "Step forward."

The god and goddess fairly raced to where Pandy stood and placed their hands upon the wreath; all three immortals lowering the shiny band of leaves onto her brow. As Hermes ever so gently squeezed her shoulder and Athena kissed her on the forehead, Zeus stood and spread his arms wide, presenting the group of four adventurers to the assembly. In later years, when she would repeat the story to her grandchildren, Pandy would say neither before nor since had she heard such noise, such a clamor as the one that arose at that moment. The crowd went absolutely wild. Not only with relief that their world was safe from evil but that one young maiden and her two—three—best friends had succeeded when everyone thought they would perish.

"And speaking of those closest to you, Pandora," Zeus said, rising and quieting the mob. "It is my turn to make something right. Aphrodite!"

Aphrodite rose up and out of her chair, took something handed to her from a nearby dryad, and sauntered to where Zeus stood.

"There, I think," Zeus said, pointing to a spot on the floor in front of the dais.

"Excuse me, please. Pardon me," Aphrodite purred as the crowed parted. She walked to the spot and set down the item in her hand. Thinking she couldn't be surprised any further, Pandy gave a start when she realized it was the small clay jar containing her mother. She tried to catch her father's eye, but his focus was locked and it wasn't on her.

Zeus held both his hands high as if to make a grand, sweeping gesture, but instead he merely flicked his wrists. The jar cracked open and instantly a swirl of ash spiraled up three meters high. Then it quickly compacted into the shape of Sybilline. Dazed, a little light-headed, and slightly achey, she tottered on her feet for a moment and would have fallen had Prometheus not raced to grab his wife. With a respectful nod of thanks to Zeus, Prometheus held Sybilline close and just stroked her hair as the woman's eyes adjusted to actually seeing for the first time in six months. Finally, she stood steady on her own two legs, leaned back, and looked at Prometheus.

"Hello, handsome," she said, groggy. "Why are there so many people in our living room?"

"Well, they're not, honey." Prometheus laughed. "But I'll explain everything later."

"Hi, Mom!" Pandy called, completely unsure how or even whether to approach her mother.

"Hello, Pandora. Honey, look," Sybilline said, "Pandora's onstage with her friends. Did I miss something? Was this a school performance? Oh, Artemis's little finger, and me not dressed for the occasion at all. And how could you let her go onstage looking like that, Prometheus! She looks like she hasn't combed her hair in weeks!"

"Shhh. Shhh," Prometheus said, putting his finger to her lips, slightly embarrassed. "Just stop talking for a moment. I'll fill you in later."

Alcie and Iole shot sideways glances at Pandy, wondering how she would handle her mother's comments. Pandy, however, just smiled from her place on the dais and it was in this moment that she knew she'd left, willingly, a part of herself behind for good.

"Some things never change," she thought, "so I guess I'll have to."

She turned to Zeus, craning her neck to see his face.

"Thank you, great . . ."

"But wait, there's more," Zeus whispered. "You also have someone here who wishes to reacquaint himself."

Pandy turned to face the crowd but, as if there were

a bright light shining from somewhere high above on his face alone, Pandy could see only one person.

Douban.

He walked slowly through the throng, his gaze never leaving hers until he finally had to shield his eyes. Looking up, Pandy saw that Eros actually was operating a kind of spotlight made from several candles and a mirror and was training it directly on Douban's face, blinding him.

"Aphrodite," Zeus said, "mind your son."

As Aphrodite scolded the child and the spotlight went out, Douban continued through the crowd until he reached the dais; he stood, like Crispus, looking fixedly at his girl.

"Who's that?" asked Sybilline.

"His name is Douban," Prometheus answered. "He's the son of a very famous physician and quite the physician himself. And he's mad for our daughter."

"Uh-huh," Sybilline said, staring at the striking dark-haired youth.

"Our little girl is growing up rather fast, isn't she, Syb?"

"Yes, fine, whatever." Sybilline grinned acerbically, mentally calculating the ease and comfort of her old age with the new information. "Oh, Prometheus, I'm so happy! My prayers to Hera have been answered. We're going to have a doctor in the family!"

CHAPTER TWENTY-THREE
Punishment

Prometheus shook his head and turned back to the dais only to find Zeus looking at Sybilline, as if Zeus had heard something out of her mouth that had made him remember something else almost forgotten.

"As joyous as this celebration is," Zeus called out, his voice commanding instant attention, "I'm afraid we have now come to a rather unpleasant portion of the proceedings. I must . . . It is now time to . . . to . . . Oh, for My sake, I don't know who I'm trying to fool: this is the best part of all, and many of you have been waiting your entire lifetimes to see this. Gods and goddesses, immortals and humans, if you will turn your attention out the windows to your left. I give you she who is without shame, she who is without conscience. She who was *once* the pride of the Olympians and the light in my life. The bearer of all female gifts and treasures; quite a catch when the world was young; now—not so much. She who was one of the sharpest and smartest, who could even outmaneuver me on occasion and yet, she who now finds herself having been soundly trumped at every turn by a mortal, albeit extraordinary, maiden. Put your hands and hooves together and let's have a big round of applause for the thorn in my side, the worm in my ambrosia, the pit in my nectar, my wife . . . Herrrrrrrrrrrraaaaaaaaaa!"

As the crowd watched the sky—which was the only thing to see beyond the terrace—two tiny objects appeared in the very far distance. For a long time, they were only black specks in an otherwise blue heaven. Then, quickly, the specks began to grow larger with each passing second.

"I think," said one of the pirates, "I think those are cages!"

"He's right," said King Peleus. "I see bars."

"But why two?" said Dionysus, waking for a moment, from his chair.

"Oh, right," said Zeus, as everyone could now easily recognize a large form in each cage. "And Demeter."

The floating cages sailed toward the terrace doors of the great hall and just before they would have crashed through, they stopped, sending both Hera and Demeter smashing against the bars. Then, as the doors opened magically, the cages floated through slowly, almost stately, and came to a stop directly over the dais.

Demeter was frantic and, had she not been gagged with a silver cloth, Pandy guessed she would have been wailing and pleading with Zeus or anyone to release her. She was hopping and tripping from bar to bar—the floors of the cages were also only bars—trying to make eye contact with any of the Olympians but especially Persephone, who was busy, deep in conversation with Hades, and avoiding her mother.

Hera, on the other hand, was gagged with a scarlet cloth and sitting calmly in one corner of her cage, like a beast waiting for its caretaker to turn his back. She glared at Zeus—until she spotted Pandora, then, even though her body remained motionless, her eyes narrowed into thin black lines of hate and rage. Pandy stared back and allowed herself the barest hint of a smile, before she turned back to look at Douban and her father.

"How long were they up there?" Hermes asked Zeus.

"Since Pandora and the rest were brought here."

"Two and a half days, father? You had them hanging over Greece for two and a half days?"

"They weren't in the flame pits," Zeus said with a shrug. "They weren't somewhere cleaning out lavatoriums. I gave them a sweet deal, because, hey, I'm a sweet guy."

Someone threw a ripe tomato with perfect aim through the bars and it landed right on Hera's cheek. At that point, she made a move to stand and Zeus held up his hands.

"All right, believe me, I understand, but let's leave the punishments to me, shall we?"

He turned and gazed up at Demeter, her hair changing from spring buds to the dried grasses of summer. That and the fact that she'd been up in the air for a while, exposed to the elements, caused the goddess to look incredibly old.

"You fool," Zeus said. "I know I applaud loyalty but you, my dear, are ridiculous. For six moons you had all the clues, all the signs that you had chosen the losing side and yet you stayed. You fought alongside the most moth-eaten of minds, the most petty, jealous, and smallest of hearts, and for what? Was not your power over the earth one of the greatest in my universe? Was not the worship you received and would have continued to receive enough for you? You wanted more and now you'll have nothing."

Again, whatever low chatter and whispers there were fell into silence and everyone seemed slightly confused. What did Zeus mean by "nothing"?

"For your disloyalty to me and my commands, for your general treachery and dishonesty and for conspiracy to commit murder—four counts of it—I sentence you, Demeter, *not* to the flames of Tartarus. *Not* to the outer reaches of the known world. *Not* to the highest known mountains or to a desert island to live out eternity on a scaly peak or burning sands. I do this: I relieve you of all your powers over agriculture, nature, and the seasons. You, goddess of the tangible earth that you love so much, shall have nothing save the *gift* of immortality and I sentence you to live the rest of the ages with no ability to help, correct, or punish mankind in any way. I doom you to watch what the mortals will do to your precious earth with no ability whatsoever to change their course. I, personally, have looked into the future and have seen how human beings will treat many areas of this planet—it's a planet, by the way, and it's much bigger than we think—and, while I do not rejoice at their actions, I feel that justice will be served in watching your heart break."

Demeter wailed underneath her gag and shook her head wildly, pleading with Zeus. Zeus waved his hand and the next instant, Demeter looked like she'd been hit from all sides by something huge and hard. As all her great powers vanished, her eyes rolled back until only the whites were showing, then she slumped forward, her cheek smashing hard into the cage bars. With another flick of Zeus's finger, the bottom of the cage dropped out and Demeter went crashing to the floor, landing on top of Hermes' empty chair, where she lay for many moments. Finally, taking pity on her mother, Persephone helped her to stand and led the shaken not-quite-a-goddess out of the hall.

"Buster!" she whispered, as she passed by her husband. "Now I can spend all year with you!"

Then, there was nothing but silence in the hall; not even a breeze from the edge of the terrace to distract as everyone turned to the second cage.

"Hello, wife."

If Hera could have spat at Zeus, she would have. Instead, she just made a spitting motion with her head and snorted, like a cow, through her nostrils. The pressure in her head from the rage and hate now building up, causing small blood vessels in her eyes to rupture, turning her eyes red.

"I would list all of your offenses for those who haven't really been following, but your crimes have been page one of our news-parchment, the *Olympus Outlook,* every day since Pandora left, so I think everyone here is pretty much up to speed. I just want to cover the highlights. Dog-napping. Attempting to exercise unauthorized powers in a different country. Illegal placement of serpents in an immortal's stomach. Coercion—let's not forget Aeolus. Conspiracy—that covers both Demeter and Juno. Attempted murder of Pandora—how many times? And, of course, murder itself: you actually did it."

Hera looked at Alcie. Alcie gave a little wave.

"I don't know why you did what you did, really," Zeus went on. "Yes, yes, you wanted power. More than mine. You wanted revenge for everything I've ever done, or things you think I've done. And everything everyone else has ever done to you. Pandora, what's the phrase you humans use? When someone just goes on and on?"

" 'Blah, blah, blah,' " Pandy answered.

"Blah, blah, blah. Exactly right. But it goes much deeper than just wanting power, my hefty bowl of cheese curds. Your revenge dictated utter destruction. Me, our universe, our way of being. Our very existence. Well, sorry, love, but you see, I just can't have it. I do feel sorry for you, wife. A little. But frankly, I don't care. Nobody cares anymore, Hera. Your problems, your jealousies, your insecurities, your legendary pettiness— boring now. All of it. You've been swallowed up by your minuteness. The once great Hera has reduced herself to living within a tiny box in her own mind, stuffed with hate, poison, and putrefaction. You're puny and perverse. As far as I'm concerned—and I'm the only one who really matters, my oafish oatie cake—you're too *small* to be a goddess."

A single tear coursed down Hera's cheek, soaking into her ruby-red gag.

"I'm sending you away, lambie-kins. Far, far away.

Another place and another time. As I said, I've looked into the future, roughly two thousand years, and found the perfect spot for you. The country is called the United States of America. One state goes by the name of Nevada. There's a little town in the middle of its wide desert: Las Vegas. It is, according to all reports, the biggest little city in the world, whatever that actually means. Legal gambling, endless feasts big enough for even the Roman appetite, singers, dancers, and circus performers. It's a real swingin' place. They have enormous inns there called 'hotels' and one in particular is modeled after . . . hey, where's Caesar? Is Julius Caesar in the hall? I know I saw him earlier."

"Here, mighty Zeus," Caesar said, waving his laurel wreath above his head.

"Well, Jules, my boy, you'll be happy to know that you made quite the impression on world history. There's an enormous inn with your name on it—Caesar's Palace—right in the middle of what's called the Strip. Guess how many rooms for guests? Guess? You never will. Are you ready for this—nearly four thousand!"

A gasp went up from the crowd.

"I KNOW!" said Zeus. "And Hera, *you* get to clean them!"

Hera's eyes went wide.

"You will be placed as a servant on the 'housekeeping' staff. For your labor you will be given a weekly payment and with that you'll eat, dress, and keep a roof over your head. Or not. In short, honey-pie, you're going to work. You, too, will be stripped of all your immortal powers, except for the fact that you'll never, ever, ever die. And, from what I understand, neither will Las Vegas. Oh, I almost forgot to tell you; Jupiter has arranged the same fate for Juno and Ceres, so who knows, you gals might run into one another at the Palace. You can talk about old times and how you all messed up so baaaaaddddd! All I have to say is bye-bye, baby, bye-bye."

Zeus turned to the stunned crowd.

"And so, since we have much celebrating still ahead of us, let us now raise our hands in a final farewell to a great gal. Not so much in personality but in girth . . ."

Before everyone's eyes, Hera slowly started to disappear; with every word from Zeus, she became more and more transparent. Zeus and Pandora were the only ones really waving good-bye; everyone else was riveted.

"We had some good times, me and this little chicklet. And We'll try to remember her only with fondness, for the goddess she used to be. A long, long time ago. . . ."

Pandy could now see the back walls of the hall through Hera.

"And We'll try to keep the poets and bards from speaking of her too harshly. Operative word being 'try.'

Oh, certainly, We'll miss her for a little while, but soon We'll forget she was . . .

Hera was almost completely gone; only her face was still visible.

". . . ever . . ."

Her eyes leveled at Zeus for a moment, then began to dart about the hall.

". . . even . . ."

With one last terrified blink, Hera disappeared completely.

". . . here."

The realization that Hera was no longer a threat to her or anyone caused Pandy to involuntarily collapse. Zeus caught her with his little finger and bent down to her ear.

"All gone, my dear," he whispered. "All gone."

CHAPTER TWENTY-FOUR
On the Terrace

Pandy, Alcie, Iole, Homer, Douban, and Crispus stood in a line at the terrace railing. Homer, Douban, and Crispus had really wanted to stand by their girls, but each had determined privately that distance and prudence was the best course. After all, there was a lot of waiting left to do and each youth knew he'd better get used to it.

Crispus had explained his story. That even though he was supposed to be six years old at present, he'd already lost years when he'd met Iole. After the group had left Rome, before Hermes had a chance to put everything back into the past, Crispus had personally prayed to Zeus and Jupiter, pouring his heart out on the altar of Jupiter's temple. Both gods had appeared to him. After a very short conversation in which Crispus had managed to convince both supreme rulers that he knew exactly what he was asking, they granted his wish and took him back in time ten years, completely preserving his memory of all his adventures with Iole and the others, then added back ten years to his age, making him as Iole knew him: sixteen.

After digesting this tale, no one was really saying much of anything. It was as if, by talking about their adventures in detail, they would all either collapse with exhaustion or that the moment of celebration would reveal itself to be a mirage and the great palace would fizzle away into the clouds.

"Immortals at two on the sundial," Alcie said.

Prometheus and Hermes were walking toward them.

"Hi, everyone," Prometheus said. "Alcie, your mother and father can really tear up the dance floor. Even with his ivory toes, your dad's terrific. And Iole, your parents are heading home but they wanted me to tell you that Crispy here . . ."

"Crispus," said the youth. "Crispus, sir."

"Crispus may stay in your stables for one night when you two return, but then it's off to the quarry with him—you—Crispus. I think your dad said something, Iole, about finding him a job with the press, inscribing the daily news. It was either that or construction. He'll tell you, I'm sure."

Then Prometheus turned to Pandy, very obviously not looking at Douban.

"Listen, honey, I'm going to take your mother back to Athens on the next Morpheus-Express. She's been trying to dance, but she keeps falling down; she's just not used to her legs yet. And apparently all the children are having such a good time in the toddler room, we're going to let Sabina bring your little brother down later, after she finishes talking with her sisters. Give your mom and me a little time to chat about . . . things. So . . . what time can we expect *you*?"

Pandy hid her smile as best she could.

"We're heading back soon, Dad. We'll all probably be right behind you. I want to show my wolfskin diary the view from the terrace and I want to say good-bye to everybody. And when we get back to the city, I want to help Douban find a place to live, even if it's temporary— just for the night. Until he can find someplace really groovy."

"Ah," Prometheus said. "So you're going to be staying in Athens, then?"

"Sheesh, Dad."

"There are those who need healing everywhere, sir," the young man replied, extending his hand. "And Athens is a city with many wonderful things to recommend it. I hope this meets with your approval."

Prometheus smiled wide and shook Douban's hand, then his face became very serious.

"It does. It will meet with more of my approval in three or four years, but yes, it does. Okay, then . . . I'll just see you later, then."

"Bye, Dad," Pandy said.

"See you at home."

"*Bye*, Dad."

"Bye, Dad," said Hermes.

Prometheus shot Hermes a look, then waved his hand in resignation and farewell.

"Hello," Hermes said to Pandy.

"Hello." She smiled.

"Still mad at me?"

"For what? Oh, you mean for omitting the fact that you'd taken us ten years into the future when we were in Rome and my father didn't know what had happened to me and was sick to the point of being senseless, which caused me so much stress that I may have already started getting gray hair? That?"

"Yes, that."

"Completely forgotten," she said.

Then she threw her arms around the god and hugged him as tightly as she could.

"And it wouldn't matter anyway," she mumbled against the soft silver fabric of his toga. "I wouldn't be alive today if it weren't for you. I'll never, ever be able to thank you for everything that you did, no matter how many sacrifices I make to you."

"What about me?" came a voice at her side.

"Or you," Pandy said, hugging Athena. "Of course you."

"Me too?"

Pandy turned to wrap her arms as far as they would go around Aphrodite, feeling the bliss that came whenever Aphrodite spoke. Then she looked around; they were all there. Ares, Artemis, Apollo, Dionysus, Poseidon in his traveling tank, Hephaestus, and Hades. As Pandy hugged each of them in turn, as best she could, Alcie, Iole, and Homer began their own rounds of hugging, cheek kissing, and hand shaking. Douban and Crispus stood a little off to the side, not wanting to get in the way.

"Wait!" came a shout and a flurry of pink and fuchsia. "I want in on this fun!"

Persephone tore across the terrace and caught Pandy up in such a hug, Pandy thought her eyes might pop from their sockets. Then Pandy stood apart and cleared her throat.

"I want you all to know that, while I still respect, honor, and fear each of you . . ."

"Oh, pshawwww," said Hermes.

"Quiet," Athena chided him.

"I also *love* each of you—more than you'll ever know."

"That goes double," said Alcie.

"And me," Iole said.

"And me," Homer finished.

"We know," said Persephone. "Borrowing from that

nice exchange you have with your dad: us you more, dear ones."

"I know!" Pandy laughed.

"I KNOW!" Persephone said, hugging her again.

"So," Pandy began, sniffling slightly. "Will I—we—see you again? This isn't really good-bye, is it? I mean, are we going to have to go through high priestesses and stuff to get to talk to you?"

"Yes," said Hades.

"Buster!" Persephone yelped, playfully hitting his arm.

"Do you really think we'd just let you go like that?" asked Hermes. "Like you're so grown up now you won't need us? Puh-leeze. We'll be around. Just whistle."

"Okay, Zeus is about to cut the 'Happy Trails To Hera' ambrosia cake," said Apollo, "and I'm not missing out on a corner piece. Who's with me?"

The immortals sped to the doorway so fast, several got stuck trying to squeeze through at the same time.

"Coming?" called Hermes.

"Be there in a moment," Pandy answered, to which Hermes gave her a huge grin.

In less than the blink of an eye, the terrace was clear and quiet and everyone turned back to the majestic view. Pandy stood at one end, only slightly apart from the rest, feeling connected and interdependent to those at her side, yet very much her own person at the same time. A light breeze came up off the rocky peaks as the six friends gazed out at the clouds in silence.

"You know," said Homer, addressing Crispus and Douban, "if the three of us shared a couple of rooms, we could save a few drachmas."

"And keep an eye on our girls," said Douban.

"*Your girls?*" asked Pandy, mock indignant. "Keep an *eye* on?"

"As if," Alcie grinned.

"Seriously," said Iole.

"One can hope," Douban responded.

"I'm in," said Crispus.

"Then it's a go," Homer said, as silence settled back onto the terrace.

A long silence.

"Glad you took the box to school?" Alcie asked finally.

"Yes," Pandy admitted after several beats.

There was another interminable pause.

"Would you do it again?" asked Iole.

After a wait that made everyone think Pandy might have gone to sleep, she turned and looked down the line at the best friends anyone could ever have.

"Well, I'll tell you . . ."

EPILOGUE . . . THE FIRST

"And that covers bed-making basics, ladies. Most of you did splendidly."

The short, thin man with a ferret face glared for the twentieth time in four days at two rather large ladies in the back of the hot, muggy training room. One of the women raised her hand.

"Oh, heavens. What is it now . . . which one are you?"

"I'm June," she said, then she pointed to the other woman, who could easily have been her twin, smacking a large wad of chewing gum between her lips. "She's Harriet."

"That's my name, don't wear it out," said Harriet casually.

"What is it, June?"

"I'd just like to put in my request, once again, for a new . . ."

"And for the millionth time," said the man, "no, you cannot have a new partner. You've all been paired up expressly to complement each other's skills. Get to know your partner and like 'er. That's the way it's going to stay."

" '*That's the way it's going to staaaay,*' " June mimicked under her breath.

"Shut up," said Harriet.

"You shut up," hissed June.

"Both of you, be quiet," said the man, his pinched nostrils flaring and beady eyes narrowing. "Now, ladies, if you'll move down the hall to our toilet demonstration room, Inga here—who has been with Caesar's for over twenty-seven years—will show you how to get the bowl bright. Everyone follow Inga. That's right, ladies. Fourth room on your right. Keep the chatter to a minimum, please. Thank you. There you go . . ."

Then the smarmy little man stretched his arm across the door just as Harriet and June were about to exit.

"And exactly where do you think you're going?"

"Gonna go get a bowl bright," said Harriet drolly.

"Oh, are you? Are you really . . . 'Sandtrap'?"

"What?" asked June. "What sandtrap?"

"Oh, no," whispered Harriet.

June and Harriet each took a step back as the man's ferret face began to melt and shift. The next moment, standing between them and the hallway, was the official Hera had dealt with at the Bureau of Visiting Deities in Persia.

"Remember me, you bright girl? And the little nickname we had for you? Your husbands, both of them, asked me to come and supervise your employment because they heard about how well you and I got on so long ago, *Harriet*. Never got around to introducing myself at the Bureau, did I? I guess that's because you left so fast after you killed those monkeys. Name's Mirrikh. Now, I don't really expect a dullard such as yourself—make that two dullards—to be able to pronounce it; I just think you two might like to know what it means. Loosely translated, it means death, slaughter, that type of thing. For you two brain trusts, however, it means I'm gonna be on you both like a cheap suit . . ."

"But I didn't really do that much!" June wailed. "I certainly never did most of the things she did! I mean I . . . I . . . I didn't kill those monkeys! I don't really deserve to be here. I actually *liked* Pandora!"

"You venomous little traitor!" screamed Harriet. "It was fine letting me do all the work, roaming all over the known world, carrying out the plans, wasn't it? And then you were just gonna come in and share the power, weren't you?"

"*Shaddup!*" Mirrikh exploded. "All you need to know is that the rest of eternity is gonna be one big toilet bowl for the both of you. You're gonna be up to your big necks in scrubbers and cleanser till the end of time!"

But June had grabbed a pillow from the newly made demonstration bed and began to swing it at Harriet like she was brandishing a club.

"Hey, are you two listening to me!"

"I'm going to scrub *you*, is what I'm going to do!" June cried, landing a blow to Harriet's head just as Harriet picked up another pillow. "I'm going to spend eternity smashing you to a pulp!"

"We'll see who pulverizes who, you little snake!" Harriet bellowed, hitting June in the stomach and sending a plume of goose feathers spurting from the pillow. "I'm going to make your life so miserable you'll wish you'd never been formed!"

Mirrikh folded his arms and, with a smile, stepped out into the hallway, locking the door behind him. With a blink, he soundproofed the room so that the hallway was silent to those passing by.

"We'll leave them right there for a few days. Give or take. And then, it's toilet time!"

EPILOGUE . . . THE SECOND

The pretty naiad was too distracted, thinking about Apollo . . .

"He's soooooo dreamy!"

. . . and grumbling to herself about actually having to babysit the immortal infants and toddlers instead of getting to participate in the festivities to have noticed that one especially speedy young man had crawled out of the room.

As Orpheus and his orchestra were playing their smash hit "Gimme Goat" for the third time and dancing had erupted in the great hall, Xander, of the great house of Prometheus, was wandering hallways, bustling in and out of anterooms and sleeping chambers. He raised himself to stand at Aphrodite's dressing table, pulling down a pot of lavender lip paste on top of his head—which he promptly ate. He crawled underneath Tyro's perch in Athena's rooms, covering himself in owl droppings—which he promptly ate. He found Artemis's not-well-hidden-at-all stash of ginger-orange oatie cakes—which he promptly ate.

Sated, he was crawling back toward the sounds of "big people," when a glint in a storage room caught his two-and-a-half-year-old attention. It took him a few moments to knock the object off the table and onto the floor. It was a plain brown wooden box, with a shiny lock and a really shiny hairpin keeping it closed.

Wiggle, wiggle.

It was fun. He could play with the box all day.

Maybe he could even get it open.

ACKNOWLEDGMENTS

Thanks to the lovely Samantha Fabisch for being the last first reader and for declaring the manuscript "perfect!" Thanks to my brother Scott Hennesy for reading them all, Zac Hug for being a wise taskmaster, Ron Davis for the brilliant line, Denise Isabella for her marvelous insight, and Ruth Percival for pushing in other directions. Thanks to Erika Carle for all she's done for the past four years. Thanks to Dan Mailley and Trish Alaskey for keeping me sane and laughing and being the best of the best. Thanks also to Michelle Nagler and Brett Wright for their sublime edits/notes/margin LOLs. Special thanks and love to my husband, Donald, who stayed up late and read and read and read. As always, deepest gratitude and love to Sara Schedeen . . . for pretty much everything.

DONALD AGNELLI

Carolyn Hennesy

is the author of all of Pandora's Mythic Misadventures, as well as the *New York Times* bestseller *The Secret Life of Damian Spinelli*. As an actress, her work can be seen on both big and little screens (prime-time and daytime). In addition to her full-time acting and writing careers, Ms. Hennesy also hosts the online show "Animal Magnetism," teaches improvisational comedy, is an avid shopaholic, and studies the flying and static trapeze. She lives in the Los Angeles area with her pups, Sophie Tucker, Liza Jane, and Arbuckle, along with Ella and Buster, the Wonder Cats.

www.carolynhennesy.com

Calling all modern goddesses!

Don't miss Pandora's adventures as she and her BFFs try to collect the seven evils before Pandy becomes the most unpopular maiden in Athens . . . *and* goes down in history as the girl who ruined the world.

www.pandyinc.com

www.bloomsbury.com
www.facebook.com/bloomsburykids